Loxley: A dish served cold

By Neil Hallam

© Lauman Media and Publishing 2017

Other titles by Neil Hallam

Between stone and a Hard Place

Stone Paper Bomb

Chapter 1.

Again and again the heavy blades crashed together.
The combatants lunged forward and drew back,
their broad swords whirling in the air as if
weightless.
In any other company the defender would be a big
man, but in this match, he was dwarfed by his
attacker.
Time and again the smaller man defended against
his opponent's blade coming down on him, with full
assistance of gravity. Despite his size, the attacker
was fast, stepping back from each blow to cover his
own body from counter attack.

As one blow fell, the smaller man moved into the
glissade or glide, as their swords met, he put in
more force, sliding his sword along the length of his
larger opponents blade, pushing it aside. This left
the bigger mans belly undefended for a thrust.
But the big man stepped back and using his gloved
hand to support his blade, fended off the attack.

Seeing the blade horizontally above him, the smaller
man moved in for a cut, which he swiftly turned into
a thrust. His hand came onto his blade, using his
thick glove to avoid injury. Then, in one move, he
transferred the weight of the sword to his left hand.
Turning it on its end and gripping the blade in both
hands, he used the upturned sword like an axe.
Swinging at his taller opponent's horizontal blade, he
hooked the cross bar over the blade and pulled back
hard. This destabilised the tall man, pulling him off
balance.

In the moments it took the big man to regain his balance, his opponent swung his sword around the right way and struck again. This time, the heavy blade swung towards the big man's neck. His balance was so far off that he could do nothing to stop the swing. It looked like certain death for the big man, then, right at the last second, the blade turned so the flat of its side struck. The big man would have a huge bruise, but he would live.

Putting down their swords, the two men shook hands.
"Good contest John", said the smaller man. "You almost had me".
"One day Robin", he replied. "I only have to get lucky once".
"We'll see", replied Robin. "Now we had better shower and hit the road. I don't want to be late for Dad's funeral".

One week earlier, Robin had inherited his family title as the Duke of Loxley. Despite not having spoken to his father in two years, it was a title he had not wanted, since it could only come from his father's death.
Major Robin Loxley and his sword play opponent, Sergeant Major John Little had spent most of the last two years in North Africa, with their Special Forces unit.
His unit's official home was at Hereford, with the more famous SAS Regiment. But Robin's secretive unit was rarely in Britain, a fact that had suited Robin well over the last couple of years.
Officially known as the Special Incursion Unit, their

speciality was long term incursion into hostile territory. They lived secretively behind enemy lines, for months at a time, with no outside support. Their job was to observe and to feed back intelligence on the world's pariah regimes.

On the rare occasions that his unit was spoken of, their official title was rarely used. Those in the know had come to call them Outlaws, based in their ability to stay hidden from the enemy, steeling what food and provisions they needed to survive.

Now, two years after his last visit to his family's Nottinghamshire home, Robin was driving the once familiar route north east, from the Welsh borders to the English Midlands.

John knew that Robin's mind would be very mixed by the complicated relationship with his father so he kept the conversation on their shared love of historic weapons.

Firearms were an absolute last resort for the Outlaws on a covert incursion. The noise of a shot would be an instant give-away, while a shooting victim would attract the highest level of police scrutiny. Instead, they favoured weapons such as knives and clubs, which would pass for local disputes.

Robin and John had carried their unit's training a step further, becoming masters in many historic weapons. Their favourites were the broad sword and long bow, but they eagerly researched and practiced with any historic weapon they could discover and replicate.

Despite John's efforts, Robin's mind continually drifted to the funeral and the inevitable meeting with the remainder of his family.

His last visit to the family estate had been for his mother's funeral. Robin had never quite seen eye to eye with his father, but he loved his mother dearly and her loss to cancer had cut him deeply.

After her death Robin took a month's leave from the army, out of a sense of duty to his family.

He thought his main task would be in consoling his bereaved father, but the time together just widened the rift between them. The old Duke had long enjoyed a reputation for gambling and womanising. The loss of his wife seemed to push him even further over the edge, and further apart from his only son.

Without his wife's steadying influence, the Duke turned Loxley Hall into a continuous party venue. Casino companies were brought in to ply their trade, while music, drink and unsavoury visitors filled the hall throughout the night.

Unable to watch his family's ancestral home treated that way, Robin returned to the army, hoping it was just a phase for his father.

Estranged from his father, Robin had thrown himself deeper into soldiering, volunteering for one back to back tour after another.

Now, after his father's death, Robin was again driving back to his family estate out of duty to his family and to put the estate in order.

Robin lived for the army and had no intention of being an active Duke. But, as the only heir, he had a responsibility to sort out his father's affairs. "Ironic", thought Robin. "It was dad's affairs that drove us apart".

Trying to take his mind from his father, Robin thought about another irony of his trip home. Through his love of historic weapons and battles, Robin knew of his own family's long history with warfare.

In the ancient Forest of Sherwood, legend and history were often intertwined. One of the stories involved a former Duke of Loxley returning from the crusades in the Holy Land to find Nottinghamshire a very different place to the one he left.

Robin had spent most of the last two years in what was once known as the Holy Land. Although he was not on a Christian Crusade, most of his enemies had fought under the banner of an extreme form of Islam.

Robin's irony was that the problems in his legendary ancestor's world were caused by Prince John. In Robin's world, they were caused by his own father.

That afternoon, Robin and John stood together as the late Duke's coffin was carried into the chapel at Loxley Hall.

"Something seems wrong", whispered Robin to his friend. "The staff are all new, and Dad's bimbo seems to hold too much sway".

Like many estates in the Nottinghamshire Dukeries, Loxley Hall had retained a core of long time, loyal staff. Many of whom had helped raise Robin. But none of them were at the funeral. There were plenty of staff wearing the estate's distinctive tweed uniform, but they were all much younger and had nothing of their predecessors bearing.

Dressed in an expensive black gown and taking prime position in the parade of mourners was Dad's bimbo, Helen Loxley. She was the final straw that drove Robin away from his father and deeper into being a solider.

Twenty years the Duke's junior, Helen was in her early 40's, an obviously peroxide blond, with paid for breasts and too much makeup. She was every inch the stereotype trophy wife. But, wily as a fox, she had used her very obvious charms to enchant the old Duke.

Her expensive appearance was no surprise to Robin, Helen had always been able to loosen his father's wallet. But it was her influence around the estate staff which surprised Robin. When he last visited Loxley Hall, she was just a dazzling accessory to his father, a bit of expensive bling. But now, among the new staff and her own hangers on, Helen seemed much more comfortable in the role of Duchess.

"Who's the heavy?" asked John. He was looking at the man standing beside Helen Loxley. There was something familiar about the man. Aged in his mid 50s and powerfully built, the man was impeccably dressed in an expensive suit and accessories. But, despite his obvious wealth, he did not fit with the titled country set.

"I don't know", replied Robin. "But he looks like an extra from a Kray Twins movie".

Robin would soon learn how accurate his parallel with the vicious London gangsters would be.

"I'm sorry Robin", began the solicitor. Robin had visited the family solicitor directly from the funeral. He wanted to the estate running itself as quickly as possible, so he could rejoin his regiment.

"Aside from your trust fund and the South Lodge cottage, the Duchess inherits everything", continued his solicitor.

Robin neither wanted, nor needed, the family money. But he had clung to the hope that Loxley Hall would have been protected from Helen's clutches. Tradition in the Dukeries would have seen the estate pass, along with the title of Duke, to the eldest son. But, it seemed his father was too smitten to make the pre nuptial agreement Robin had hoped for.

Robin had loved his childhood playing at Loxley Hall, then as he grew, exploring the wider area of the Dukeries. Now, he feared his father had given away his family's 400 year history in the area.

The area known as the Dukeries is twenty miles north of Nottingham, and extends about ten miles further north, towards Yorkshire. One of the last remaining sections of the ancient Forest of Sherwood, and now one of the largest combinations of park and forest in England.

Along with Robin's family estate, the Dukeries also contain the estates of: Welbeck, Clumber, and Thoresby, belonging to the Dukes of Portland and Newcastle, and Earl Manvers; and to these we can add Worksop Manor Park, part of the Duke of Newcastle's estate; and Rufford Abbey, the seat of Lord Savile. The owners of the Dukeries trace their descent to the famous Bess of Hardwick, who had a passion for house-building and the creation of great estates. Before her death in 1607 she had married four times, and on each occasion managed to vastly increase the territorial influence of her family. Hence this huge Dukery has been kept in one piece, the owners of its various sections all co-operating to maintain its primeval simplicity. Now, Robin feared, Helen could break up the historic estate.

Apart from his own home, Welbeck Abbey held the warmest place in Robin's heart. Until 2005 it was leased to the Ministry of Defence and occupied by the Army Sixth Form College. Robin spent his youth watching the students train, then, as soon as he was old enough, he signed up himself.

The more that Robin got into the detail with his solicitor, the more he understood how deeply Helen had influenced the old Duke.

His father had spent his life drinking, gambling and womanising. But with Helen, recreational drugs entered the Duke's life. Stories of cocaine use at their many parties abounded. The post mortem had shown that at some point he had begun to use opiates, possibly contributing to the shortening of the Duke's life.

His father's expensive lifestyle and high maintenance wife had depleted the family fortune considerably. Although Helen had inherited the Loxley estate, it came with a massive, recently incurred, mortgage.

"Sheriff Leisure holds most of the paper", advised the solicitor.

It was then that Robin realised why the tough

looking man at the funeral with Helen looked familiar. "Clive Motte", said Robin, finally recognising the Nottinghamshire night club owner.
"Yes", replied the solicitor. "The Sheriff of Nottingham", he continued, referring to Motte's nick name as the company boss.

Motte had started out running a small city centre bar. But his holdings and wealth had grown suspiciously fast. Motte now owned many of Nottinghamshire's busiest bars and night clubs. There was no doubt that Motte's vicious and ruthless style of management had contributed to the success of his company. But, there was always suspicion that he had also fought his way to the top of the county's organised drug trade.
Other than a few convictions for violence, the police had never proven anything against Motte. He was always clever enough to put others into positions of risk.
Robin could not think of anyone worse to have a controlling stake in the Loxley estate. If Helen did not keep up the mortgage repayments, then Motte would gain a significant jump in his ambitions of social climbing.

Robin spent the next hour going through all the possible legal challenges to Helen's inheritance. Several had some merit, but for now, the Duke of Loxley had no estate. Through his trust fund, he was still a wealthy man, but the money seemed a little worthless if he could not pass Loxley Hall to another generation of his family.
So, with little more they could do that evening, Robin

and John relaxed in the way soldiers the world over
have done for decades.

Chapter 2:

"Over to our reporter at the scene", announced the BBC news anchor.

The reporter stood in the shadows, on the edge of Nottingham's Lace Market area. The area had once been the industrial heart of the city's thriving lace industry. Now it's Victorian buildings housed bars and residential apartments.

"The police are describing this attack as brutal", began the reporter. "The unnamed man has been taken to Queens Medical Centre for treatment of his injuries. An eyewitness told me that one of the paramedics had commented she had never seen anyone so badly beaten before".

The reporter passed on the description of the suspects, with a plea for the public to consider them dangerous and not to approach them.

"Witnesses saw two men running from the scene. Both are described as very big men, with one of them well above average height. They both wore hoodies, with the hoods hiding their faces. The taller of the two wore blue; the other had a green hooded top".

Despite the drink inside them, Robin and John had slipped effortlessly back into their training.

The south and east of the city remain undeveloped. Much of its former industrial buildings abandoned, emptied for a redevelopment that was stalled by the recession. The two commandos had no difficulty slipping out of sight.

Nottingham is famous for its tunnels and caves. The commandos had used remnants of the old Victoria railway tunnels to ease their way out of the Lace Market. The huge Victoria shopping centre stands on the site of the very grand city centre railway station. Its tracks had run south through tunnels cut into Nottingham's soft sandstone bedrock. Now, mostly filled in, some sections remained around Weekday Cross and the Contemporary Art Gallery. It was here that Robin and John caught their breath before moving deeper into the urban decay of Nottingham's south side. While they rested and planned, Robin thought back on how he had now become an outlaw in his own home city.

The evening had started in the way many off duty soldiers' evenings had done for decades. Two battle hardened comrades, full of adrenalin from their latest war zone, letting their hair down.
Robin could add to this dangerous mix, a raging hatred for what had happened to his father and their family estate. But all of that hatred was bubbling away below the surface, for now, Robin and John were just two mates out on the town.
They drank steadily, their huge frames reducing the effects of the alcohol. Those same huge frames, military bearing and Help for Heroes hoodies provided a steady stream of female admirers. With three universities, Nottingham city centre is often said to have at least two women to every man. Robin and John were taking full advantage of this in enjoying their night out.
Although, they were not following the female students to some of their more obvious haunts. Most of Nottingham's busiest venues were owned by Sheriff Leisure. Robin would not bring himself to put

money in Clive Motte's pocket.

Instead, they followed their love of history, to some of Nottingham's oldest and most interesting pubs.

Their evening started in the Old Trip to Jerusalem. This 800 year old inn, cut into the Rock below Nottingham Castle, is the oldest in England. Robin never tired of hearing the tales of Crusaders and ghost stories told in the inn's caves.

Next, the friends crossed the road to Ye Olde Salutation Inn. It is said to date back to 1240, when a tannery was built over a mediaeval ale house. Like many of Nottingham's old buildings, the Salutation is built over a network of caves. Here again, Robin and John listened to tales of the building's history. They had heard most before, but the story tellers always seemed to find another interesting tidbit.

With a few drinks inside them, Robin and John started to want a bit more lively location, so they walked into the city's Old Market Square. Once the home of Nottingham's famous Goose Fair, the square is still a focal point for the city centre. Here their choice of hostelry was the Bell Inn. Dating from 1437, the Grade Two Listed building began life as part of a Carmelite monastery.

As the evening turned into the early hours many of the smaller venues started to close, as the revellers moved into the bigger night clubs.

With Motte having a stake in many of the bigger clubs, Robin had no interest in following the crowds into them. So, they wandered the older parts of the city centre, watching the groups of girls moving between the clubs and generally taking in the city's history.

Their walk took them into the Lace Market Quarter, the area of the original Saxon settlement that became Nottingham. This historic quarter-mile square area went on to become the centre of the world's lace industry during the British Empire and is now a protected heritage area.

It was never a market in the sense of having stalls, but there were salesrooms and warehouses for storing, displaying and selling the lace. Most of the buildings are typically Victorian, with densely packed 4-7 story red brick building lined streets. Its iron railings, old gas lamps and red phone boxes helped give Robin a sense of going back in time to Victorian England.

Robin loved the Lace Market's architecture, the best of it designed by Watson Fothergill, a prolific local architect responsible for some 100 buildings in the area between 1870 and 1906. His Gothic style was very popular in Victorian times, meaning that many shops, banks, houses and even churches are decorated with turrets and gargoyles.

They did not know it at the time, but their walk around the historic Lace Market would be a life changer for Robin and John. It would soon lead to them running from the police and hiding in the shadows of the former railway tunnels.

The exercise and fresh air was starting to remove the effects of several pints of real ale as they walked along High Pavement, a handsome Georgian street and one of the few non Victorian parts of the Lace Market.

They stood admiring the Galleries of Justice,

formerly Nottingham's jail, Crown Court and site of the city's gallows. Then, something caught their eye in the shadows around the 15th century St Mary's Church.

Something about the gathering looked wrong. The expensive American car should not have been parked in the pedestrianised area. The four people on the outside of the group leader looked to be typical, young clubbers. But the man in the centre looked very out of place among them. Dressed in designer sports ware and dripping in gold jewellery, everything about the man was screaming drug dealer. Then, Robin saw one of the clubbers counting out money, which turned his assumption into a near certainty.
"I'm not watching him peddling that crap", said Robin as he broke into a run. John was a fraction of a second behind him, running to back up his commanding officer and best friend.
As they ran, both men pulled up their hoods, casting their faces into shadow.

The small group of clubbers scattered in panic as soon as the hooded men reached them. None of them were the least bit brave or streetwise. The dealer on the other hand, had fought his way through the ranks of Nottingham's street gangs. The gun in his jacket pocket made him much braver about the uneven odds.
Had a trained soldier like Robin been carrying a gun, it would have been holstered for easy access. The street thug was not that well organised and struggled pulling the pistol from his pocket.

That delay was all that Robin needed. A chop from the side of Robin's hand rendered the thug's gun hand useless, his arm snapping painfully at the wrist.

John reacted instantly, following Robin's lead. They each took one of the dealer's arms, swiftly dragging him into St Mary's churchyard and away from CCTV and passers by.

In the shadows of the gravestones, they had the dealer stretched out, expertly searching him for weapons drugs and cash. Soon he had nothing of value left about him.

Then Robin started his search for information. He knew that Clive Motte had links to Nottinghamshire's drug trade and was desperate to prove those links and have Motte removed from being a danger to his family.

Robin and John were very persuasive in their questioning.

The habits you develop to keep you alive are the hardest to break. Even out enjoying himself, Robin always had some form of weapon to hand. As he started questioning the dealer, he began to remove his belt. From the thick leather belt, he removed the ornate metal buckle. Away from its mounting, the buckle could be seen for its other purpose. The once confident dealer suddenly looked very afraid as Robin slipped the knuckle duster onto his hand. They extracted a lot of information on the supply of drugs in the area and how the various gangs carved up their turf. But in comparison to Motte, this was a very minor player. He simply did not have the information that Robin wanted.

Satisfied they had got everything they could from the dealer, Robin and John set about disposing of his drugs down the nearest drain.
"You know his suppliers will hold him liable for the cost of this lot, don't you?" asked John.
"I really don't care", answered Robin. "Drugs cost Dad his life and will probably have cost future Loxleys their birthright. He deserves everything he gets".
They were just tipping the last few bags when they saw telltale blue lights reflecting off nearby roofs.
"Leg it", ordered Robin, as the two friends sprinted in the opposite direction to the police lights.
This was how Robin and John came to be hiding in the old railway tunnel.

The Lace Market is so close to Nottingham's BBC News centre they had a reporter on scene almost as soon as the police arrived.
Robin was monitoring the news on his smartphone, to see how much of a stir they had caused. It had been the drug buying clubbers who had rung the police, bitter that they had handed over money, but received no drugs because of Robin's intervention. They had assumed that Robin and John were rival drug dealers and wanted the police to exact revenge for them.
The BBC website reported the incident as a dispute between the rival street gangs. The beaten gangster was a regular in the Lace Market. The revellers did not know his real name, but knew he was part of a gang who called themselves MPR, or, Money,

Power and Respect. They were a vicious street gang who controlled most of the street level drug trade on this side of the city.

Witnesses had seen John and Robin running from the churchyard, but with their hooded tops, they had been taken for street gang members. In truth, they looked nothing like the wannabe hoodlums who terrorised the Nottingham estates. But, in the dark and the heat of the incident, the witnesses saw what they thought fitted best.

"They won't be looking for anyone our age", thought Robin. So, burying their hoodies in the debris of the cutting, they worked their way through the shadows into the derelict south side of the city.

Here, many of the factories and warehouses had been demolished to make way for a development that never happened. But, there were still enough empty buildings to attract the homeless and the two fugitives.

Robin and John decided to spend the night here and slip away when the morning's workers started to come into the city. They knew from the news coverage that any search would concentrate on the two estates to the south and east, which were the turf of the two biggest rival gangs.

After a less than perfect nights sleep they made the short walk to the railway station and their train north to Worksop, where they had left their car.

On the train, they watched the BBC morning news on Robin's phone.

"This was a particularly brutal attack", began the police Inspector. He explained that, on the face of it, the beating had the hallmarks of a drug feud. But, there was something which did not quite fit. "I was in the army before the police", continued the Inspector. "This looked like a torture. The victim will recover, but there is hardly an inch of his body that has not been beaten".

The news anchor went on to report that the, as yet unnamed, victim was stable, but still in considerable pain.

Robin allowed himself a wry smile, knowing he and John had used their training well.

As Robin and John relaxed on the train, a charity shop manager was opening up for the day. She always tidied the shop and took pride in preparing for her volunteers and customers to start arriving. The shop had been in darkness and barely drew any attention when the commuters had scurried past a half hour earlier. No one noticed the two figures briefly stop by the letter box before moving on.

On the doormat inside the shop, was a tatty looking carrier bag. She instantly wondered what rubbish had been pushed through by last night's drunks, but needed to sit down when she looked inside. Her charity was going to have a very good day, as there was over £1000 in cash inside the bag.

Robin tried to imagine what the charity would do with their windfall. He tried not to dwell too long over what would happen to the drug dealer over his debt for the missing drugs and money.

Chapter 3.

The walk through Sherwood Forest relaxed Robin. There was a possibility they could have been identified for the previous night's incident, so they decided to take a long walk back from Worksop's railway station. Robin knew all the tracks and trails through the Dukeries, so they could easily avoid roads and people.

Robin had in an ear plug, monitoring the Nottingham news channels. There were regular updates on what the police were treating as a serious incident. But, the descriptions of two hooded men could have been anyone.

Still, the cautious commandos surveilled Robin's South Lodge cottage until they were sure no one else was paying them any interest.

While John, as his guest, took first turn in the shower, Robin's thoughts drifted back to the previous night.

What the two friends had done was nothing they had not done hundreds of times before to insurgents and terrorists. But, this felt very different. On one level, using his very specialised skills on the streets of Nottingham felt wrong. Robin's Outlaw unit had enjoyed very little down time since its creation. They seemed to be moved constantly between one far flung theatre of war and the next. But the overriding theme was the states of war, conflict or oppression that they were fighting against.

Using guerrilla tactics in a British city that was supposedly at peace should have offended all of the army officer's morals. But it did not.

Nottingham was at war. It was a long time since the regular shootings had earned Nottingham its nickname of Shottingham. The police had gained control of the more obvious gun crime, but the menace of drugs and gangs still bubbled away below the surface.

Three of the city's large estates had their own homegrown street gangs, who still fought fiercely for the turf in which to sell their drugs. Occasionally, innocents also got caught in the cross fire of their turf wars, to say nothing of the lives ruined by their drugs.

Each of the city's gangs had aligned themselves with bigger gangs from Birmingham and Manchester. These heavier players had brought a whole new level of viciousness to Nottingham's drug wars and the gangs demands for "respect".

Clearing away the traditional organised crime that created the Shottingham problem had left a void in Nottingham's drug trade and the street gangs had grown into the void.

Before the current street gangs, several traditional crime families had ruled the drug trade with a rod of iron. All were modelled on the East End gangsters, like the Kray twins. The Dawes and Hardy families had controlled the north of the county, while the much higher profile Gunn brothers had run the city. All now languished in jail, thanks to a sustained police operation over several years.

There was always rumoured to be a godfather figure who sat above these crime families. The underworld referred to him only as the Tax Collector, as his organisation rarely handled the drugs, they just sold permission to operate. This godfather was still said to be in control, selling protection to the new, younger breed of gangster.

Robin was certain that Clive Motte was the Tax Collector, but the police had spent 30 years trying to build a case against him. Robin wondered if he could succeed where the police had failed.

When both friends had showered and changed, Robin started to talk through the information they had beaten out of the drug dealer.

In the scheme of things, and despite his fancy car and jewellery, he had been a fairly minor player. He had named the youngsters he employed to sell his deals around the estate. He also knew the safe house at which he picked up his wares for the evening.

Beyond this, the dealer knew very little of any importance. His gang's supplies came in from the Birmingham connection, but he was too small a fish to know any real detail.

He had been able to give a detailed description of his gang's turf boundary. Whatever your position in a drug gang, that is the sort of information that keeps you alive. None of the street level dealers wanted to stray onto another gang's turf, so they learned their territories by heart.

Robin dug out some maps of Nottingham and the two of them began to transcribe the geographical detail they had got from the Dealer. As the turf boundaries started to take shape, Robin realised that if their map was seen by none else, it could connect them with their previous night's activities.

He did not get many visitors at South Lodge, but he could not afford the police, or Motte's people, seeing the map.

"Shall we take this downstairs", suggested Robin. John knew that Robin had a large and ornate wine cellar beneath his cottage, but there was more to the cottage's cellars than met the eye.

Once in the cellar, Robin moved towards the rack holding the older, more valuable bottles. This was a side of the cellar that was only visited on very special occasions.

Robin gripped the corner of the wine rack, then slowly and gently slid it to one side on hidden rollers, to reveal a brick lined tunnel.

"Welcome to my childhood playground", said Robin. He explained that an earlier and eccentric Duke had dug the network of tunnels, but their location had been lost to the family over the last several generations. Robin's boyish curiosity had led him to rediscover them in his early teens. It became a matter of great pride for Robin to keep his hidden world a secret.

The nearby Thoresby Hall is quite famous for its tunnels and catacombs. But the Loxley estate's underground world remained completely unknown. Now a luxurious spa hotel, Thoresby had been built as a home for the Pierpoint and Manvers families. The families' connections with Thoresby predate the Battle of Culloden. But the current hall was built in 1868.

The catacombs and underground apartments are at least as beautiful as the grand house above ground.

A labyrinth of tunnels also joined Thoresby with various parts of the Welbeck estate and Robin had played in them with the Thoresby children.

Robin remembered when, as a small boy, he accompanied his family to lavish parties held in the Manvers' underground apartments. One of the local guide books described them far better than Robin could put into words. "The underground apartments are nobly planned and proportioned and for elegance of decoration could hardly be surpassed. All the workmanship is curiously perfect. The walls are not only of vast thickness, but so treated with asphalt as to make the penetration of damp next to impossible. The doors, of enormous size and weight, are so perfectly hung that a child could open or shut them, and they close with the beautiful precision of those in the private drawing-rooms of Windsor Castle.

Even by the comparatively dim light of a winter afternoon this magnificent suite of apartments is perfectly lit from above, and an effective side-light is obtained from a glass-roofed corridor running on one side. Library, writing-rooms, billiard - rooms, and reception-rooms are lit by gas in the night-time. Equally notable is the magnificent ballroom, 160 feet long, lit by day by gigantic bull's-eyes, and at night by gas. It is difficult to imagine a more perfect apartment for the purpose of festivity. Its tasteful decorations have a light and elegant effect, and the arrangement of corridors, conservatories, and refreshment - rooms, and the devices which secure efficient ventilation, are as well and carefully thought of as the spacious lifts for raising weary visitors to the upper air."

In contrast to the very grand Thoresby catacombs, the underground world of the Loxley estate was much simpler.
A previous Duke had ambitions to emulate his neighbour's subterranean world, but his ambitions had fallen far short of his abilities or finances. The Loxley tunnels were finished in their structure, lighting and ventilation, but there had been no money left to decorate them with anything close to the grandeur of Thoresby.
Feeling intense shame at his failure to match his neighbours' project, Robin's ancestor had ordered the tunnels sealed, never to be spoken of again.
But the adventurous young Robin had found Loxley's hidden world. Never tempted to boast of his find, Robin kept the tunnels and underground rooms as his own secret world.
Then, on turning 21, Robin's father gifted him the South Lodge cottage and Robin set about secretly joining it to the tunnel network.

The underground rooms vastly increased the space Robin had in his modest cottage. The practicalities of his military life meant that he had decorated much more simply than the earlier Duke had intended, but the rooms were comfortable and functional.
One wing of the catacombs housed Robin's extensive collection of historic weapons.
Another section had become his garage. Originally intended as stables, they had been built to accommodate the grand and very large carriages

common in the Dukeries. So, the room and access tunnels were plenty big enough for Robin's collection of cars and motorbikes.

"Wow", exclaimed John. "How have you kept all this hidden?"
"Practice", replied Robin. "Hiding is what we do, isn't it", referring to their military life in the Outlaws.
"So, what do you think?" continued Robin. "Will it do as a base to go after Motte?"
John agreed it would suit their purposes very well indeed. "But, we'll need more than just the two of us", suggested John.
Robin agreed they would need help to fight the Tax Collector's huge empire. "But who could we trust?" asked Robin.
"Tuck is home on leave with his family", replied John.

Francis Friar was a childhood friend of Robin's. His parents had both worked on the Loxley estate, his father as a gamekeeper and his mother as a cook in the Hall. Now retired, his parents lived in one of the houses owned by the estate in Sheffield's Loxley Village.
Friar had followed his mum's vocation as a cook, earning him the nick name of Tuck. He had followed Robin into the army, then later into the Outlaws as a Sergeant and their unit cook.
"Excellent", replied Robin. "I can't think of a better ally and we will eat well too".
So, later that evening, Tuck joined his two comrades in passing through the wine cellar to the Loxley tunnels.

Over the next few days, the three of them set about the transformation of Robin's private museum into a war room and control centre.

They secretly moved in computers, communication systems and TV monitors. So adept were they at living covert lives that no one on the estate suspected they were doing anything other than enjoying some well earned leave.

Just as they had hoped, they also enjoyed some wonderful meals, prepared by Tuck in Robin's cottage kitchen.

Over dinner, John and Tuck started discussing how they could obtain a stock of weapons to use in their war against the Tax Collector.

There were several options open to them. The estate had a large stock of legally held shotguns and hunting rifles. The black market was a possibility. But the best option was to borrow from the local Territorial Army units.

But Robin had other thoughts, "Never", he exclaimed. "Not on the streets of our own country". Robin was firmly against using firearms on home ground. "These thugs might use guns, but we have more gentlemanly means", he said, referring to his huge collection of historic weapons.

"Off with his head", exclaimed Tuck, in a feigned royal accent. Like all of Robin's Outlaws, Tuck was deadly with most hand to hand weapons. He did not share Robin and John's passion for their history, but he agreed they should not lower themselves to the level of the gangsters they were going after.

Robin's next key job was to free himself up to work on Clive Motte. He had only returned from the Middle East on compassionate leave for his father's funeral. Any time soon, he and John would be expected to rejoin the Outlaws in spying on fanatical insurgents.

In the end, it was easier than Robin had expected. His team had not been rotated back to Britain in the last two years. Their Colonel was becoming worried about them burning out, so quickly agreed to a UK posting, training Special Forces candidates.

Even better for Robin's plans, he had been allowed to resurrect the disused Proteus Training Area, which sat within the Dukeries.

Now, Robin could remain within Nottinghamshire and the rest of his unit would soon be traveling to join him.

Chapter 4.

Crash, crash, crash, sounded the axes on the reinforced door.

Despite Robin's love of ancient weapons, these were modern tools, from his cottage's woodshed. He knew the crack house door would be reinforced against a police raid, so needed to quickly destroy the door and its frame.

The door had been designed to withstand the police mini battering ram, or Enforcer. But few of Nottingham's police were the size and strength of Robin and John.

Blow after blow, the two huge men rained on the door, until, with no structure left, the whole thing collapsed inward. Three men in hooded tops moved with purpose into the hallway.

The flat was a nondescript, privately rented flat in the Radford area to the north of the city centre. This was the home turf of the MPR, or Money, Power, Respect street gang.

The drug dealer they had interrogated in the Lace Market had given up its location. Robin had just needed a plan and some reinforcements to mount an assault.

The plan had been put together in the catacombs under Loxely Hall. Robin, John and Tuck had painstakingly prepared maps and satellite imagery of the estate and its surrounding area.

They supplemented the maps with live reconnaissance. All good soldiers know that time spent on recon is never wasted.

They had driven through, covertly photographing CCTV cameras and routes away from the flat. Before moving on the crack house, they knew every comer in the area and every route in from the area's two biggest police stations, along with logging the police response times.

They had a preferred plan, but they also had three other contingency plans to fall back on. The Outlaws wanted to achieve their objective, but most of all, they needed to get away.

Reinforcements had arrived in the form of one of Robin's most trusted Outlaws. Aside from his best friend John, Robin was closest to the Corporal who had risked his own life to save him in an almost suicidal mission in a Baghdad suburb.

Robin and Corporal Mitchell Miller had been working alone, trying to locate one of Sadam Hussain's many safe houses. The job had been rushed at the orders of military command. The intelligence had come in late and needed to be acted on quickly. The Outlaws were the only unit close enough to respond.

The assignment did not fit the mission profile of Robin's team and they were poorly equipped to work as regular infantry. But they were at heart soldiers and they headed out to follow their orders.

But the intelligence was poor and Sadam's Republican Guard was waiting for them.

Robin's small team was vastly outnumbered. Their infantry support had become pinned down by hostile fire. The Outlaws were left to beat an unplanned and unsupported retreat.

The American led coalition had airdropped them a

weapons package before they left for their mission, but it was nothing close to what Robin would like to have taken on such an assignment.

They carried only lightweight carbine rifles, had no body armour and only their own sabotage explosives. Even regular infantry would have been better equipped. If they had been acting as a standard Special Forces unit, they would have been provisioned above and beyond the usual infantry level.

In their covert role, they were actually less equipped than the insurgent Iraqi guerrilla forces, but they fought bravely, moving from cover to cover.

Robin took a protective lead. Feeling responsibility for his men, he took responsibility for providing covering fire as the unit moved position.

It was in one of these many moves that Robin became separated and pinned down by the Republican Guard.

Corporal Miller then did something that would earn him the lifelong gratitude and respect of his commanding officer.

Those who witnessed his actions described it as being like a cartoon. Miller ran from cover, zig zagging across the street. As each foot lifted from the road, a bullet sent a plume of dirt into the air. Every one of the shots could and should have hit Miller, but he continued to run like a cartoon coyote or Road Runner bird.

With the two of them to cover each other's moves, Robin and Miller were able to rejoin their team.

In any other circumstances, Miller would have been

a candidate for a Victoria Cross. None who saw him start his run believed he had any hope of reaching Robin. It was, they thought, a suicidal attempt. But somehow, he pulled it off.

But, the Outlaws knew when they volunteered that there would be no medals. Their very existence was covert; the British army could not afford the publicity of a medal ceremony.

In Robin's tightly knit team, the respect of each other meant far more than a medal. It was this trust in Miller that put him working with Robin and John on their crack house raid.

"Much", with me, shouted Robin, as John's final axe blow shattered the door.

Mitchell Miller's younger brother had difficulty pronouncing his name as Mitch, so like many childhood names, Much had stuck to him into adulthood.

Side by side, Much and Robin stormed into the flat, while the huge "Little" John prevented anyone from leaving.

The two Outlaws worked as one, side by side, their backs turned slightly towards each other, as they fought their way further into the flat.

First came the minor gang members, armed with knives. None came close to the Outlaws as they swung out with their own weapons, shattering bones and removing their ability to stand or fight.

Robin had picked the mace as his weapon of choice for the crack house raid. The blunt clubs with their heavy metal head on a wooden handle were ideal

for the close quarters of the flat.
The heads of the military maces that Robin collected were shaped with flanges or knobs to allow greater penetration of plate armour. But here, the flanges, like blunt blades, served a different purpose. Each blow splintered a bone on the advancing gangsters. With their arms and legs shattered, the fight soon drained away from the Outlaws' opponents.

The length of combat maces varied considerably. Robin and his team carried foot soldiers' maces which were always quite short, at about two or three feet long. The maces of cavalrymen were longer and better suited for blows delivered from horseback, but would have been useless in the tight corridors of the crack house.

Robin had maces in his collection dating back to ancient times. He had some genuine antiques, but these were mostly from the Middle Ages. He had many replicas made, either for practice, or because the originals were no longer available.
But Robin also collected ancient literature, in which the weapons that fascinated him were used. Maces featured in the ancient Indian epic Ramayana and a magical talking mace named Sharur appeared in the Sumerian myth of Ninurta.
Persians favoured maces for their heavily armoured cavalry. For a heavily armed Persian knight, a mace was as effective as a sword or battle axe.
Maces were very common in Eastern Europe, especially medieval Poland and Ukraine. Eastern European maces often had pear shaped heads. These type of maces were also used by the

Moldavian king Stephen the Great.

All the Outlaws had learned in military history classes, about the trench raiding clubs used during World War I. These were modern variations on the medieval mace. They were homemade mêlée weapons used by both the Allies and the Central Powers. Clubs were used during nighttime trench raiding expeditions as a quiet and effective way of killing or wounding enemy soldiers.

The mace chosen by Robin for today's raid was much closer to the weapon's roots in what is now Eastern Europe.
The Pernach is a flanged mace developed during the 12th century in the Eastern Slavic kingdom of Kievan Rus. It was later used widely throughout the whole of Europe. The name comes from the Slavic word pero meaning feather, because of the Pernach's resemblance to a fletched arrow.
It was the metal fletches which were doing so much damage to the gangsters' limbs.

One by one the gangsters fell to the heavy maces of Robin and Much. They knew the real players would have guns, but so far none had appeared.
Then, they finally fought their way to the door of the flat's main room. Here, they were met with a very different scenario to the youngsters they had so quickly neutralised.
Two much older, more confident men faced them. Both wore military surplus body armour, which looked completely out of place with their sportswear and gangster bling.

It was the guns that caught Robin's attention. One waved a rather old looking pistol at him. Robin quickly wrote this off as a fairly minor risk. The pistol's age and condition alone reduced the likelihood of it being a reliable and accurate weapon. But it was the gangster's stance which most amused Robin.

"Classic video game", thought Robin as he watched the man in front of him. He stood square on, as if to start a street brawl, rather than the steadier side profile of a trained marksman.

It was the way he held his pistol that amused Robin the most. Held in the stereotypical street gang style, he held his pistol sideways; at 90 degrees to the position it was designed to be fired from.

"Couldn't hit a bull's backside with a banjo", thought Robin, as he turned his attention to the other man. The second gangster looked by far the more serious of the two. He wore the same odd mix of gangster bling and combat body armour, but he oozed danger.

His stance was far more steady, his face controlled and menacing. The twin barrels of his sawn off shotgun pointed directly at Robin.

This man was Robin's target. His training and instincts triggered instantly as Robin leapt to the left, away from the front of the shotgun.

As he moved, Robin's arm circled high, his mace arcing like the sail of a windmill towards the gangster.

The heavy mace crashed down, destroying the gangster's collar bone.

The man's Kevlar armour covered his torso well, but

Robin's choice of weapon took account of this. The mace was primarily designed to tackle armoured adversaries. In most cases, a sword was more effective against an unprotected man, but their blades could rarely pierce armour. So maces were developed to do their damage through chain mail and armour plate.

As the blunt force of the heavy mace head crashed down on the gangster, the feather like flanges transferred that force through the Kevlar and into his collar bone.

Robin knew this was a particularly painful break, but it also had the advantage of rendering that arm useless. Robin now faced a one armed adversary.

Much saw that Robin had swung high, so he moved low to avoid their blows colliding. With his body stooped below the pistol's aim, Much swung his mace at the gangster's shins.

With no Kevlar protecting his legs, the lower leg collapsed under the shattered bone.

When the gangster fell to the floor, Much's second blow came swiftly down on the gangster's wrist. The arm sandwiched between the floor and the heavy mace head was also instantly destroyed.

Much cared nothing for the man's screams as he put plastic handcuffs onto the gangster's shattered wrist.

The older man was putting up more of a fight. With only one arm, he could not aim his shotgun. In fact, he could not even get off a shot, as he needed the gun to protect him from Robin's mace.

The man was good; he fended off most of Robin's blows. But those that did connect were causing him damage.

As each blow took its toll, the gangster became less steady on his feet. Then, once Much had secured his man, he helped Robin by duplicating the blow which had disabled his own adversary's legs.

With his shin bone destroyed, all of the gangster's fight left him and he collapsed to the floor.

The two Outlaws quickly secured him, with plastic handcuffs to his wrists and ankles, and duck tape over his eyes and mouth.

This man was coming with them. They had made too much noise to remain in the flat, but they needed information to plan their next attack on the Tax Collector's empire.

While Robin and Much finished securing the gangsters, Tuck brought in their anonymous looking van.

Carrying their prisoner by his shattered arms and legs, the Outlaws cared nothing for his pain. This was drug dealing scum, and not a sound would come from his taped over mouth.

Deep in the Dukeries, but far from the Loxley estate, the Outlaws worked on their prisoner.

Just like the dealer in the Lace Market, this man's shattered bones made interrogation easy. Any pressure on the broken areas caused excruciating pain.

Soon the gangster was telling Robin everything he knew about his gang's drug trade.

But, yet again, he was too small a fish to have any direct connection to Clive Motte.

Chapter 5.

For over half an hour the gunshots echoed through the air. The shots were coming so fast Robin imagined being back in the war zone, confronting rapid fire.

All around them lead fell like rain, making Robin glad of his wide brimmed leather hat that was protecting his face from the falling shot.

"You lot have too much money", observed Much. There was no correlation between the amount of shot being put into the air and the few game birds that were falling from the sky. Much knew how much the shotgun cartridges cost and he could guess at how many were fired.

"The regulars are better", replied Robin. "This is the estate's grace and favour day. Most of them have borrowed guns, then spent a fortune on country clobber to look the part".

Like many of England's country estates, Loxley made a significant income from its shoots. Syndicates of "guns" clubbed together to pay the exorbitant fees for a few days shooting each season.

The shoots gave welcome employment to country areas devoid of any real industry. A small battalion of full time game keepers bred the birds and managed the shooting grounds. Farm hands looked after the crops that provided cover for the birds to roost in. Then, on shooting days, a small army of part time beaters and dog handlers were hired for the day.

The grace and favour day was the estate's showcase to the world outside the Dukeries. The wealthy guests had all either been of benefit to the estate, or were being cultivated to do business with them.

Robin hated being among the estate's new regime, but as the new Duke of Loxley, his presence was expected.

Robin John and Tuck had been raised among the shooting and fishing of the Dukeries' estates. But, for Much Miller, this was a whole new world. He was used to seeing army officers' pomp and posturing, but the class of the landed gentry and the ostentatious wealth of the nouveau riche was something new to him.

He had been in culture shock since arriving at the farm on which the Loxley shoot was based.

"They look like Jeeves and Wooster", thought Much as he watched the gamekeepers going about their preparations. Whenever the estate was open to the public, they wore the estate's very distinctive uniform of country tweeds. Their suits had changed little in decades, with a very bold check to the jackets, waistcoats and knee length breeks.

Activity at the farm picked up in pace as the start of the shoot approached. The beaters, who would drive the game birds into the air, gathered around their trailer. Other estate workers gathered the plastic crates in which the birds would be collected for the game dealer.

"What?", asked Much. "They don't get to keep the birds they shoot?"

"No", replied Robin, explaining that the clients paid to shoot a set number of birds in the day, but the estate kept ownership of the birds. A local game dealer, with connections to the estate collected the 300 or so birds at the end of each day's shoot, to sell on to local butchers and some bigger prepared food manufacturers.

All of the shoot's staff seemed relaxed and happy in their work, but one group stood out among the rest. The dog handlers chatted among themselves, while their dogs played happily among their owners' 4x4 vehicles. The dogs' job was to collect the fallen birds and bring them back to their handlers. To this end, they used soft mouthed Labradors and Spaniels, who would not damage the birds they carried.

Like the estate workers, many of the dogs were related. A proud mum was reunited for the day with her litter of four Springer Spaniel pups. Coming from a strong line of working dogs, the owner had no difficulty in finding buyers among the shoot's dog handlers. Robin smiled as he watched them run and tumble about in the farm yard.

The beaters were first to leave the farm yard. For all the money and luxury around them, their day would be much less luxurious. They were dressed for walking through thick undergrowth and were quite obviously a different group of people to the Dukeries gentry and their wealthy clients. But they all enjoyed being paid to be part of country life, they would be fed well during the day and get to take home a couple of birds for the pot.

The beaters transport was less than luxurious too. Their large covered trailer was drawn behind a tractor. Outwardly the trailer was beautifully painted in the estate's livery. Inside, the beaters sat on rough wooden benches, protected by a mix of surplus cushions they had brought in from home. But their mood was high, they all knew each other and were being paid for a very sociable day out.

With the beaters on their way to the first game drive, the gamekeepers could turn their attention to the clients who had now started to arrive.
"A lot of expensive new kit", observed John.
The shooters, or guns, as they were known, were always smartly dressed. But the regulars always looked somehow different from the grace and favour crowd. The regulars were country people, who had developed their own style over many years.
Today's clients were a much more urban group, who had visited a country outfitter especially for today's event. They never quite suited the tweeds, checks and waxed cotton that had cost them so much money.

"Wow", said Much. "What's that?" The Loxley Estate's transport for the guns was something very impressive.
The huge military surplus 4x4 truck had undergone an extensive face lift since its former life.
The truck retained its rugged go anywhere appearance. But the guns were cosseted in an elegantly coach built passenger compartment.

Robin, John, Much and Tuck did not ride with the guns, as every seat was full for this rare opportunity to mix with the gentry.

Robin drove one of a small number of vehicles that came with his inherited title. The Duke of Loxley's fleet comprised a Bentley, a Jaguar and the Landrover he drove today.

All three vehicles were now quite old, but had been beautifully cared for by the estate staff. Robin knew the mechanic's and valet's attention would cease with the passing of the estate to Helen Loxley. But Robin was well used to maintaining his own collection of vehicles, hidden away in the tunnels beneath the estate.

His Landrover followed the estate's huge truck, out of the farm yard and into an unmade lane.

They were on their way to the opposite end of the drive that the beaters had already reached.

"Up, up up", came the shout of the beaters as they moved into the crop. Several of them waved plastic flags, making yet more noise to drive the birds into the air.

Robin and his Outlaws joined in with the seemingly endless volleys of shot rising into the airborne flock.

Robin in particular was bringing down a huge amount of birds. He was far less wasteful with his shot, each discharge of his gun bringing down a bird, precisely where Robin wanted it to fall.

Robin's rate of fire was doubled, as he had hired one of the regular beaters to act as his loader. He used a pair of double barrelled shot guns, bringing down two birds, while his other gun was being reloaded for him.

When the shooting ceased and the dogs started running out to the fallen birds, Robin saw a familiar figure walking towards him.

"Coming to gloat?", thought Robin, as the man he currently despised most in the world headed across the field.

"Nice guns", said Clive Motte, as he reached Robin's side. "Purdeys", he added, "and quite old too, if I'm not mistaken".

Motte was not mistaken. Robin's love of historic weapons extended to his shotguns. The matched pair of antique guns were from what is arguably the world's finest gunmaker.

Motte's next words were shut out by Robin remembering some of the history of the famous London gunsmith.

James Purdey & Sons have been making the finest quality guns in London, since 1814, when James Purdey the Elder opened in a small shop off Leicester Square.

In 1831 Charles Darwin paid a visit, ordering guns and supplies for the voyage of HMS Beagle.

Queen Victoria ordered her first Purdeys in 1838: a pair of pistols, as a royal gift to the Imam of Muscat. Her eldest son the Prince of Wales, later King Edward VII, granted his Royal Warrant to the founder's son, James Purdey the Younger, in 1868. Each succeeding monarch since than has placed their faith in Purdey's, including our present Queen. Before long, Purdey moved into Audley House, a specially built property in Mayfair. Its famed Long Room, originally built as a working office, is today revered in the game-gun community.

Every Purdey 'Best' gun is handmade in London.

Purdey's stockers, actioners and engravers still hand-craft their own tools at the beginning of their apprenticeship, before using those tools to create the world's finest guns.

Looking down into a 'well' in the Long Room, James Purdey the Younger could follow the progress of the craftsmen below. Robin had seen photographs of the time, where piles of wooden 'blanks' could be seen alongside it, waiting to be turned.

Robin, along with the greatest shots of the past two centuries had visited the Long Room, and seen his predecessors immortalised in portraits and memorabilia.

Although Robin favoured the antique guns for public display. He also owned several Purdey's which were hand crafted for him.

One of the joys his Purdeys brought him was the knowledge that, from the very first fitting, every element of the gun was made entirely for him. When Robin placed his order he started a process of hand-crafting that took two years to complete.

To properly understand his requirements, the gunsmiths took Robin to the West London Shooting Ground where they have been fitting their customers since the 1930s. There, he was fitted with a 'try-gun', and spent time shooting as they took his stock dimensions. The try-gun has an articulated and fully adjustable stock, allowing fine alterations to be made by the instructor, in order to achieve the perfect fit.

Then, back at Audley House, Robin was able to select the walnut stock blank for his gun.

Robin knew that many of today's guests had bought a Purdey. But most would not have allowed the time to be properly fitted at the Shooting Ground. These wannabes would have opted to have their stock dimensions taken in the Long Room at Audley House, with an electric try-gun originally devised to aid the convalescence of King George V.

Coming back into the real world, Robin registered what Motte had asked him. "Sorry, yes they are quite old".
One of the things that helped Purdeys retain their value was the company's meticulous record keeping and the craftsmen's habit of engraving each section of their work.
The ledgers contain all the intricate measurements taken from the customer. They also list every change of owner, who registered the transaction with them, providing an unbroken line of provenance for many of their most historic guns.

The very earliest ledgers are now lost. But from 1818 onward Purdey have a complete record of the daily transactions of the firm. These include James Purdey's comments on customers who failed to honour their debts, noted alongside the main entry as 'BAD' in a fine copperplate script.
But the line of provenance for Robin's guns did not lead to a bad debtor. They were made for one of Purdey's best customers.
This was the original matched pair of guns which Queen Victoria's son, who became King Edward VI, ordered in 1868, leading to Purdey's first Royal Warrant.

Robin delighted in telling Motte the history of his guns. It seemed that the Tax Collector was well on the way to seizing the trappings of his family history, but he would never have their class or tradition. The Loxley's enjoyed a close relationship with the Windsors and the Saxe-Coburg Gothas, as they were called before George V changed the Royal Family's name after World War I. It was this friendship that had secured Robin his prized pair of guns. Wealthy as Motte had become, some things would still elude him.

Robin tried to goad Motte further, by asking about the drug related beatings which dominated the news.

"Nothing to do with me Robin", replied Motte. "I'm an honest business man".

"Like hell", thought Robin. But he could not help but be impressed by Motte's calm way of dealing with Robin's veiled accusation.

"In fact", added Motte. "I'm thinking of diversifying into casinos. Maybe I can win those fancy guns from you".

While Robin and Motte sparred with each other, John Little guided Tuck and Much away. He could tell that their loyalty to their Captain was ready to boil over. The last thing Robin would want was a scene on his family estate, in sight of all their guests.

The yelping of one of the dogs drew Robin away. Motte seemed not to notice the distressed animal, but Robin had grown up around them.

He saw that one of the spaniels had become caught in some bailing twine attached to the hedge.

Robin ran towards the dog, overtaking the estate workers as he put his special forces training into practice.

He already had out his knife as he reached the hedge. The knife had been a present from his mother and he knew the animal loving Duchess would approve of the use it was now getting.

Like Robin's guns, his knife was far from ordinary. It came from the same gunsmiths as his shotguns. Robin's mum had accompanied him to London when he collected his custom made guns. She had taken the opportunity to quietly buy Robin a present.

Purdey knives range in price from £250 to £500, with a choice of bone or wooden handles. But, for the limited edition of eight Sentinel Knives, the price rose to £900.

Just like the rest of their range, the blades have the unusual pattern formed in the Firestorm Damascus Steel, which is as individual as a fingerprint.

But most incredible of all, are the limited edition handles crafted from the tusks of a prehistoric woolly mammoth.

The discovery was made in northern Russia, where the mammoth was recovered from the permafrost. This impressive, long-extinct creature would have roamed the tundra 10,000 years in the past.

The handle is made from the outer edges of the Woolly Mammoth Tusk known as the Crust, recovered from the permafrost in Northern Russia. The mammoth tusk handles are fixed to the blade using nickel silver bolts. The hand sewn sheath is made from vegetable tanned leather and moulded to ensure a perfect fit.

With the dog free, Robin knew that his presence at the shoot had been well noted by all those attending and he had done his duty to the family. So, when they moved to the next drive, Robin's Landrover slipped quietly away from the convoy.

Chapter 6.

Bicycles cut in and out of Nottingham's estates and alleyways. Some were just kids having fun, but many were an integral part of the city's drug trade. This was how the youngsters first entered the gangs. Speed on their bikes and knowledge of the cut throughs kept their deadly product flowing through the city's estates. Using the kids to make their deliveries also kept the more senior gangsters removed from risk of capture.

They started them young too, the ruthless dealers knew that 10 was the cut off for doli incapax, or criminal responsibility. The eight and nine year olds at the bottom of the food chain could not be prosecuted. If caught, they would spend some time with a social worker, but would very soon be back making their deliveries.

Robin had never been a father, but he could not tolerate kids being drawn into the drug trade so early. This was to be the focus of the Outlaw's next hit on the Tax Collector's income.

Much of their information had been persuaded out of the dealers they had already encountered. Like all good military units, the Outlaws had supplemented this with their own surveillance. They now knew where most of the drug houses were, so it had just been a matter of watching where the bicycles went when they left to make their deliveries.

Robin and John both used cycles for exercise, but Much was far more interested in the sport for its own right. He noticed how the quality and value of the cycles fluctuated among the kids. You could tell how successful, and thus how experienced, the kids were, by looking at their bikes. Most favoured small wheeled BMX bikes, rather than the mountain bikes the Outlaws rode in the Dukeries. But despite the apparent simplicity of the bikes, a hierarchy could be seen if you knew what to look for.

The bottom end was obvious, the youngest of the street kids had the tattyest old bikes you could imagine. Held together with black tape and zip ties, most had no brakes, causing the rider to use his shoe on the back tyre to stop.

Once they had some money behind them, the kids soon upgraded to flashier models. Then, with each pay day, came more bling and accessories for the bikes.

"They won't be easy to catch", counselled Much. "The BMX bikes wouldn't be my choice, but they spend all day on them and they know the area too". During their surveillance, they had seen how quickly the kids made their way through the city estates. They always seemed one step ahead of both the competition and the police.

But Robin had a plan, one that involved an intense period of training for his Outlaws.

All four were very fit cyclists. But even Much, who had the highest skill level had to work hard mastering the technique Robin wanted to use.

Again and again they fell to the ground. They were trying to master controlling their bikes without the handlebars, keeping their hands free for Robin's weapon of choice.

With each fall they bounced back and practiced harder, gradually increasing their speed and manoeuvrability. The Outlaws knew the falls were much softer in the fallen leaves of the Dukeries than it would be in the city estates. There, would be concrete surfaces, kerb stones and cars to manoeuvre around. A fall on the operation could also lead to facing the knives and guns of the local gangs.

They needed to become flawless in their bike control, while maintaining velodrome levels of speed and acceleration.

Eventually, the day came that Robin was confident in his team's ability to execute the plan. Without hands, the four friends could race each other, slalom style, through the trees. Then, flawlessly hit their targets every time.

Dressed in their almost trademark hoodies, the four Outlaws rode into the Meadows area on Nottingham's southern edge. Robin's mind was drifting to Patagonia, but aside from the wind whipping across the flood plain, no one else would have grasped the connection.

Bordering the River Trent, the Meadows had always played some part in the city's flood defences. Initially just as a large flood plain, the Victorians added an ornate embankment in 1901.

Beyond the embankment lay Victorian terraced housing. This was built for the railway and factory workers of twentieth century Nottingham. But now, thanks to the nearby river and National Watersports Centre, houses many of Britain's brightest paddle sport stars.

But, it was the area beyond the remaining Victoriana that interested the Outlaws.

Like many inner cities of the1970s, housing in the Meadows was deemed unsuitable by the council and large parts were demolished to make way for a new development of modern council housing. This was an approach common to many local authorities at the time, which saw the dispersal of often tight knit communities and replacement with public housing projects of variable longevity. The new development was based on the modern model of planning which involved segregating traffic and pedestrians by constructing cul-de-sacs, feeder roads and underpasses.

This was where Robin knew that he needed cycling skills to combat the young drug couriers' mastery of their environment.

The grey concrete of the Meadows' underpasses was a far cry from the granite and basalt screes of Patagonia. But as the Outlaws rode into the paths and tunnels, Robin could not help imagining they were the Tehuelches Indians who once inhabited the southernmost tip of Chile and Argentina.

Steadily they crisscrossed the estate, on the hunt for the first of the young drug couriers. The kids were all over the estate, showing off their bike handling skills, hopping on and off the kerb, bouncing on one wheel, riding the concrete benches and performing a range of other tricks.

Robin's surveillance had shown that the kids' behaviour changed markedly when there was a delivery to be made. Fired with adrenalin, they became singularly focused on their job of exchanging drugs for cash and getting the cash back to their dealer.

Whatever they were doing, the kids showed immense skill with their bikes. But it was their focus that was the tell tale for Robin. Rather than the playful arrogance in showing off their skills, when making a delivery, they became like professional racers. Nothing stood in their way, their small legs pounded immense amounts of energy into the pedals. They were fearless in the way they took the corners and rode high on the underpass walls.

Then, after seemingly endless patrols of the estate, the hooded Outlaws spotted their first mark. The young boy leapt from the roof of the underpass, landing expertly on his back wheel, before speeding off into the network of paths leading deeper into the estate.

"Now", shouted Robin, as the four friends starburst into the formation they had practiced so hard.

With Tuck and Much racing ahead of the youngster, Robin and John settled into a rhythm behind him. Reaching into the pocket of his hoodie, Robin prepared the reason for his hard training, and for his dreams of Patagonia.

Robin's weapon of choice for this mission had been the Bolas, a South American weapon, whose name came from the Spanish bola, or ball.

The bolas is a type of throwing weapon made of weights on the ends of interconnected cords, designed to capture animals by entangling their legs.

They were most famously used by the gauchos, or Argentinean cowboys.

But it was the much earlier versions of the weapon that most interested Robin.
Early examples had been found in excavations of Pre-Columbian settlements, especially in Patagonia, where indigenous peoples used them to catch the 200-pound llama-like guanaco and huge ñandú birds.

There is no uniform design; most bolas have two or three balls, but there are versions of up to eight or nine. Some bolas have balls of equal weight, others vary the knot and cord. Gauchos use bolas made of braided leather cords with wooden balls or small leather sacks full of stones at the ends of the cords to capture running cattle or game. The thrower grasps the bolas by the nexus of the cords. He gives the balls momentum by swinging them and then releases the bolas. The weapon is usually used to entangle the animal's legs, but when thrown with enough force might even break a bone.

Robin favoured a more ancient technique than the one adopted by the Gauchos.
Whether they were using two or three weights, when working from the ground, the Argentinean cowboys held tight to the cord, while swinging the weights together.
But the pre Columbian Patagonian Indians used a different technique from horse back. They held one of the weights, while swinging the other two. This technique needed more space to execute than the modern variation, and the speed and range was reduced because the two moving weights had to transfer their energy to the weight which was held.

These disadvantages were less important from horse back, where the extra stability of the throw was more important.

So it was for Robin and his Outlaws. They were working from the moving platforms of their mountain bikes, and the old ways suited them best.

While Tuck and Much kept the boy central to the path, Robin started his swing.

Expertly controlling the mountain bike with his thighs and body weight, Robin began to put momentum into his bolas.

The trick was to put enough energy into the swing to propel the weapon, but not to send it into an uncontrollable windmill motion.

Once, twice, then away. Robin put two big rotations into his swing, then let go.

Robin's Bolas had three weights, designed with two shorter cords attached to heavier weights, and one longer cord with a light weight. The heavier weights fly at the front parallel to each other, to hit either side of the legs, and the lighter weight goes around, wrapping up the legs.

This technique worked perfectly with the BMX bike. The first cords going either side of the bike, then the following cord encircled the boy, fetching him from his bike.

"Gotcha'" exclaimed Robin, as the boy hit the floor. Quickly, they moved into the next phase of their plan, which involved the local school.

Like many inner city schools, this one was fortified like a prison, with high metal fences. On one of their earlier surveillance trips, the Outlaws had loosened some of the bolts, allowing them easy access into the school grounds.

Inside were two things that interested Robin. First was a bank of cycle lockers, in which the students could safely secure their bikes. Robin was going to secure the couriers' bikes in them, along with their drugs, to await collection by the police. Any cash would, as usual, be retained and handed over to charity by the Outlaws.

There were other pieces of school equipment that appealed to Robin's sense of irony.

Part of his justification for this particular operation had been a sense that the drug dealers were robbing the kids of their childhood.

"Time this kid learned about playtime", said Robin, as he dragged the kid across the school yard.

Outdoor gyms had become popular in parks and school playing areas. The Meadows School had also been equipped with the heavy duty, exercise bikes, ski machines, sit up benches and other robust pieces of gym equipment.

Robin took the boy to the ski machine, and then deftly used a roll of Duck Tape to secure him to the machine. With both feet and hands fixed firmly to the machine, and more tape around his mouth, the kid could go nowhere.

The more frustrated the kid got, the harder he fought against his bonds. But all that happened was his struggles put motion into the ski machine.

"Keep skiing kid", said Robin, as they walked away.

Back on patrol, the Outlaws had their eye in for spotting the young couriers at work.

Again and again the bolas swung. With each kid brought down by the weighted cords, Robin's exercise class grew.

All the young boys were fighting hard against the tape holding them on their machine. But this just gave the impression of a competitive bunch of kids playing together.

Before long, the machines were full of furiously exercising boys, and the lockers were full of bikes and small bags of drugs.

An anonymous call brought the police to the school yard, where they found enough evidence to disrupt a small part of the estate's drug trade.

True to form, the police were just as interested in who had fastened the boys there, as they were in their illegal activities.

What few witnesses would come forward, described four hooded men on mountain bikes.

The press had arrived, drawn in by the police activity at the school. The journalists too were beginning to register the regular sightings of hooded men around the growing number of drug take downs.

"Is this a war?" asked the reporter, towards his cameraman. "Or, does Nottingham have a group of vigilantes?"

This reporter was the first to realise there was an orchestrated campaign being fought against the city's drug trade. But he had no way of knowing if it was a rival gang moving into new territory, or if the city's residents were starting to fight back.

Robin and his Outlaws knew the truth was slightly more complicated. But they were not about to help anyone, press or police, with their enquiries.

The next morning, the school received an anonymous envelope of cash in the post. There was no note and no indication where it had come from. Although the cash taken from the kids were quite small amounts, taken together it made a reasonable contribution to school funds. Robin hoped it would help compensate for any disruption the police CSI teams caused to the school.

Chapter 7.

John had never seen such anger on Robin's face before. He knew the phone call was from the Loxley family solicitor, so guessed their conversation had something to do with Loxley Hall.
Robin said very little, but a great deal of information was obviously flowing from the solicitor. It was clear that Robin was very unhappy with what he was being told.

As Robin put down the phone and turned towards his friend, the anger seemed to drain away, to be replaced by a flat sadness.
"Motte has the Hall", said Robin.
Sheriff Leisure had foreclosed on their mortgage and Clive Motte was planning to move into Loxley Hall.
The legalities of the Loxley Estate were complex. Although Motte now owned the Hall itself, the estate as a whole was held in a complicated family trust. Along with his step-mother and a number of family members, Robin still had a seat on the board of trustees. The trust controlled the estate's tied housing, the shooting rights and most importantly to Robin, use of the Loxley name.
This was how the solicitor had been able to brief Robin on what would normally be protected by solicitor / client privilege.

"He's applied for a casino licence too", added Robin. The solicitor had explained the procedure for objecting to the application. But, with nearby Thoresby Hall having been allowed to go down the hotel and leisure route, the Loxley Hall application was likely to succeed.

And succeed it did, at a pace that suggested to Robin that Motte had been greasing palms to speed it through.

Barely had the ink dried on the licence, than Motte had builders in converting Loxley Hall's ornate banqueting hall into his casino.

When opening night arrived, Robin was left with no choice than to attend the opening.

Much as Robin despised both Motte and gambling, it was expected of the Duke to attend any major event on the Loxley Estate.

Robin had no difficulty in securing invitations for John, Tuck and Much. Despite the animosity between them, Motte was clever enough to know he had to carefully navigate his way around the aristocratic traditions of the Dukeries.

As well as keeping up appearances, Robin wanted his team there to assess the increased security. It stood to reason that a casino would need much greater security than a family home. Should the Outlaws need to take action at the Hall, then their surveillance would be vital.

Given the large amounts of currency handled within a casino, both patrons and staff may be tempted to cheat and steal. Most casinos have security measures to prevent this. Security cameras located throughout the casino are the most basic measure. It took Robin a matter of minutes to locate all the overt cameras, and a great many of the supposedly hidden ones too.

Like most modern casinos, Motte's security was divided between a physical security force and a specialized surveillance department. The physical security team, drawn from the doormen at his many nightclubs, patrolled the casino and responded to calls for assistance and reports of suspicious or definite criminal activity.

Motte had also recruited specialised surveillance staff to operate the casino's closed circuit television system, known in the industry as the eye in the sky. Both of these casino security departments worked very closely with each other to ensure the safety of both guests and the casino's assets.

Motte had also built catwalks into the ceiling above the casino floor, which allowed his surveillance personnel to look directly down, through one way glass, on the activities at the tables and slot machines. Robin had researched casino design and this could be the only reason to lower the banqueting hall's ornate ceiling with a false glass ceiling.

"He's really gone to town", thought Robin. "If we ever have to move on the Tax Collector here, it will take a lot of planning.

Soldiering involved a lot of down time and Robin's Outlaws were used extensively by the British Army and their NATO allies. Their training regimes were intense and regular, to keep them capable of their dangerous work. But, it was a fact of human physiology that the soldiers needed down time for their bodies and minds to recover.

Like many soldiers, Robin's team enjoyed a great

many DVD movies while they rested and recuperated between missions.

A particular favourite of Robin's had been Martin Scorsese's 1995 thriller,
Casino, starring Robert De Niro, Joe Pesci, and Sharon Stone.
Although fictional, the movie was based on the non-fiction book Casino: Love and Honor in Las Vegas.

In Casino, De Niro stars as Sam "Ace" Rothstein, a gambling handicapper who is called by the Italian Mob to oversee operations at the Mob's Las Vegas casino. His character is based on Frank Rosenthal, who ran the Stardust, Fremont, and Hacienda casinos in Las Vegas for the Chicago Outfit from the 1970s until the early 1980s. Robin could see a little of Motte in De Niro's character.
There were many of Motte's heavies with similarities to Pesci's character. Nicholas "Nicky" Santoro, was based on real-life Mob enforcer Anthony Spilotro, a made man. Nicky was sent to Vegas to make sure that money from the casino was skimmed off the top before declaring to the tax assessors and the mobsters in Vegas were kept in line.
But it was Sharon Stone's character that gave Robin the greatest cause to smile. He saw much of his step-mother Helen Loxley, in Stone's Ginger McKenna. She played Ace's scheming, self-absorbed wife, based on the real life Geri McGee.

Robin watched his late father's trophy wife circulating around the gambling tables. She seemed a natural at convincing the male gamblers to risk ever bigger piles of chips at the tables.

Scheming and self-absorbed was a description that fitted Helen Loxley well. But it was the irony of Helen's cocaine habit which amused Robin the most. Ultimately, it had been Ginger McKenna's drug use which had proven her undoing. Ginger fled to Los Angeles and ultimately died penniless of a drug overdose in a motel.

Robin hoped such a drastic fall from grace might also become true for his step-mother.

In Casino, the FBI moved in and the casino empire crumbled.

But Robin knew that without a great deal of evidence, the British police would not move against Motte.

He had long ago legitimised all the parts of his business that touched him. Much of the money skimmed in tax from Nottinghamshire's drug dealers would be laundered through Motte's casino. But Robin would have to work very hard to build anything the police could act on.

Robin had equipped his Outlaws with chips bought with his trust fund, so they could circulate among the tables.

But they did not waste their chips. Each choice of table gave them a different view of the casino. Playing slowly and carefully, close to the table minimums, they could watch how the cash flowed around the casino and learn the routines of the security.

Robbing Motte in the home he had taken from Robin was an attractive target, but it was one that seemed impossible.

Each time one of the Outlaws thought he had spotted a weakness, one of the others saw how it was covered.

The big problem was the overhead gallery. Robin knew the Hall, along with some of its secrets unknown to Motte.

He also knew that once out of the Hall, no one could stop them, as Robin's knowledge of the estate and the wider Dukeries was extensive.

John was at the roulette table when Helen Loxley walked over to him.

"Little John", said Helen, using the nickname the old Duke had given Robin's huge friend.

"I never expected to see you back inside Loxley Hall, but it's a very pleasant surprise".

"I can't believe she's actually flirting with me", thought John.

"Where Robin needs a friend, you will usually find me", replied John. "But I don't get called Little John very often these days", he added.

Helen continued trying to charm the huge soldier. But, although polite, John remained on task, steadily placing bets and watching the activities of the casino staff.

Eventually Helen began to realise that her charms were not working on John, and she turned her attention to Robin.

Robin spotted her approaching in his peripheral vision, but did not give her the satisfaction of acknowledging her approach. He could see that she was using her best cat walk strut, which was getting the attention of many of the gamblers.

But attractive as Helen Loxley was, Robin knew what lay beneath the surface and it was not pretty at all.

"Have you a hug for your mum", asked Helen. Robin's reply was delivered with a smile which did not match the venom of his words. "I think not Helen. I have very fond memories of my mum, and I'm afraid Dad's widow really can't come close to her".

Helen was not used to men being cold towards her, so it came as something of a shock.

But she very quickly regained her composure, leaving Robin with "I'm a trustee Robin. You are going to have to work with me for the good of the estate".

Despite her bimbo appearance, Robin knew there was something clever and calculating beneath the surface.

"I'm going to have to watch her closely", thought Robin, as Helen walked over to another gaming table.

As more junior NCOs, Much and Tuck did not have quite the same bearing as their Major and Sergeant Major. They both looked slightly out of comfort in their dinner jackets and bow ties, in the same way that many of the security staff did.

Both were much happier in the less formal surroundings of the Seniors' Mess at camp, while Robin and John spent their time in the pomp of the Officers' Mess.

But, despite their discomfort with the formalities, they were both superb soldiers. Between them they never missed a move of the guards or the cameras.

Of particular interest to them was the cashiers counter. In keeping with modern designs, the counter did not use any sort of bars or screen. The smiling cashiers accepted the money from the customers across an open bar counter, counting out chips from ornate racks on the counter top.
Much and Tuck knew the chips had no value outside the casino. Guards watched the racks, but only so that the gamblers could not sneak a few extra chips or the staff could not collude with the customers.
It was the cash that interested the Outlaws. They knew that Motte's primary motivator was greed. For them to hurt Motte, it needed to be in his wallet.
Cash went into fairly standard looking cash drawers, fixed below the counters.
Security guards stood behind and either side of the caches and a bank of CCTV cameras watched their every move.
The Outlaws watched carefully each time the full cash drawers were moved out of the cashiers counter. With the door open, Robin could work out how Motte had built the security area behind the counter.

What really caught Robin's eye were the many posters advertising Goliath.
Motte had convinced Grosvenor Casinos to bring Loxley Hall into their giant poker event called the Goliath. Designed to attract up to 1,500 players, the Goliath had an initial buy-in at £120 and offered a guaranteed prize pool of £100,000, with 25% of the registration fee going to the Marie Curie Cancer

Care charity.

The event grew year on year, with the 2014 Goliath event becoming the largest poker tournament ever held outside of the USA with a total of 3,394 players entering.

For this year's event the posters predicted over 4,000 participants would enter.

"I think the charity deserves more than 25%, don't you?", asked Robin.

John provided a voice of reason, "I don't know Robin, security is very tight".

The longer they watched, the more their opinions swayed. Publicly robbing Motte's new casino would cause huge damage to his reputation and his business. But it would be the most risky operation they had ever conducted. Security looked excellent and it was much too close to home.

Robin wanted badly to pull it off, but he was realistic enough to know they needed much better intelligence and very careful planning.

"It won't be something we put together in a hurry", concluded Robin.

As the Outlaws left Loxley Hall, Robin's thoughts drifted to the end of Scorsese's film, hoping that it might foretell Motte's future.

With the mob out of power, the old casinos were demolished and purchased by big corporations, who built new and gaudier attractions, which De Niro lamented were not the same as when the mafia were in control.

Sam Rothstein subsequently retired to San Diego and continued to live as a sports handicapper for the mob, in his own words, ending up "right back where I started".

Walking out of the front doors, Robin could not help but say "and that's that", echoing the words De Niro used to close the film.

Chapter 8.

This time, the Outlaws were going into battle without their hooded tops.
The four friends needed to blend in, not just be anonymous. The hoods disguised their identities, but would make them more obvious than sore thumbs in Nottingham's Lace Market night life.

Often, when operating overseas, the Outlaws needed to alter their appearance, so they had all developed some proficiency in make up.
As they walked into club land, hair pieces gave their hair a different style and colour. False beards disguised their features, while fitting with the fashion for young men at the time.
Their clothes had been specially chosen to meet the clubs' strict dress code, while allowing them the freedom of movement needed for the expected fight.

Bar Sheriff was a long way off being the biggest of Clive Motte's clubs, but he considered it the flagship of his portfolio.
The bigger venues were profitable on size and attendance. But this boutique venue was much more exclusive. Its 200 person capacity would not be profitable under any of Motte's usual business plans. But here, the cost of admission and the expensive drinks kept the clientele very exclusive.
Bar Sheriff was the place to be for footballers, the leaders of Nottingham's gangs and any of the city's wannabes.
It was the gang leaders that Robin wanted to target. Motte's security kept drugs out of his favourite

venue, but it was obvious that much of the cash spent in the club was drug money.

Here, on their own turf, the gangsters would take any hostility very personally.

Security was much more evident than for other clubs of a comparable size. Motte used the cream of his Door Supervisors and spared nothing in the numbers on duty there.

The Outlaws were silently evaluating the doormen as they approached the door. In keeping with its Hollywood image, a red carpet and red silken ropes guided their way to the entrance. But, unlike Hollywood, there was no guest list. In Nottingham, ability to pay the exorbitant entrance fee was considered recommendation enough.

With Robin's trust fund behind them, money was seldom a problem for the Outlaws.

Leaders from four of the city's main gangs could regularly be found in Bar Sheriff.

Ordinarily, if these gangs were together, there would be tensions, caused by their constant demand for "respect".

But here, under the gaze of the Tax Collector's security they kept an uneasy truce.

The Brewsters Road Crew and the Certified Marmion Gang or CMG from St Ann's, rubbed shoulders with the Meadows Estate's Waterfront Gang and Radford's MPR, or Money Power Respect Gang.

These were not the kids who the Outlaws encountered cycling through the Meadows. Neither were they the lieutenants who ran the Radford drugs den. The gangsters in Bar Sheriff were another level entirely. Here were the men of violence who had fought and intimidated their way to the top of their estates' hierarchy, along with their minders and entourage.

If Robin's plan worked, the delicate truce between the gangsters would soon be a thing of the past.

The Outlaws passed easily through the club's security. A handful of cash spoke volumes at Bar Sheriff.

It also helped that their faces were not known. Anyone of significance in the drug world was known to Motte's key people. The fact that Robin and his friends were not recognised just put them in the rich wannabe category, possibly with their athletic builds; they could be sportsmen on a night out.

The big risk was the metal detector arch built into the club's entrance. Robin knew the weapons they carried would not trigger the alarm, but he could not be sure that it would not be supplemented by a random pat down.

As it was, their relaxed easy manner saw them swiftly through security and into the opulent club.

Inside the club, the Outlaws mingled among the clubbers. The atmosphere was strange; this was a place to be seen, not necessarily a place to relax in. The four drug gangs had adopted opposite corners of the club as their turf. Rarely did they stray to each other's corner. But the wannabes moved constantly around the club, desperately trying to bask in the gangsters' notoriety.

This allowed the Outlaws to mingle freely around the

four corners. The real players paid no attention to anyone outside their own entourage. But they liked the attention from outsiders, in Robin's case, mistaking his interest for the respect that the gangsters craved.

Then, there was movement among the gangs that Robin hoped might provide the catalyst to start his plan. The leaders of MPR and Waterfront gangs moved to a booth in a neutral area of the club. Surrounded by minders and hang arounds from both gangs, the leaders clearly had some business to discuss.

One by one, the Outlaws drifted to the toilets, or shadowy areas of the club to assemble their weapons.

The choice for this operation had been a hard one. Everything inside the club would be at very close quarters. Add to that, the need in Robin's plan for them to act with stealth and they needed a weapon that was easily concealed and effective at close range. Then, Robin knew he had to consider a contingency that they might need to fight their way out of the Lace Market, so could need something suited to a melee.

The weapon Robin had chosen was the most used weapon across almost every culture and people, whether they were knights, tribal warriors or samurai, and for good reason.

It was the AK47 of medieval times. It was easy & cheap to manufacture, easy to maintain and simple to use. It was a good balance between weight, speed, handling and striking power. And when used correctly, it was just as deadly as a sword.

Robin had chosen the spear. When explaining his choice to the Outlaws, Robin used the example of the samurai.
Everyone has heard of the samurai, a warrior class who adhered to a strict code that dictated what they should do in and out of battle. Everyone believes their iconic weapon was the katana. Popular opinion considers the katana the very soul of a samurai.
But the katana did not gain its romantic legend among the Japanese until long after its bloodiest wars had been fought and won. It was only under the Tokugawa Shogunate, a time of relative peace and prosperity that the katana became the symbol of the samurai.
Before this the samurai's weapon of choice was not a katana but a spear. It was one of the fields of mastery on which a samurai was judged on his martial prowess.
Their katana were treated as a sidearm, and only used if they could no longer use spears.
With a spear, they were expected to be able to strike just as fast and kill as efficiently as if they were holding a sword or bow.

The weapons the Outlaws carried were no ordinary spears. They knew traditional weapons would not make it through Motte's strict security.
Any metal would set off the detectors, designed to find guns or knives.
No bags or bulky jackets were allowed past the reception area, to reduce the chances of smuggling in weapons or contraband.

So, Robin's spears were made especially for this task and were very different to the historic items in his collection.

The shafts, which split into two threaded sections, were made of a super strong nylon composite that was almost as hard as steel. They were completely undetectable when passing through metal detectors. The nylon composite was ideal for the shaft, and many manufacturers of covert knives also used it for the blade. But Robin needed something much sharper for the blades of his spears.

He settled on ceramic blades, the world's second hardest material, right after diamonds. After it has been sharpened, it will keep its razor sharp edge and will not wear out.

Ceramic material also had the advantage of being very light. The lighter the weight, the less strain you feel on your arms and shoulders. Any advantage when they were likely to be outnumbered had to be taken.

As the Outlaws started to move in, they saw that the gang leaders were well protected inside the booth, but their minders were spread around the outside of the booth in easy reach.

It helped that some of them were so overconfident, that they were barely performing their role of minder. Many of these posturing gangsters were so busy eying the opposition that they were hardly taking in anything happening around them.

One crucial thing that passed them by was the short, stocky Tuck moving in on them through the crowd. With Tuck's low centre of gravity it was a simple matter for him to put one of the MPR minders off balance. With the minder fighting for his balance, Tuck was able to send his drink flying towards a Waterfront minder standing nearby.

In the violent world of the drug gangs, disrespect cannot be tolerated, and despite Motte's security, the now soaked Waterfront member had to front up the MPR man and demand respect.
The two gangsters were nose to nose, desperately trying to find a way out of conflict in Motte's club. They were both terrified of the Tax Collector, but neither could be seen to lose face in front of so many gang members.
That was when Mutch moved in to help things along a little.
Mutch delicately threaded his spear through the crowd gathered around the two gangsters. Swiftly and firmly, he drew the ceramic blade of his spear across the MPR member's side.
Instantly blood spread across the gangster's white shirt. It was a superficial wound, but the expert soldier had placed it accurately to bleed heavily.

Mutch had withdrawn his spear and blended into the crowd before the gangsters saw the blood.
They jumped to the obvious conclusion, that the slighted Waterfront man had cut the man who thrown beer at him.

Motte's security started to move in, but tensions were now too great for the gangsters to acknowledge the door men's presence.
The club erupted into a sea of violence. Apart from

the Outlaws spears, there were no weapons inside Bar Sheriff. But Robin's plan was to make it appear that the gangsters had brought weapons into the Tax Collector's club.

As the fighting continued, the Outlaws expertly inserted their spears into the melee, cutting the gangsters.

The thrusting spear usually has the advantage of reach, being considerably longer than other weapon types. Exact spear lengths from ancient history are hard to deduce as few spear shafts survive archaeologically but 6 ft. to 8 ft seems to have been the norm. Robin kept his specially made spears to 3 ft long, to cope with the close confines of the night club.

This meant his Outlaws had to get in close, but it allowed the spears to be easily concealed.

As always with his historic weapons, Robin had meticulously researched the construction and use of his chosen weapon.

Despite the adrenaline fuelled fight, Robin's mind could not help drifting to his knowledge of the spear. In some way, it helped make him one with the weapon.

Robin knew the name came from the Old English spere, meaning pole.

They are divided into two broad categories: those designed for thrusting in melee combat, just as Robin and his team were now doing and those designed for throwing, which his composite spears were not designed for.

The spear has been used throughout human history both as a hunting tool and as a weapon. Along with the axe, knife and club it is one of the earliest and most important tools developed by early humans. It has been used in virtually every conflict up until the modern era, where even today it continues on in the form of the bayonet, with which the Outlaws were very proficient.

It amused Robin to know that the use of spears is not confined to human beings. It's use is also practiced by Chimpanzees in Senegal. They create spears by breaking straight limbs off trees, stripping them of their bark and side branches, and sharpening one end with their teeth. They then used the weapons to hunt galagos sleeping in hollows. Orangutans also use spears to fish, presumably after observing humans fishing in a similar manner.

Robin saw a line of gangsters line up, pushing at the opposing gang. To do this, they had their back leg stretched backwards, providing their Achilles tendons as a target. Robin did not waste the opportunity, with their exposed tendons cut, three of the gangsters fell quickly to the floor.

Robin had used the samurai to explain his choice of weapon to his Outlaws. But in his head, he identified more with the Zulu people of South Africa. They were known for their skill with short thrusting spears called iklwa. These spears were designed for close combat and often were wielded in conjunction with a large oval shield. Advanced skills in close combat allowed the Zulu military to conquer much of southeast Africa. Robin liked the underdog and it was easy for him to liken his small team's fight with that of the Zulu.

The melee seemed to last for ages, but in reality it was mere minutes before Motte's men composed themselves.
No weapons were allowed in Bar Sheriff, unless you were the Sheriff's men. They had a ready supply of baseball bats, which they now swung indiscriminately at the gangsters.
John's height made him an obvious target on the edge of the fight. The powerful man had to shrug off several blows across his back and shoulders.
The crowd of gangsters started moving as one towards the exit. As they moved with the crowd, Robin saw an opportunity to really annoy Motte's men.
At just the right moment, as one of the doormen moved close to the Waterfront boys, a ceramic spear tip drove deep into the bouncer's thigh. As he fell to the floor in pain, the other doormen made the obvious, but wrong, conclusion. They were sure the Waterfront Gang had stabbed one of their own men.

This had the effect that Robin expected. The violence offered by the doormen moved up several notches. No longer were they just trying to clear the club, they wanted blood.
Time after time, wooden bats fell onto gangsters' heads. The move towards the door became a stampede, in which the Outlaws allowed themselves to be pulled along.
By the time they reached the cobbled street outside,

their spears had been disassembled and returned to the pouches inside their clothing.

As the gangsters fought with each other and with the doormen, the Outlaws slipped quickly out of the Lace Market before the police could arrive.

"That should hurt the profits", said Robin as they walked out of the city.

"Can't be good for business, if you are looking over your shoulder", added John.

This was the first of their raids in which the Outlaws had not brought away some money for a charity. But the tensions they had put into the drugs market would cause much more damage to the Tax Collector's profits.

All in all, Robin and his team were very satisfied with their night's work.

Chapter 9.

The four guerrilla insurgents sat silently among the trees. They had been out before first light, preparing for their deadly mission.

All along the forest road, they had already laid their explosives. Some of their bombs could be triggered by mobile phones, while others were booby traps, set to explode when a vehicle passed by.

They had chosen their spot well. They were deep within the forest, where very few people ventured. But they were at a junction of tracks, which gave them a choice of escapes with their hidden 4x4.

In the silence of the forest the guerrillas listened for the earliest sounds of their prey. They already knew that the first rumblings would give them just over a mile in which to begin their attack.

Several miles away the convoy rolled out of the military base. The trucks contained the troops and supplies that would leave such a base every day on patrol. But there was also a VIP element to today's convoy, as the Defence Minister was visiting the troops.

The soldiers escorting the convoy expected that some time or another they would be tested and all hoped their training would prepare them.

Only the guerrillas knew exactly when and where the soldiers would be attacked. They too hoped the convoy's training would pass the test, as it was the guerrillas who had delivered the training.

"If they're on time, we've got about 40 minutes", said Robin.

"Everything's set", replied John. "There's only four of

us, but it should seem like there's many more".

The forest was part of the British Army's Proteus training camp, set deep within the Dukeries. Robin and his team had been using the area to train the local Territorial Army, or TA regiment ready for overseas deployment.
Today was the culmination of this phase of their training. The soldiers would put into practice the convoy protection duties that Robin and his team had trained them in.
Only this time they would not have their instructors along to guide them. Robin and his Outlaws were playing the role of insurgents, who would attack the convoy and put their students to the test.

Modern warfare has changed dramatically in recent years. In both World Wars, the Falklands, even Vietnam and Korea, our forces were fighting a defined, uniformed army. But in recent times the conflicts are often with disparate and not so clearly defined guerrilla forces.
Robin knew that protection of military convoys is a critical issue for military planners facing modern guerilla warfare threats.
The major concern has always been the security of the drivers and passengers, while maintaining the vehicle's mobility under attack. Along with advancements in arms or technology, this is achieved in part by adding armour to the cabin and engine compartment.
Robin had taught his students the additional measures, such as tactical driving and the active protection equipment, required when facing RPGs

and other weapon threats.

Where there are known high risk areas, convoys are usually secured by heavily armed escort vehicles. These vehicles are armored more heavily than the trucks, and will be the first to be equipped with active countermeasures, used to secure the platform as well as other vehicles from RPG attack. But, to suit his training scenario, Robin had not provided these specialist vehicles.

Although his convoy did not have the specially equipped escort vehicles, the troops did have some of the typical convoy protectors, such as acoustic firearms and sniper detection systems and stabilised remote operated weapon stations.
This integrated sensor-system can instantly return fire in the enemy direction, while on the move.
They were also equipped with electronic countermeasures, to jam radio-controlled improvised explosive devices, or IEDs. These jammers are designed to pre-activate IEDs, by mimicking the command signal, or disrupt the communications channel when the convoy passes nearby.
This equipment was fitted to much lighter armoured escort vehicles than a high risk convoy would usually require.

The convoy soldiers were monitoring for enemy activity along the road from the air, by unmanned vehicles.
The more famous tactical UAVs are tasked primarily with intelligence gathering and are rarely available for such missions; Robin had provided miniature

UAVs or, MAV to his students. These were a more robust version of the mini remote helicopters which have now become popular.

Using an on-the-move control system, the MAVs were operating as an advanced guard, securing an area ahead of the convoy lead element. Sensors employed by these MAVs are programmed to detect recent changes in the terrain indicating the existence of an IED or ambush on the roadside. The drones provide the capability of generating a video image in real-time to the convoy's command truck and to the event commander in his front command room.

The Outlaws had assisted in security for U.S President Obama's visit to Israel. Robin had drawn on some of their experiences in planning this training exercise, to add a VIP element to the test. The special preparations for the Obama convoy included concentric security circles. There, increased levels of security were allocated to each circle around the VIP.

Standard VIP protocol is for at least four vehicles to be on the move in the convoy. Robin's scenario exceeded this, as he also had lorries and troop carriers in the formation.

The lead and rear vehicles had electronic blocking devices installed to disrupt and block different types of transmissions for triggering IEDs.

The convoys include two VIP vehicles; both appear identical and will often even carry exactly the same license plate. Robin had also used this subterfuge; he and his Outlaws did not know which truck carried the VIP, so working out the right one formed part of

his ambush plan.
In Israel, they used a second identical convoy, departing on a different route but maintaining the same tight schedules. This is another deception and camouflage convoy, again using identical vehicles. But Robin would not face that challenge in his exercise, where only one convoy was in play.

"Contact", said Much, as he heard the first rumblings of the convoy.
Much's warning put the Outlaws on high alert. They knew what equipment and tactics were available to their students. They also knew the minimum number of vehicles needed for the transport objectives, and he also knew the maximum number that was available to the unit's officers. But how they put their convoy together was up to the unit's commanders. Robin's team needed to be vigilant, to gain information as quickly as they could.

Tuck had climbed one of the tallest trees and camouflaged himself into a lookout position.
He had already heard the approaching convoy as Much shouted his warning, so he had his binoculars trained on the furthest limits of the road.
The Outlaws new the convoy had radio detectors, so they were exercising radio silence until their operation went tactical.
Their students would not be able to break the Outlaws encryption, but they would detect any transmissions, giving away Robin's position.

Then, on first sight of the convoy, Tuck gave a long whistle to alert his team.

Then came a series of whistles, in a pre defined order, to inform Robin of the convoy's make up.

"Two whistles", counted Robin. "That's two escort vehicles". Then, "one troop carrier, two lorries and two VIP vehicles".

"Interesting choice", thought Robin. "Let's see how that pans out".

Robin had engineered several strategic choices into his exercise scenario. One of them was in the use of specialist convoy escort vehicles.

It was standard practice to put an escort at both front and rear of the convoy.

A third escort vehicle was available and would have been expected with the VIP within the convoy, specifically allocated to the VIP. But the only option to crew it was to draw from the fighting unit in the troop carrier. The commander had opted to keep his ground troops as a strong unit.

Much had moved closer to Tuck's tree, so he could relay verbal messages from their lookout.

"Eyeball", said Tuck, on first sight of the convoy. Then, as the convoy came to a halt, "stop stop". Within minutes Tuck saw the reason for the halt.

"They've spotted the first mine", observed Tuck. He guessed the UAV had spotted the disturbed terrain, where the Outlaws had planted their first mine. The soldiers came out of their troop carrier in a well rehearsed formation. Soldiers with metal detectors searched for the mine, while their comrades formed a protective group around them.

"That's the first mine down", reported Tuck as the convoy resumed its journey.

"Ok, now they know we're here, let's see how good their jamming is", thought Robin. He sent the signals to remotely activate three of his mines. These multiple signals would test how well his students had set up the jamming equipment.

They were not found wanting, as the convoy passed over the series of mines unharmed.

With the remote mines proved useless, and the UAVs detecting the buried pressure mines, Robin needed another plan.

"Stinger deployment", announced Robin. He had named his ambush plan after the police technique of pulling a spiked mat across the road to puncture car tyres. But the plan he was about to use was far more technical and complex.

As the convoy rolled into the ambush zone, John pulled hard on a thick cable. This single cable ran through a pulley system, to ten almost invisible lines. These lines lay unnoticed in the dirt of the forest road. As John pulled, the lines brought their weapons into position. Attached, but hidden in the opposite undergrowth, were five heavy duty stinger mats and five specially prepared mines.

"The ten pieces of equipment should be enough for seven vehicles", hoped Robin, as he watched John deploy the trap.

The convoy was moving slowly, but it was still moving too fast for them to avoid the stinger mats, which punctured five pairs of tyres.

Just as the convoy commander was registering what was happening to the tyres, John flicked a switch. The other five cables carried an electrical current and were attached to some very carefully prepared pieces of ordinance.

When John detonated the mines, powerful explosive charges sent five flat projectiles upwards towards the underside of the vehicles.

Robin had modelled his mines on pieces of Hollywood stunt equipment. Similar devices were used to throw vehicles into the air, simulating much bigger explosions.

Robin's designs worked perfectly, and five convoy vehicles were thrown over, onto their sides.

Tuck was next to react. With his observation post now obsolete, Tuck was ready to join the attack.

Using a pre positioned rope, Tuck abseiled out of the tree, onto the roof of the troop carrier.

The moment he hit the roof, Tuck switched on a powerful magnet, fixing another of Robin's creations to the armoured roof.

Seconds later, a shaped charge blew a hole through the roof. Tuck immediately followed this with a CS gas grenade. The CS was intended to mimic something much more deadly, and took the convoy's fighting troops out of the exercise.

Tuck's mission success was about to turn into personal failure.

Just as he had demonstrated with the signal jamming, the convoy's young commander had mastered all of the technology available to him.

The acoustic firearms detection system had reacted to Tuck's explosion and the commander quickly activated his stabilised remote operated weapon system. This automated gun fired hundreds of blank rounds in Tuck's direction, taking him well and truly out of play.

Much and John moved quickly and together, darting behind sandstone outcrops. This was all part of Robin's plan, as they had pre placed their rocket propelled grenade, or RPG launchers.
They knew the acoustic sniper detection system would instantly lock onto their RPG launchers. But the rock would save them from the same fate as Tuck.
The instant they began preparing to fire on the convoy, volleys of blank rounds surrounded the outcrops.
The Outlaws had hidden CCTV cameras in the trees to give them sight of the convoy, without becoming targets. Using the camera images, Much and John launched their grenades.
They did not know which of the two VIP vehicles carried their target, but the RPGs ripped off the doors from both of them.

Robin then swiftly brought an end to the exercise. Stepping out of the undergrowth, Robin assessed the scene as he moved. Recognising the soldier he had detailed to play the VIP, Robin let loose his own volley of rapid fire blank rounds.
"Endex", shouted Robin. Using the universal command to end the exercise.
"Clear this lot up, then back to base for tea, medals and a debrief'" continued Robin.

All in all, Robin was very satisfied with his day's work. His students had taken in most of his training.

Where they had been found wanting provided Robin with learning for them during the debrief.
But, importantly to Robin, some of the tactics he had practiced would be used again in his personal war with the Tax Collector.

Chapter 10.

The four conspirators sat silently among the trees. They had been out since dusk, preparing for their ambush.
All along the tree lined road, they had laid their explosives and other sabotage equipment.
They had chosen their spot well. They were deep within rural Nottinghamshire, where very few people ventured. But they were at a junction of tracks, which gave them a choice of escapes with their hidden 4x4.

Several miles away the convoy rolled off the A1 trunk road. Robin was experiencing a very strong feeling of deja vu. But there was a reason that today seemed so like the recent TA convoy exercise. Robin had designed the exercise to test some of the tactics his Outlaws would use tonight.

Tonight Robin would need to direct the convoy away from the busy A road they would be using.
This was John's task, he was ready in the hedge line with signs and lights to create a diversion.

Tuck was again in a high tree, overlooking the ambush location. But this was also a spot from where he could see the main road.

"You're up John", said Tuck into his radio, alerting John to the approaching convoy. This time the Outlaws felt safe using their encrypted radios, as Motte was unlikely to have advanced enough decryption kit.

Once the last innocent car passed by, John quickly pulled out his barriers and switched on his lights. The simple rouse worked perfectly as the convoy of lorries, trucks and caravans rolled onto the rural lane.
John knew the drivers would be cursing yet more road works on this notorious stretch of road. It was now late and the drivers and passengers would be eager to arrive and set up their caravans for the night.
But the Outlaws had other plans for them.
As quickly as he had set up his diversion, John packed it away behind the convoy.
Then, jumping on his small, off road motorcycle, he raced across country to rejoin the Outlaws at their ambush.

If anyone had been on this remote country lane, in the early hours of the night, they might have wondered what a convoy of brightly painted fairground wagons were doing on such a quiet country road.
Under normal circumstances there would be no reason for such a convoy to be on this lane. It was far from suitable for such large vehicles, many of them towing trailers and caravans.
Robin knew this was no ordinary fairground convoy. The drivers were not interested in providing innocent

fun. But rather they were using the fairground rides as a cover to transport their deadly drugs.

As the travelling fair season began, fairground workers from all over Britain were heading out on to the road. It was this one group in particular that interested Robin, one of the dealers he interrogated had given information about them

Robin at first disbelieved the information.
When people think of travellers, it is usually the heated evictions at traveller sites, or the TV series Big Fat Gypsy Wedding. Because of this misconception, Robin could not understand how Motte could have infiltrated such a tight knit ethnic group.
But the travelling community has a distinct subsection of which little is reported, the showmen or fairground people.
Unlike Irish Travellers and Gypsies, showmen do not view themselves as an ethnic group but a cultural one united by the fairground industry.

Robin's research had shown how easy it must have been for Clive Motte to infiltrate the community of showmen. Unlike other travellers, fairground people were not necessarily born into the life. Robin had read about Edward Silcock, for whom the choice to become a showman was a way of avoiding a life down the mines.
Edward, and his four brothers, operated a games stall in Wigan in the early 1900s. They then branched out with a set of swings, a barrel organ, a children's ride and a carousel which they took all

over Lancashire.

Edward's grandson John Silcock is the present owner of JE Silcock Amusements. He gained his own experience of the fairs while still at boarding school. His parents travelled with the fairs on a weekly basis and he spent his weekends working with them.

This news story showed Robin that you did not need ethnic breeding to become a showman. Just sufficient money to buy a ride, and the Tax Collector could provide plenty of money.

In fact, the chairman of the Showmen's Guild expressed frustration at misconceptions people hold about the showman. In the article he wrote "We spend millions of pounds on equipment and yet the showmen are always portrayed as Gypsies."

Reading about the decent people, like the Silcock's who worked hard within the fairground industry, Robin could see how the lifestyle would suit Motte's purposes for the transport of drugs.

In the article, Robin read that John Silcock said "It was very good as a child. You see a different location every week". He explained "A good site is crucial to a showman. They must be close to areas like town centres where people congregate to ensure high footfall, with space for the caravans many showmen stay in when they are on the road." Robin knew this was just the sort of situation that would suit infiltration by Motte's people.

Robin had also read about David Wallis, president of the Showmen's Guild of Great Britain. The 69-year-old Liverpudlian, who cut a striking figure in his

Crombie coat and trilby, is a fifth generation showman. He has taken fairs all over the world, to places including Hong Kong, Singapore, China, Iceland, Norway, South Africa and Dubai.
Robin could see from the article that the international interests of the travelling showmen would provide an ideal cover for the importation of Motte's drugs.
This was what he expected to find in this particular showman's convoy which was on its way home from Amsterdam.

As the convoy rolled into the ambush zone, just like at Proteus, John pulled hard on a thick cable. This cable ran through a pulley system, to ten almost invisible lines. These lines lay unnoticed in the dark of the country road. As John pulled, the lines brought their weapons into position. Attached, but hidden in the opposite undergrowth, were five heavy duty stinger mats and five specially prepared mines. The stingers were identical to the ones from their exercise, but the explosive charges were much smaller, as the fair ground vehicles were not armoured.
Just like the army convoy, the showmen were moving slowly, but they were still moving too fast to avoid the stinger mats, which punctured five pairs of tyres.

While the showmen were still registering what was happening to the tyres, John flicked a switch.
The other five cables carried an electrical current and were attached to some very carefully prepared pieces of ordinance.

Unlike the Hollywood equipment Robin had used in his exercise, these mines were not designed to topple the lorries. Here, the Outlaws only needed to immobilise the lorries, by snapping their axels.

Just like he had practiced, Tuck was next to react. With his observation post now obsolete, Tuck joined the attack. Using a pre positioned rope, Tuck abseiled out of the tree, onto the roof of the biggest lorry. This time, he didn't plan on gassing the showmen, he was providing top cover for the other Outlaws.

Much and John were the next to react, moving quickly and together, they moved forward with their weapons.
There were no sandstone outcrops to hide behind, but they would not be facing any advanced military technology.
They could expect the convoy to carry guns, so they still moved with the trees as cover, but they would not face sustained automatic fire.
It was not just the showmen who were without advanced weapons. In keeping with their self imposed rules of engagement, the Outlaws carried much more primitive weapons than their targets.

Robin's weapon of choice for this mission was the English longbow.
The longbow was the machine gun of the Middle Ages: accurate, deadly, possessed of a long range and rapid rate of fire, many mediaeval sources likened the flight of its missiles to a storm.
The longbow was one of the few historic weapons

Robin had been taught through his military training. There is a record of the longbow in action as late as WWII, when Jack Churchill was credited with a longbow kill in France during 1940.

This piece of military legend kept the weapon within the consideration of many Special Forces units.

Outside of his official training, Robin had studied the English longbow with interest. The powerful medieval bow was used for hunting and as a weapon in warfare.

Longbows proved very effective against the French during the Hundred Years' War, particularly in the battles of Sluys (1340), Crécy (1346), and Poitiers (1356), and most famously at the Battle of Agincourt (1415).

Longbows are difficult to use. Medieval bowmen trained from boyhood to master their powerful weapons. So difficult were the bows to pull, and so much training was required, that the skeletons of archers became recognisably adapted. Archers were left with enlarged left arms and often bone spurs on left wrists, left shoulders and right fingers. The Outlaws had not been able to put in years of practice, but their training for this mission had been the most intense they had undertaken so far.

Most important in Robin's training was to teach his Outlaws the difference between bending and drawing their bows.

Because of the high draw weights Robin taught them how to lay their bodies into the bow, not to draw with strength of arms as other nations do.

Robin told them that Englishman did not keep their left hand steady, and draw the bow string with his right. Rather, he keeps his right at rest upon the nerve, pressing the whole weight of his body into the horns of his bow. Hence the English phrase "bending the bow," and the French of "drawing" one.

At the height of the English longbow's use, practice was demanded by law. Henry III passed his Assize of Arms in 1252 requiring all "citizens, burgesses, free tenants, villeins and others from 15 to 60 years of age" to be armed. The poorest of them were expected to have a halberd and a knife, and a bow if they owned land worth more than £2.
This made it easier for the King to raise an army, but also meant that the bow was a weapon commonly used by rebels during the Peasants' Revolt. From the time that the yeoman class of England became proficient with the longbow, the nobility in England had to be careful not to push them into open rebellion. Robin silently chuckled at the irony that, just like his forbears, his longbow was fighting against a Tax Collector.

The tactics that Much and John used in the army exercise involved a small number of grenade launches against the convoy.
They did not have the luxury of heavy ordinance against the showmen's convoy. All they had were arrows to keep the crews under control.
With the valuable cargo they knew was hidden in the trucks, the Outlaws expected to face gunfire, but their tactics had been designed to minimise the opportunities for a return of fire.

Robin had planned this phase of their attack to be one of a rapid fire of arrows, to discourage any resistance.

He had described the longbow as the machine gun of the Middle Ages, but knew it would take skill and effort to be anything like as effective as a modern day automatic weapon.

Under most circumstances archers would not shoot arrows at maximum rate, as it would exhaust even the most experienced man. Their rate of fire was usually around six arrows a minute.

Not only do the arms and shoulder muscles tire from the exertion, but the fingers holding the bowstring become strained.

But Robin did not expect this phase to last anything like as long as a Middle Ages battle, so Much and John would be going for many more than six per minute.

Their medieval forbears would have been provided with between 60 and 72 arrows at the time of battle. These would be stored stabbed upright into the ground at their feet, reducing the time it took to notch, draw and shoot.

Historically young boys were employed to run additional arrows to archers in their positions on the battlefield. The Outlaws did not have this service, so they had pre-placed their arrows in tactical positions around the ambush site. Planted into the ground, the arrows looked like very strange feathered bushes. Biggest of all were the bushes now at Much and John's feat, their tactics involved an early show of force to discourage any heroics against them.

Robin would usually hand make his own arrows, but for the volume needed in this operation, he had been shopping. To avoid detection, the purchases had been small and from many suppliers.

He had bought his war arrows in the thousands. But Robin knew his purchases did not come close to the numbers bought for medieval armies.

He had read that in the 18 years between 1341 and 1359 the English crown bought 1,232,400 arrows.

Much and John's bombardment of the convoy was working as planned. The sustained hail of arrows kept the showmen firmly inside their vehicles.

Then, as always happens, one man became brave and a hand holding a shotgun appeared out of one of the truck Windows.

This was where Tuck, standing on one of the truck roofs came into the plan. Before the gunman could think about pulling the trigger, Tuck put an arrow through his hand.

With opposition subdued from the ground and above, Robin moved forward for his role in the plan. Unlike Much and John, Robin was not loosing his arrows in rapid fire.

His shots were aimed to get very close to their adversaries and further increase their fear of the outlaws.

Fourteenth century war arrows were capable of penetrating the battle armour of the time. So Robin had no trouble puncturing the bodywork of the show men's vehicles. Each shot missing a human body by less than an inch.

Before long, the showmen willingly complied with Robin's instructions to get out of their vehicles.

The Outlaws ushered their captives to the largest of the convoy's caravans. Much and Tuck kept the caravan doors and windows covered, while Robin and John systematically searched the convoy.

It took very little time for the skilled Special Forces soldiers to find what they were looking for.

Cash and jewellery were spread among the vehicles and caravans. But there were a limited number of hiding places, and the Outlaws soon had quite a haul.

The drugs were the easiest to find, as they had already beaten that information from one of their earlier conquests.

Before the Outlaws finished, they dragged out the showman they saw as the leader. Their rather persuasive interview techniques extracted more very useful information.

Then, to end their operation, Robin deployed the only modern weapon in his armoury. The incendiary grenade soon had the ride containing the drugs alight.

Driving away Much could not help giving their prisoners the classic British two-fingered salute. Robin had told him that this salute dated back to the Hundred Years War. The French hated the English archers who used the Longbow with such devastating effect. Any archers caught by the French had their Index and middle fingers chopped off from their right hand- a terrible penalty for an archer. This led to the practice of the English archers, especially in siege situations, taunting their French enemy with their continued presence by raising their two fingers in the 'Two-Fingered Salute' meaning "You haven't cut off my fingers!"

Chapter 11.

Robin's feet pounded hard against the forest trail.
Harder and harder he pushed himself towards a
better time for his regular lap of the Loxley estate.
It was a route he had been running since boyhood
and could almost navigate it blindfolded.
Robin particularly liked to run early in the morning,
when the low sun worked its way through the
estate's forest. He knew practically every tree on his
circuit, having watched many of them grow, as he
himself aged.
But today, as he pushed hard up the trail towards
the Hall, there was a new tree, silhouetted against
the morning sky.
"Impossible", thought Robin. "That wasn't here
yesterday".
Perhaps he had pushed too hard up the hill. Maybe
the oxygen debt was playing tricks with his eyes. But
it certainly looked like a strong, young tree.
Then, as he closed in on the tree, the edges of the
silhouette began to break. Something wisped
around the treetop that didn't quite fit.

The more Robin's eyes focused on the tree, the less
tree like it appeared.
As the morning breeze whipped up the hillside, it
blew the dark, silk like leaves sideways.
Gradually, Robin realised that it was not a tree at all.
"It's a girl", he exclaimed.
Robin was part right in his assessment of the
silhouette as a tree. Aside from her long dark hair
blowing in the breeze, the beautiful young woman
stood motionless in a yoga tree balance.

One foot placed firmly on the floor. The other placed gently against the opposite thigh, its knee bent at a sharp angle. Her arms curved upwards in a perfect semi circle. Most importantly, not a muscle twitched to spoil her balance.

"She's good", thought Robin. She had been on the skyline for at least ten minutes of Robin's run, and he had not seen her so much as twitch.

Robin knew enough about yoga to know she must be a very experienced practitioner.

21st century Britain typically associates the term yoga with Hatha yoga and its asanas, or postures, as a form of exercise. Robin would learn that the girl had delved much deeper into yoga's spiritual roots.

"Good morning", announced Robin as he ran closer to the girl. "I'm Robin. I haven't seen you around Loxley before".

The girl brought herself out of her tree balance, stretching her arms high overhead into mountain pose. Then she put her hands together in what has become the Christian prayer posture, but had its roots in ancient India. She brought her hands slowly down her centre line to rest beside her heart, before relaxing and acknowledging Robin.

"Morning", she replied. "I'm new around here".

"Marion", said the girl, as she offered her hand to Robin.

"Nice to meet you Marion", he replied, shaking her hand. "Sorry, but I need to finish my run, or I'll be late for work. Hope our paths cross again soon".

"I'm sure they will Robin", replied Marion. She had recognised Robin as the Duke of Loxley, but he was nothing like the stuffy aristocrat she had expected.

Marion really did hope their paths would cross again soon.

The next time that Robin ran his familiar circuit was the weekend, so he was a little later reaching the point he had first seem Marion's tree pose.
He felt disappointed running uphill towards Loxley Hall, as he could not see Marion on the skyline.
Then, as he reached the top of the rise, his spirit lifted as he saw the beautiful dark haired girl. Marion was further through her practice, and was seated in a body twist.
"Hello again", said Marion, as she saw Robin approach.
This time, as Robin was in no hurry, he sat cross legged on the grass in front of her.

"What brings you to Loxley", asked Robin.
"I ran out of things to study", replied Marion. "And now that home is big enough to avoid dad, I've come home".
It was then that Robin realised that Marion did have a familiar look about her. "You're Clive Motte's daughter", he exclaimed.
"For my sins", replied Marion.
Robin and Marion moved to Robin's cottage, to continue their conversation over tea.

Marion explained how, as a young girl, she had been sent off to boarding school by her father.
"Dad built his business on violence", explained Marion. "Home wasn't the best place for a kid, with a steady stream of angry competitors at the door. So I was sent away. But I got lucky with Millfield, and

school felt much more like home.

School was where Marion was first acquainted with yoga and eastern mysticism in general.
Millfield School, in Glastonbury was founded by Rollo Meyer in 1935, following his return from India with seven Indian boys, six of whom were princes.
The first Hindu teacher to bring aspects of yoga to a western audience, Swami Vivekananda, toured Europe in the 1890s.
But it was not until the 1960s that western interest in Hindu spirituality reached its peak. A number of Neo-Hindu schools specifically focused on a western public, grew out of this interest.
Unsurprisingly, Millfield's sport mad teachers, already primed by the school's Indian links, became heavily involved.

As it grew, Millfield stood by its founder's ethos of attempting to discover and nurture whatever talent a young person has. It gained an international reputation for sport and achieved success with dyslexic pupils, but it also excels in music and the arts.
Successful Old Millfieldians include former British Lions and Wales rugby captain Gareth Edwards; BBC chief political correspondent John Sergeant; Olympic Gold medallists Duncan Goodhew, Peter Wilson and Helen Glover and drummer of rock group the Police, Stewart Copeland.
Marion proudly told Robin that her old school had more Olympic representatives in London 2012 than any other school.

Marion enjoyed the boarding environment at Millfield.
The houses were the focal point of Marion's life at school; the boarders were highly supportive of each other's achievements and she enjoyed going to sports matches, concerts and plays where her friends were performing.
The houses are run by a team of resident houseparents and tutors, who provided Marion with a much warmer, supportive atmosphere than she was getting at home.
As Marion described her school life, Robin saw parallels with his own time at Welbeck Army School and the Sandhurst Military Academy. This explained to Robin why he was so quickly feeling comfortable in Marion's company.

Morion's use of academia to avoid her father's violent world did not end with Millfield. The school's academic record easily assisted her in acceptance at Cambridge University.

Cambridge University appealed to Robin's sense of history, and also, as he would discover, to Marion's. Cambridge itself dates from the first century AD, when the town grew alongside the River Cam. Learning at Cambridge had its roots in ecclesiastical institutions. The Convent of St Radegund, for example, was founded in 1135 on the site which eventually became Jesus College.

Then, in 1209, scholars from Oxford migrated to Cambridge. Before long they were numerous enough to set up an organisation, represented by a

Chancellor, and arranged regular courses of study, taught by their own members. So Cambridge as a university town was born.

In these early years, most of the scholars were clergymen, in holy orders of some sort, and expecting careers in the Church or in the Civil Service. Marion was pleased this had changed. Although she talked freely with Robin about the spiritual beginnings of her yoga, Marion had little time for organised religion. In fact, Marion was quietly a fan of 16th century alumni, Erasmus of Rotterdam, who encouraged new learning, in Greek and Hebrew, helping to clear the way for the half-theological, half-philosophical speculations leading to the reformation of the church and the dissolution of the monasteries.

Marion talked with Robin about her studies. A Bachelor's Degree in Indian history began her extended time at Cambridge. An MA in Indian Studies and an MSc in Psychology followed. But still Marion could not face going home to her father. With money no object to the Tax Collector in keeping his daughter happy, he kept the money flowing.

It was the massive expansion of the University's teaching accommodation in the 1950s and 1960s that provided Marion with the drive towards her Doctorate.

A huge new regional hospital replaced the ancient Addenbrooke's Hospital in the city centre, and provided the nucleus for a wide range of medically related departments and institutes, including a new

School of Clinical Medicine.
It was in this school that Marion started her work towards helping cancer patients through yoga.
Her research found no scientific evidence to prove that yoga can cure or prevent cancer. But she found that it helped people with cancer to sleep better and cope with anxiety.

"So, after all that clinical work, what was the draw of Loxley?" asked Robin.
That was a simple question for Marion to answer.
"Horses", she replied, a huge smile breaking at the thought of her beloved animals.

In common with many of Marion's lifelong interests, she started riding at Millfield.
Riding is part of the Millfield activities programme, so she started with lessons as part of the school curriculum.
But with a team of 20 equestrian staff, there were many more opportunities to ride at Millfield. She progressed to become a sessional rider, taking extra riding lessons throughout the term.
Then, when dad was convinced to write a cheque, she became a full time rider, one of an elite group of pupils who have a horse at livery in the stables.

Robin had been to Milfield many times, as the school hires out its facilities during school holidays.
So Robin's Outlaws had often held training camps there.
But Robin was enjoying listening to Marion talk and let her continue excitedly describing her old school's riding facilities.

She described; stabling for 53 horses in a mix of American style barns and traditional stables, a large Indoor arena, an all-weather outdoor arena and a second new outdoor arena. There were show jumps and portable cross country jumps, an off road canter track, gallops and a polo pitch. All in all, Marion had plenty of opportunities to develop an obsession with horses at Millfield.

Marion was such easy company, that a post work out cuppa became a leisurely brunch. Although Tuck did most of the Outlaws' cooking, no Special Forces soldier could survive without becoming proficient at such a basic, life preserving skill. So, standing at his cottage's wood burning range, Robin soon filled the cottage with smells of sausage and bacon.

What became apparent to Robin was that, with the exceptions of riding and yoga, Marion appeared to have few fond memories outside of school or university. Even her yoga had become inextricably entwined with her academic work.
She made no mention at all of family life. Where her dad was mentioned, it was almost always in the context of paying for something.
Her only other surviving memories were of violence. Marion remembered with horror the many challenges made to her father over aspects of his business. They seldom ended well for the challenger as, when it came to violence, Motte was notorious for not having an off switch. He would always go well beyond what was needed simply to win a fight. It was this almost psychopathic streak that gained Motte his reputation, and made it unheard of for

anyone to inform on him.

Robin was pleased that this beautiful, interesting woman had found an escape from her father's life. But he could not help but wonder if she knew that her academic life had been funded by the drug trade.

Marion seemed oblivious to this fact. She talked freely about her father's ruthless and violent business practices and clearly disliked Clive Motte intensely. But she appeared oblivious as to where her family fortune came from.

Then came the story that convinced Robin that Marion really did not know the truth about her father.

Marion had become very relaxed with Robin and was opening up to him in ways she seldom did with anyone else.

She began to tell Robin about the loss of her first and only real love. This was when Robin knew she could not know her father was one of the country's most successful drug lords.

Marion spoke softly about her freshman year at Cambridge. Within the first term she had met Paul, a chemistry undergraduate, who shared her love of horses. She had quickly fallen head over heels in love with him.

Paul was fun to be with, and like her, he never seemed short of money. Also like her, he seldom spoke about his family. Marion assumed that like her, he had reasons to forget his family. But the truth was, Paul's family income didn't come close to supporting his horses, car, clothes and party lifestyle. Paul made his own money, in ways he could not talk about.

Paul had a secret, and that secret lived in a rented flat, well away from the splendour of the university. It was where he went when Marion thought he was putting in extra time in the lab.

As it happened, Paul's explanation was not far from the truth. The talented chemist was misusing his skills to provide many of Cambridge's undergraduates with a steady supply of designer pharmaceuticals.

But, talented or not, Paul had chosen a very dangerous trade.

The process of cooking methamphetamine can be deadly for the chemist, as it involves poisonous, flammable, and explosive chemicals. Aside from the ever present risk of explosion, the main danger in producing methamphetamine comes from anhydrous ammonia.

Paul's criminal partners stole his supplies from farm sites, where it is used as fertilizer. Without the specialist storage available to the farmers, Paul kept the chemical in a standard household fridge not designed to hold this volatile gas.

His substandard storage procedures failed and Paul inhaled the gas, causing him severe lung damage.

Marion reported Paul as missing, when he did not turn up for their early evening ride together. But, as he was an adult, the police needed more than a missed date to launch a full scale search.

It took three days before police forced entry to his secret flat, following reports of a chemical smell.

Paul was just alive, having spent the three days in agony, but unable to shout or raise assistance.

Paul died in hospital the following day, in Marion's arms. That was when she developed her lifelong hatred of the drug trade.

Chapter 12.

Robin spent as much time as he could manage with Marion, over the next few weeks. They ran together, Marion began to teach him some yoga. Luckily, Robin could also ride. In some of the countries where his Outlaws had operated, horses were the most easily stolen forms of transport they could find. But much as he enjoyed her company, there was something far more pressing on Robin's mind.

As the calendar moved towards October, Robin had to find more regular excuses to be away from Marion. He and his Outlaws had another mission to prepare for.

The Showman boss who the Outlaws interrogated had tried his best to defy Robin's questions. But Robin had been subjected to torture in some of the world's most despotic regimes. So, tough as the Showman was, he eventually yielded to the methods Robin had learned through experience.

Clive Motte funded several traveling showmen's rides, because they provided such a fantastic cover for the movement of his wares.

The Showman told Robin that all of Motte's traveling families would be heading for the same place in October.

It was the highlight of the Showmen's year. What they describe as "coming back to the holy city". All of their families gather here, otherwise they would only see one another at weddings and funerals.

It angered Robin knowing the Tax Collector was tainting an event he had loved as a child, rarely missing the annual treat with his mother.

Nottingham's Goose Fair is one of Europe's largest travelling fairs with a history dating back more than 700 years, starting around 1284, with permission granted by the Charter of King Edward I.

The Goose Fair was only cancelled due to the bubonic plague in 1646 and again during the two World Wars.

Historically held in Nottingham's Old Market Square it moved to the Forest Recreation Ground after 1927, because of redevelopment of the Square.

Like everyone of Robin's generation, he had only known the Goose Fair for its 500 attractions, from the latest white knuckle rides to the popular family, children's and old-time rides.

But, like many historic fairs, it started as a trade event with a reputation for high-quality cheese. Its name is derived from the thousands of geese that were driven from Lincolnshire to be sold in Nottingham.

With the area around the site so busy with traffic, pedestrians and police, this was a mission the Outlaws would have to escape from on foot. Just like the local gangsters, they would lose themselves in the urban maze of Radford and Hyson Green.

Walking onto the site, they got their first reminder of the fair's history. A huge fiberglass goose traditionally stands guard on the nearby roundabout, welcoming visitors to Nottingham and its famous fair.

The Outlaws walked amongst the array of Roller Coasters, Water Rides, Giant Wheels, Bombers, Dodgems, Twists and Waltzers. They were looking

for one ride in particular, that was financed by Clive
Motte and from which his men would wholesale their
drugs to the street dealers.

It was not just the noise and lights of the rides that
kept Robin's attention.
Food and smells are synonymous with the world
famous Goose Fair.
Ask some what culinary delights "make" the fair, and
they say it's the traditional mushy peas. Ask others
and they say it's the home-made brandy snaps.
For many, you haven't been to Goose Fair until you
have tried cock-on-a-stick. The boiled sugar lollypop
dates back to 1872, when Nottingham Showman
Ben Brooks created the first brightly coloured
lollypop in the shape of a cockerel.
Tempting as the many smells were, the Outlaws had
business to deal with. Drugs were being peddled at
a family event and the profits were going back to the
Tax Collector. This was something that Robin could
not allow to go unpunished.

The Outlaws separated as they approached the ride.
Robin and John pulled up their hoods as they
slipped silently into the back of the ride. Tuck and
Much waited for Robin's signal. They would enter
the ride as customers, allowing the Outlaws to
attack on two fronts.
Robin could not help but smile at the irony of the
ride Motte had chosen. An attraction designed to
mimic evil, was being used to distribute a worse kind
of evil.
Moving through the semi-darkness, the occasional
flash of light illuminated the ride's many special

effects using luminescent paint, lit by blacklights. The scenes in the ride were based on horror film characters, such as Dracula and Freddie Kruger.

Robin was in the Ghost Train, a dark ride attraction, first created at Blackpool Pleasure Beach in 1930, but now popular in travelling fairs.
The choice made perfect sense to Robin. The darkness provided cover for the dealers to conduct their transactions, and then escape back into anonymity as customers.
Robin and John also benefited from the anonymity of the Ghost Train. Hidden in the shadowy corners, they took in all the sounds and movement, but remained undetected themselves.
As they waited, Robin listened to the haunting music that has become a theme tune to many Ghost Train rides. "Impressions of Sorcerer" was written for the 1977 movie Sorcerer, by German synth-rock band Tangerine Dream.
So good are the horror credentials of the instrumental track, that the director of the Exorcist has said that if he had discovered Tangerine Dream before scoring his movie, he would have asked them to perform on that picture too.

Patience was rewarded, as in the Ghost Train's semi light, Robin spotted the exchange he was waiting for. A small bag of drugs, exchanged for a bigger bag of cash. Then, using all their Special Forces skills, Robin and John followed the Showmen to where they kept their goods and money hidden.
A silent update to Tuck and Much by text set them moving towards the queue for the ride.

"Jump off at Freddie", it had read. They had taken one ride through earlier, and knew that Robin meant the lifelike, fluorescent model of Freddie Kruger. The ride went very dark, just before turning towards the nightmare image. This would give the Outlaws chance to leave the train unseen.

The ride is in two sections, first comes a dark section, before passing though an open station, decorated with trolls, ghosts and witches. Tuck and Much kept their eyes tightly closed through the open section, to preserve their night vision.
They felt the ride travel down a small drop in the station area, before pulling up again to go into the second section, where Robin awaited them.
With all four Outlaws back together, they positioned themselves for an ambush and settled down, waiting for another deal to happen.

While he waited, Robin reflected on the ups and downs of crime at the Goose Fair over the years. The Police and Council maintained that the bad years were over and things were getting better. The previous year, out of 410,000 people attending, only seven people were arrested. The arrests were for offences including three relating to alcohol, two for possession of knives, one for possession of drugs and one for a public order offence.
Robin knew that with Motte involved at the Fair, the single drug offence was the very small tip of a very large iceberg.

Once hailed as a Mecca for thugs, gangs and pickpockets, the sheer volume of officials policing the fair would have been enough to make even the most hardened criminal think twice.

2004 was the worst year, when at the height of Nottingham's gang wars, 14 year old Danielle Beccan was returning from the Goose Fair when she was shot near her home. A car with blacked-out windows pulled up alongside her and her friends noticed a gun. They told her to get down on the ground, but she was too slow. Six bullets were fired and Danielle was hit in the stomach. She collapsed and died later in hospital.

Robin remembered Superintendent Colbeck saying "Goose Fair was traditionally a time of tension between rival groups". He smiled at the thought that another rival group was about to add some tension, his own Outlaws would certainly create a stir among the gangs.

Robin was pleased that the dealers were using the Ghost Train. The dark is the Special Forces' friend, and his team would work well inside.

But it would also keep their actions out of public view. Robin wanted to hit the dealers in their pockets. He would also shed no tears if another street gang was blamed for the robbery.

But he was also well aware of the thousands of families visiting the event, and the majority of law abiding Showmen running the Fair.

For the showmen themselves it is the biggest party on the calendar. Traditionally it is the place where many young people from the fair community meet up to choose a partner, and many marriages are set on course at the three Goose Fair Dances held each year.

The young people form a committee to organise three big midweek dances during the fair, hiring out nightclubs in Nottingham exclusively.

While the younger generation have the dances, the older ones have get-togethers too, but it's more likely to be a meal. The Showmen call it 'The Last Supper' on the Tuesday night before the fair starts on Wednesday, because for the next few days they snatch a bite to eat where they can.

Then, as they had done many times before, the Outlaws instantly moved from waiting into action. The dealers had met to conduct their deal. Like Robin and his team, the Showmen had been waiting in the shadowy corners of the Ghost Train. The local dealers had been briefed to enter though the emergency door, and then follow a cord placed for them as a guide through the semi-light.

While the dealers were distracted with their greetings, the Outlaws jumped into action.

For once, the odds were even for Robin. With two Showmen and two dealers, each of the four Outlaws had their own targets.

Almost simultaneously, four fists impacted on gangsters' ribs. In the gloom of the ride, it looked like they had struck their victims with empty fists. But the pain in the recipients' chests said differently.

Robin had chosen knuckledusters or Brass Knuckles for this mission.

With the heavy police presence, they could not be caught with anything more deadly.

They were illegal in Britain, but Robin liked the irony

that in Brazil, where they are legal and freely sold, knuckledusters are called "Soco Inglês," which means "English Punch." In the Outlaws' trained hands, they could be deadly enough.
Knuckledusters are shaped to fit around the knuckles. They are designed to preserve and concentrate a punch's force by directing it toward a smaller contact area. This results in increased tissue disruption, and an increased likelihood of fracturing the victim's bones.
The rounded palm grip also spreads across the attacker's palm, reducing the counter-force that would otherwise be absorbed by the attacker's fingers.

Robin was pleased of his Brass Knuckles' protection to his fists, as he rained blow after blow onto the dealer's body.
The steady rhythm of his punches allowed his mind to drift momentarily to the weapon's history. They are believed to have evolved from the Roman "caestus", a type of hand guard made from leather and metal used during the gladiatorial event of pankration, which literary means 'all force'. It was a combination of wrestling and boxing, where everything was permitted except biting, gouging and attacking the genitals.

18th century Sikhs used a type of brass knuckle called the Sher Panja.
The Japanese martial art of Kobudo used simple knuckles with no ring holes for the fingers but a grip for the palm. The knuckle then had a rectangular type shape with small spikes or blunt bits of metal

on the outside.

Then Robin remembered their use within the mediaeval period which interested him so much. During the 1800s in Europe, armoured gauntlets were often adorned with brass knuckles. It suited Robin to think of himself as a chivalrous knight, as he pummeled the drug dealer.

The gangsters they fought against may well have used knuckledusters, if the Outlaws had given them time to react. But unlike the Outlaws', theirs would have been made in Pakistan or China, out of steel. Truly brass knuckles are rare due to the expense of brass, which can cost over £100 for one set.

The gangsters barely had time to return a single punch, as the Outlaw's fists performed like jackhammers.
With no fresh ribs to break, Robin returned his attention to those he had already broken. He knew this would make it easier to extract information from the gangster, before they took their money and drugs, and made their escape.

Robin had followed another historical example in providing his Outlaws with their Brass Knuckles. During the American Civil War soldiers would melt the lead out of bullets to make their own knuckles. When the lead was melted, they would pour it into a mold that was dug out in the dirt and left to set. Robin had copied their technique, moulding his knuckles in the soil of the Dukeries. But unlike the Civil War soldiers, who had to use comparatively soft lead, Robin had easy access to brass. Robin was now an instructor on an active military training area, where thousands of spent rounds can be easily collected.

Brass is a commonly used shell case material because it is resistant to corrosion. A brass case head can be work-hardened to withstand the high pressures of cartridges, and allow for manipulation via extraction and ejection without tearing the metal. But Robin was interested in the hard property of brass for the damage it was now doing to his hated drug dealers.

Once the dealers were completely subdued, and all their knowledge of the drug trade extracted, the Outlaws removed the stocks of cash and drugs. "There must be over a million here", exclaimed John, looking at the size of their haul.

Robin had estimated slightly more for the combined value of drugs and money.

With a large proportion of the drugs still to be sold, Robin had a little over £100,000 to pass on to charity. The drugs would be disposed of down the first secluded storm drain they came across.

"The cash will do some good", thought Robin. "And the drugs won't be reaching the streets. The hole in Motte's pocket won't do any harm either".

But there was another string to Robin's disruption of the city's gangs. As they left the showmen and dealers, they knew they were in the heartland of Radford's MPR gang. So, as the Outlaws left, they each made a W sign with their fingers, the sign of the Meadows' Waterfront Gang.

"That will leave them fighting among themselves

again", thought Robin, knowing it would add to the tension they had created in Bar Sheriff.

Chapter 13.

The tunnels under Loxley Hall were busy over the next few weeks.

An old mountaineering friend of Robin's now ran a Scout and Guides Activity Centre. Robin had decided the Goose Fair dealers' 100K would go to help his friend's centre grow. As always, the help would be anonymous.

Robin had secretly bought two mini busses, complete with box trailers. Then, he had set about filling both vans and trailers to their ceilings with climbing and camping equipment. All of it bought quietly, in cash, from suppliers around the country. Robin was always fanatically careful about not being seen taking vehicles in and out of the tunnels. The more often he did it, the more worried he became about making a slip.

The vehicle exit was expertly hidden. Robin had used a mixture of modern technology, together with his Special Forces expertise in camouflage.

A remote control activated hidden motors and cables. A fake rock face, almost indistinguishable from the real thing silently moved to allow access to the tunnel.

Specially grown ivy and other creepers covered the artificial rock face. The same remote set cables in motion, carefully parting the curtains of foliage.

In the depth of night, the foliage and rock moved aside for the Outlaws.

Tuck and Much drove the two mini busses, while Robin and John followed in Robin's favourite personal vehicle.

Robin had always had a soft spot for that icon of British motoring, the Land Rover Defender.
He had grown up among them on the Loxley Estate. Then, on joining the Army, they had become one of his most dependable tools. So, he could not resist buying what many considered to be the ultimate Land Rover.

Like Robin, and many other Land Rover enthusiasts, Bradford based luxury vehicle designer Afzal Kahn was saddened to learn that the Defender was being phased out because of increasingly stringent emission standards.
Calling the decision an 'absolute tragedy', Kahn and his 40 strong design team could not resist developing something to help the icon live on.
Kahn's £150,000 Flying Huntsman Pickup has a heavily modified body and six wheels, but it is still recognisably related to the Land Rover Defender on which it is based.
Along with a third axle, Kahn put the tail of a pickup version of the iconic off-roader onto the back of a top-of-the-range long wheelbase model.
Robin loved the exterior styling's aggressive lines and military style detailing such as the crosshair motif featured on the headlamps and exhausts. But most of all, he loved the powerful 6.2-litre General Motors V8. The huge American engine's 550bhp gave the Flying Huntsman explosive performance which is a far cry from the steady pulling power of the original Defender.

The Outlaws quietly parked the fully loaded mini busses and trailers in the Activity Centre car park.

The ownership documents and keys went through the site office letter box, providing an early morning surprise for Robin's old friends.

Then, with Tuck and Much on board, and safely clear of the Centre, Robin put every one on the Flying Huntsman's 6.2 litres into use.

Robin took advantage of the opportunity to play with his expensive toy, while the roads were empty and the police were otherwise occupied in the towns and cities.

Very few people were on the roads of the Dukeries to see the Huntsman, but one very excited pair of eyes did watch them come home.

The young man had spotted Robin driving the Huntsman a few weeks earlier and had become fixated on the 6x6 beast.

With night turning into early morning, Robin returned the Huntsman to his underground garage, and the Outlaws drifted off to bed.

Despite their late night, the long habit of military discipline brought the Outlaws from their beds before losing too much of the morning.

Robin thought he must still be dreaming, as he walked into the garage, to clean the Huntsman after their nocturnal outing. The huge vehicle was gleaming, as if it had never left the garage.

"Are the guys trying to surprise me?", thought Robin. Wondering if the other Outlaws had got up before him.

But, as he walked around his vehicle, he saw that the phantom cleaner was sitting on the floor, polishing one of the chromed wheels.

Instantly on his guard, as this was among Robin's most private of places. "Who are you", asked Robin of the young man polishing his car.

It was not one of his Outlaws. In fact, Robin had never seen this young man before.

18 or 19 years old, and impeccably dressed in a suit and tie, he was the most unlikely car valet that Robin had ever come across.

"Polish polish, shiny bright. Polish polish, shiny bright", repeated the young man, over and over. Never taking his attention away from the wheel.

"Who are you", asked Robin again. Then the encounter got even stranger.

"Who are you", repeated the man, back at Robin. He was about to reply, "I'm the Duke", but he was interrupted by the man repeating "Who are you", over and over.

Robin was on the verge of losing his temper with the young trespasser. But again, Robin's love of old movies stirred something in his memory about the young man's behaviour. "Rain Man", thought Robin, remembering the 1988 Dustin Hoffman film.

The film tells the story of selfish wheeler-dealer, Charlie Babbitt (Tom Cruise), who discovers that his father had died and left his multimillion-dollar estate to his other son, Raymond (Hoffman), an autistic savant, who Charlie did not know about.

Raymond actually lived with the family when Charlie was young, and Charlie realises that the comforting figure from his childhood, whom he thought was an imaginary friend named "Rain Man", was actually Raymond, who was sent away because he had burned Charlie by accident as a little boy.

Because he had memorised every airline crash Raymond refused to fly, so they set out on a road trip together. During the journey, Charlie got to know Raymond, learning that he was a mental calculator, able to count hundreds of objects at once, and make nearly instant calculations, far beyond the normal human range.

After a car deal went wrong, Charlie found himself $80,000 in debt and took Raymond to Las Vegas, hoping to win the money at blackjack by counting cards.

When the casino bosses realised what they were doing, they asked Charlie and Raymond to leave, but Charlie had made enough to cover his debts.

The more Robin challenged the young man, the stranger his behaviour became.

He stopped his polishing chant, and moved into an encyclopaedic description of the Flying Huntsman.

"Kahn Flying Huntsman", began the young man.

"Made by the Chelsea Truck Company, named after the Chelsea Tractor 4x4s. Designed by Afzal Kahn, born 1974, from Bradford. Based on the Mercedes G63 AMG 6x6, cost £370,000. The first six wheel Mercedes since they built one for the Nazis in 1930s Germany".

Every time Robin thought the man had stopped, and he himself tried to speak, the man began another string of facts about the Huntsman.

"Mr Kahn will only build 20 Flying Huntsmen per year. Each has a plaque with the names of the team who have coach-built your car. 880mm longer than a standard Defender and 150mm wider".

Then, he launched into a string of quotes that Robin recognised as being from Afzal Kahn. "These days it's not what you wear, it's what you drive", and "The Road Is My Catwalk".

Robin realised that he could see something of himself in this young man's fascination for facts. Robin obsessively studied the history of his ancient weapons and could recite the facts at will. But here was someone who had encyclopaedic knowledge of Robin's car, yet appeared to be quite high on the autism spectrum. But most important for Robin, he had found his way through the camouflage and security of his tunnel entrance.

Robin's diagnosis of autism was strengthened as he watched the young man's non-verbal behaviours. He seemed to have difficulty with eye contact, facial expressions and body language.

Then, as the other Outlaws entered the garage behind him, Robin noticed the man was focusing his attention on him, and ignoring the as yet unfamiliar people behind him.

Robin began to play on this, engaging the young man in conversation about his car. He remembered that children with autism often lack interest in other children, choosing to gravitate towards older children, rather than interacting with children of the same age.

Eventually Robin teased an introduction from him. "I'm Will Scarlet ", he said, punctuating his introduction with an excited flapping of his right hand.

Robin had read that higher functioning people with autism can suffer from intense loneliness compared to non-autistic peers. This despite the common belief that children with autism prefer to be alone. Making and maintaining friendships often proves to be difficult. For them, the quality of friendships, not the number of friends, predicts how lonely they feel. Robin knew that functional friendships, such as those resulting in invitations to parties, affected their quality of life more deeply. So, Robin played on this, working to Will's obvious love of cars, he began to show him around the collection.

Once Will relaxed into Robin's company, some of the symptoms of his autism seemed to lessen. Apart from the lack of eye contact and the occasional hand twitch, it became difficult to tell there was anything wrong with Will.
At each of Robin's impressive collection of cars and motorcycles, Will recited a list of facts, figures and trivia.
Robin was sure that Will was showing some of the higher functions of Hoffman's Rain Man character, but the more comfortable the two of them got, the less autistic Will appeared.

About 1 in every 100 people in Britain has autism. Of these, about 10% show unusual abilities, ranging from the memorisation of trivia to the extraordinarily rare talents of autistic savants. In 1887, the condition was named Idiot Savant, French for "learned idiot". Robin was learning that Will was a long way from being an idiot.
The most dramatic examples of savant syndrome

occur in individuals who score very low on IQ tests, while demonstrating exceptional brilliance in specific areas, such as rapid calculation, memory, or musical ability.

The Rain Man was one of these low IQ savants, but Robin was realising that Will Scarlet combined his incredible memory, with a close to average IQ.

The extraordinary mental abilities come about by savants accessing low-level, less-processed information that exists in all human brains, but is not normally available to conscious awareness. This was how Will could remember the astonishing level of automotive trivia. But, Will had another talent, one that had got him into Robin's tunnels in the first place.

As they reached the end of Robin's collection, Will started to recite facts about TV presenter Chris Evans' collection of cars. Evans is well known to be a fan of fast cars, particularly Ferraris.

Will was able to remember that Evans was banned from driving for 56 days in 2001 and fined £600 after being stopped by Surrey Police driving at 105 mph. He knew that on 18 May 2008, Evans bought a 1961 250 GT Spyder California, formerly owned by James Coburn for a world record price of 6.4 Million Euros. Then in May 2010 he toppled his own record by buying a 1963 Ferrari 250 GTO, one of only thirty-six built, for £12 million. Then, three years later the record was almost doubled when Evans sold the car for $42 million.

Robin started to realise the significance of Will's breaking and entering talents, when he took out his smart phone. Will started to scroll through photographs of Chris Evans' most prized cars, including the rare right-hand drive 1966 Ferrari 275 GTB, a 1971 Ferrari 365 GTS/4 'Daytona' Spider and, what seemed to be Will's favourite, a1964 Daimler Dart Police Car, valued at £50,000-60,000

"Wait a minute", exclaimed Robin. "Did you take these pictures yourself?"

At Robin's question, Will became flustered and started to exhibit some of the autistic traits he had earlier displayed. "Take pictures yourself, take pictures yourself", repeated Will. Then, eventually, Robin managed to calm him, and he admitted having sneaked in and out of Chris Evans' garage block. "I can get in most places", said Will.

It seemed that Will's brain processed buildings in the way most people approach a logic puzzle. There is always a way through physical, electronic and computerised security. Will's single minded approach could almost always crack the security and get him into whatever building he had set himself to.

The fact that Will Scarlet had found his way into the tunnels presented Robin with a dilemma.

The secrecy of the tunnels was crucial to his war against the Tax Collector. Will had already proven himself willing to talk about his burglary talents, so Robin needed a way of silencing the young trespasser.

The answer to many of the Outlaws' problems was often a bullet. But there was no way Robin was going to kill the autistic innocent.

In the end, it was Will himself who provided the answer. He was absolutely desperate for a job in the motor trade, but no one would take him on. So, Will Scarlet became Robin's vehicle valet and apprentice mechanic.

He had to rapidly block off the sections of the tunnels in which they planned their missions against Clive Motte. But Will never wanted to stray far from his vehicles.

Will turned up every day, on the bus from his mother's house. He worked tirelessly, alternating between cleaning the vehicles and learning the mechanics trade from Robin, and from studying You Tube videos.

In a few short weeks, Will had exhausted every mechanical opportunity in Robin's collection. So, to keep the youngster focused and occupied, Robin bought a small used car dealership, which was close enough to Loxley Hall for him to watch the talented young man.

Robin hired a manager to run the business, but Will Scarlet singlehandedly looked after the rapidly rotating stock.

Even with his new distraction, Will made regular visits to the tunnels, as Robin's collection of vehicles was far more exciting than their used car stock. Will's special favourite remained the Flying Huntsman.

The Outlaws were now well into planning their next move against Motte. But they were hitting walls in their project. John had joked about whether young Will could help with their problem. But Robin would not put the young man at risk, or compromise the secrecy of their operation any further.

Adamant as Robin was about not involving his apprentice in anything other than the cars, Will Scarlet had other ideas.

Chapter 14.

"Who are these new gangsters? asked the TV news reporter.
The reporter used a montage of CCTV clips to illustrate the point he was trying to make.
Robin knew they had not been captured on CCTV, so at first paid little interest in the report.
But, then a series of sketches replaced the moving images on the screen.
"A drug dealer beaten half to death in the Lace Market", continued the reporter.
"Then, a violent robbery at what is alleged to be one of the Radford gang's drug houses"
"We then saw a running battle through the alleyways of the Meadows, all played out with bicycles".
When the sketches of four hooded men filled the screen, Robin began to realise the report was about his Outlaws. The artist had really gone to town, arming his creations with longbows, swords and battle axes.

"This reporter has done well", thought Robin. All he was missing was the nightclub incident and the operations against the traveling showmen.
What was most impressive was that the reporter had pieced together information about their use of historic weapons.

"Most of the city's gang problems revolve around the Meadows' Waterfront Gang and Radford's Money, Power, Respect. Throw in the Brewsters Crew and a few smaller gangs and the police usually know who is responsible for a fall out among the gangs".

The reporter went on to explain that his sources close to the police were baffled over what appeared to be a developing gang war.

He detailed the gangs' traditions of identifying themselves with coloured scarves, modelling themselves on America's urban gangs. "But the new gangsters carry nothing to identify themselves, wearing nondescript, dark coloured hoodies."

"But most unique are their weapons", continued the reporter. "Our home grown gangs will use knives, clubs and machetes, and occasionally guns. But witnesses report seeing these new outlaws with mediaeval war clubs, axes and even South American bolas. No Nottingham gang has ever been known to use such weapons".

Robin had hoped that he would by now see the beginnings of a civil war among the gangs. There had been some rumblings following the deception he pulled off in Bar Sheriff. But it had not reached the level he had hoped.

Now, with this reporter's investigative journalism, the gangs and the police would all be trying to identify the new players.

Robin though it ironic that the reporter had accidentally hit on his unit's nickname of the Outlaws. "We'll have to be low profile for a while", thought Robin.

The pitfalls in planning their next operation against the Tax Collector had almost led to them shelving the objective. But now, with the need to be discrete, an assault on Motte's head office seemed less likely of attracting attention, than another head to head with the gangs.

As it happened, some of their dead ends were about to be opened up.

"I know how to get in", said Will. The comment had come out of the blue, while Will was polishing Robin's Norton Commando motorcycle.

"What do you mean Will?" asked Robin.

Will Scarlet's reply came as a shock, as Robin thought Will was still oblivious to the Outlaw's extra curricular activities.

"The Sheriff building ", replied Will."I know how to get in".

Robin was speechless. It was immediately obvious that Will had got through the additional security, into the Outlaws' most secret areas of the tunnels. Wary of giving anything away that Will did not already know, Robin encouraged him to talk.

Young Will described everything he had seen in the Outlaws' war room. He remembered all of the Tax Collector's network. But most of all, he had correctly interpreted Robin's plans for the new Sheriff Leisure HQ.

Clive Motte's pub and club business had first grown as a way of laundering the money from his criminal enterprises.

Today, Sheriff Leisure earned enough legitimate income to keep Motte a very wealthy man. But that was never enough for the Tax Collector. He needed the power and the fear he invoked at the top of the criminal food chain. So, his legitimate businesses continued to launder the tax he demanded from all the dealers operating beneath him.

Motte had been very careful to distance himself from the criminality that earned him a fortune. The cash and offshore bank transfers kept flowing towards Motte, but he was never in a position to risk arrest. Robin had been watching the construction of Sheriff Leisure's new HQ on the waterfront at Nottingham. One area in the centre of the building, seemed more secure than the rest. Robin knew this was likely to hold a vault. In the era of electronic money transfers, he hoped there might be evidence linking Motte to his untraceable transactions.

Robin's conundrum lay in the level of security in the entire executive suite of Sheriff House. It was not just the central bunker that had heightened security, it was the whole suite of offices built around the core.
Robin and Much had gained access to the building in the guise of cleaners. After all, it was supposedly only the offices of a pub management company. But they had carefully noted the comings and goings in the secure area. Access was by three locks; a traditional key, a keypad, requiring regularly changed codes and a retinal scan.
Robin was sure that if access to the suite was so difficult, it would be even harder to access the building's core.

Will outlined his plan to Robin. "Most of the security looks simple enough", he began. "It would have to be a very special lock for me not to pick it. I have written a computer program that will get through most keypad. But it's the biometrics that would defeat me". He also theorised that if a retinal scan was needed at the front door, more sensitive access would probably need further biometrics.

Will explained that was the part they would need one of Sheriff's directors to assist them with.

"No chance!" exclaimed Much. "They know Motte would kill them. Very slowly and painfully".

But Will did have a plan. "You'll like this", he said. "Not a lot, but you'll like it".

Robin recognised the magician Paul Daniels' catchphrase, and wondered why Will had chosen to use it at that particular time. He was soon to learn that the savant had a very good reason for using the phrase.

On the morning of their operation, Robin and Much entered Sheriff House with the cleaners, as they had done several times before.

Their stolen access cards still worked and eased them through most parts of the building.

As before, they pushed a cleaners' trolley. But this time, the trolley held much more than bleach and polish.

They spent much longer than necessary cleaning one of the toilets, so much so that some of the office staff were becoming impatient at having to go to the next floor. The toilet however, was perfectly placed to execute the next stage of their plan.

Unlike many of Motte's inner circle, Finance Director, Tony Wilkinson was an early bird and a creature of habit. He was almost always among the first to arrive, eager to check on the overnight takings.

Robin had watched Wilkinson arrive several times,

always punctual, always going straight to the executive suite; turning his key, punching his code and putting his eye to the scanner. He also knew it was too early for the rest of Motte's entourage, who would have been in the nightclubs with their boss. Robin moved fast, as Wilkinson reached the toilet door. His powerful arms effortlessly pulled the accountant into the toilet.

In most of the Outlaws' missions, this would be where weapons would be used to gain compliance. But today, Much stood beside the cleaning trolley, armed only with a television.

Wilkinson went white when he saw the image on the screen. It showed the front room of his house, where he had kissed his wife goodbye less than an hour before.

His wife of ten years, Carol, was still in the room, but she was now tied to a dining chair. On either side of Carol stood John and Tuck, dressed in their dark hooded tops. Each of them armed with a deadly looking commando knife.

Off to the side stood Will, his face also hidden by a hoodie. Robin had given Will a red hoodie, in honour of his family name of Scarlet. But Will saw a greater significance.

Will's autism led him to follow any interest to a fanatical level. His current obsession was with cars. But previously, he had been just as fascinated with magic. He had studied the methods of all the great illusionists, with the rigour of a PHD student.

This had explained Will's earlier use of magician Paul Daniels' catchphrase.

It also explained why he took such pride in wearing

his new red hoodie. The garment reminded him of one of his heroes, Dynamo.

Steven Frayne, more commonly known by his stage name "Dynamo", is an English magician, best known for his award-winning television show Dynamo: Magician Impossible. Frayne came from one of Bradford's roughest estates, his magic providing a way out of the bullying he suffered there as a child. This was something Will could identify with, as his autism had often prompted him to be bullied.

On stage, Dynamo often acknowledges his humble beginnings by modelling his stage wear of the urban street clothes of his youth. A red hooded top being one of the items Will had seen his hero wear on stage.

Beside Will was a tall, thin object, almost the same height as him. It was covered by a dark blue cloth, decorated with stars, crescent moons and other astronomical symbols.

At his cue, Will pulled the cloth away with a theatrical flourish. Beneath the cloth was a statue of a woman. Will had created the object in fibreglass, although the original was in metal, a unique construction from one of Germany's greatest clock makers.

She had breasts, arms, legs, and two faces, one in front and one in back. The front face was round, with oval eyes that peered down with a look filled with pity.

The eyes in the back face were closed, but the mouth was slightly open, as if she was about to whisper something.

Long blonde hair covered her head and came down in braids past her waist. Her dress was of worn velvet folded thousands of times, spilling over her feet.

Her breasts were bare, with two strands of pearls and a gold necklace with a black stone on the end draped over them.

Will opened the statue from the front, along a seam between her breasts. The trigger to open her was hidden in the black stone at the end of her gold chain. When the stone was pressed, her arms opened, revealing a hollow interior with sharp iron spikes.

Carol had not yet seen the statue, or its spikes from where she sat. But Wilkinson could see them very clearly and recognised it as an Iron Maiden, a device so fiendish it was once thought to be fictional.

Once the victim was inside, strategically placed spikes would pierce several vital organs. However, they were relatively short spikes, so the wounds wouldn't be instantly fatal. Instead, the victim would linger and bleed to death over several hours.

One of the modern world's most brutal modern regimes also appeared to favour the Iron Maiden. Towards the end of the second Gulf War, after the fall of Saddam Hussain's regime, Wilkinson had read news reports of a gruesome find by reporters in Bagdad. In 2003, Time magazine were reporting from outside the Iraqi Football Association, where Sadam's son Uday Hussein had his office.

Hidden in a pile of dead leaves, not 20 yards from

Uday's office, was that must-have appliance of every medieval dungeon: an iron maiden. It was seven feet tall, three feet across and deep enough to house a grown man. But most gruesome of all, it was clearly worn from use, its nails having lost some of their sharpness.

This was what caused the fear on Wilkinson's face. In his mind, he instantly linked the device with the Iraqi regime and could easily imagine the suffering that his wife would endure inside. "Are you going to cooperate?" asked Robin.

Wilkinson's mind was on overdrive. He loved his wife and could not see her suffer. But he also knew the suffering that Motte would inflict on him if he betrayed his boss.

In the end, he gambled on the Outlaws being unable to go through with their threat. "Go to hell", he shouted.

"Oh, I think it might be the lovely Carol who is headed for hell", replied Robin, as he signalled for Will to continue.

John and Tuck untied Carol Wilkinson and walked her towards the Iron Maiden. She too immediately recognised the device and began to scream and struggle. But her struggles were to no avail and she soon stood within the Maiden.

Her screams and pleas became more frantic, but still her husband chose to call the Outlaws' bluff.

So, Will pressed another button and his meticulously created statue started to move her arms, pulling in her victim, and then closing up, piercing her prey.

Robin was ready with a cloth to push into Wilkinson's mouth, stifling his own inevitable screams.

"It's not instant", reassured Robin. "I can tell you that, the first recorded use of an Iron Maiden was on 14th of August 1515, when a German forger was tortured with the device. As the doors shut, spikes penetrated the forger's body just enough to cause excruciating pain, but not enough to kill him. Crying in vain, the forger lived two days". "Is that what you want for your wife?" asked Robin. "Two days of agony?"

With that, Wilkinson crumpled and led the Outlaws though the security, into the building's central core.

Wilkinson would arrive home to find his wife unharmed.

Will's Iron Maiden appeared terrifyingly real, but he had studied the art of illusion.

Young Will had studied the famous Harry Houdini's Spanish Maiden escape.

To escape the Maiden Houdini gripped one of the spikes at the hinge side and lifted it upward a fraction of an inch. Each time the cover was pushed upward, the spring of each hinge worked on the pin ratchet and the pins were slowly forced out of the springs. Once finished, Houdini opened the box at the side, using the padlocks as hinges. Then after escaping, he replaced the pins by pushing them through the hinges from the bottom. The box appeared perfectly secure and ready for inspection.

But it was not Houdini's illusion that Will had replicated here, as the occupant of the Maiden was not in on the act. Rather, Will followed the example of another of his heroes, Paul Daniels.

Paul's most controversial trick, was during a live Halloween special in 1987, when the magician sparked panic among his fans by faking his own death.

In the show's climax, Daniels performed, on live TV, a re-creation of Houdini's trick in which he was chained inside an iron maiden. He had to escape before the door swung fully shut to avoid being impaled on spikes.

At the critical moment the door slammed shut, leaving viewers believing Paul had been trapped and killed inside.

Daniels failed to appear, the screen cut to black, giving the impression the trick had gone badly wrong. The BBC's phone lines were jammed with over 11,000 calls from viewers, whose concern turned to complaints when it was revealed to be a hoax.

It was the shock of seeing the Maiden close on his wife that Will was relying on for his illusion. He did not know exactly how Daniels had staged his trick. But Will had designed retractable spikes. The slightly blunt spikes dug into Carol Wilkinson, just enough to produce her reaction. But as the box closed, the spikes retracted safely away. To Tony Wilkinson, it appeared terrifyingly real and he complied with everything Robin asked of him.

Chapter 15.

Robin's big win was not to happen. With Will's help and Tony Wilkinson's reluctant cooperation, Robin had hoped to raid Clive Motte's off shore bank accounts. But the Tax Collector's paranoid security was even tighter than they expected.
Wilkinson's pass codes and biometrics had got them right to the heart of Sheriff House. They had emptied the vault of nearly a quarter of a million pounds. Wilkinson had even been able to copy flight charts and maps of landing locations that parts of Motte's network used to import their narcotics.
With Wilkinson believing that his wife was bleeding to death inside the Iron Maiden, he gave the Outlaws everything that was in his power to give. But the off shore accounts were not his to give. Motte trusted no one with the millions of pounds he held as untraceable working capital. The retina scans of three of his most trusted lieutenants, including Wilkinson, were programmed into the computers. But all of them were useless without Motte himself being present to add his own biometric check.

Tony Wilkinson was left wondering whether to tell his boss about the robbery and risk his legendary and violent temper. Or, as their business handled so much off the books cash, whether he could hide the theft from Motte.
Either way, he could easily regret what could potentially become a fatal decision.
Robin also had a decision to make about the £250,000 now hidden in his tunnels. Somehow, the

money was destined for charitable purposes, but he needed a way to distribute it without suspicion on himself, or revealing where the money came from. But for now, Robin had things to worry about as the Duke of Loxley.

The Loxley Estate Hunt was Nottinghamshire's biggest and oldest hunt. It was also one of the most respected among Britain's 179 hunting communities. Contrary to some beliefs, hunting is still widely practiced, with around 320,000 people turning out nationally.

It had been years since Robin had ridden with the hunt, but now, as Duke, it was expected of him. But Robin was also worried about whether Clive Motte had managed to influence traditions that generations of his family had built.

Fox hunting originated in the 16th century, with foxes being referred to as beasts of the chase since medieval times. The earliest known attempt to hunt a fox with hounds was in Norfolk, in 1534, where farmers began chasing foxes with their dogs for the purpose of pest control. The first use of packs specifically trained to hunt foxes was in the late 1600s.

The Loxley's ties to the Dukeries dated back to the 1500s, when Bess of Hardwick used her influence to bring so many Dukes to North Nottinghamshire. This put Robin's ancestors there, right in the early days of the hunt.

Like many proponents of fox hunting, Robin viewed it as an important part of rural culture, and useful for reasons of conservation and pest control. But he was well aware of the counter arguments that it is cruel and unnecessary. When challenged, Robin would argue that foxes are considered vermin by the law of England and Wales. He would also argue that as an agricultural and game shooting area, the Dukeries was vulnerable to the fox's tendency to commit acts of surplus killing, yet having killed many birds they eat only one.

But privately, Robin valued the tradition and the employment it provided for people like John Little's father, the former gamekeeper.

Despite his love of the Dukeries' traditions and his sense of duty as the Duke, Robin had mixed feelings about the first hunt of this season.

He was excited for the opportunity to ride again with Marion, who was certain to be there. But the certainty of Marion's attendance meant that her father, as owner of the estate and most of the hunt infrastructure, would also be there.

As always, Robin was at the start of any event promptly. John and Tuck, also having grown up on the estate were with him. But Much was no fan of hunting. In fact, his last words to Robin as he left the cottage were to quote Oscar Wilde, from his 1893 play A Woman of No Importance, who famously referred to "the English country gentleman galloping after a fox" as "the unspeakable in full pursuit of the uneatable".

Robin's punctuality meant that he was there to see the key people of the hunt arriving.

As a social ritual, participants in a fox hunt fill

specific roles, the most prominent of which is the Master, who has responsibility for the overall management of the hunt, and the care and breeding of the Hunt's fox hounds, as well as control and direction of its paid staff.

The Master also works very closely with the Huntsman who is the most highly paid professional among the hunt staff. He is responsible for directing the hounds. The Huntsman is instantly recognisable, as he carries a horn to communicate to the hounds, followers and Whippers In.

The Whippers-in, or Whips, are made up from the estate's other paid staff, such as the Gamekeepers. They are assistants to the huntsman. Their main job is to keep the pack all together, especially to prevent the hounds from straying or 'riotting', which term refers to the hunting of animals other than the hunted fox or trail line. To help them to control the pack, they carry hunting whips. It amused Robin to know that this country tradition inspired parliament to use whip for a member who enforces party discipline and ensure the attendance of other members at important votes.

While Robin was thinking about the history of the hunt, he noticed the expression on John's face change. "What are they doing in colours", exclaimed John. It was more a statement of disgust than a question.

Robin turned in the direction that John was looking. He saw Clive Motte dressed in a red hunting jacket. His wife, Helen wore a black version of the jacket, with a flash of red at the back of her collar.

"A bit early for that isn't it?" Robin knew that as

owner of the estate, Motte would eventually adopt the traditional mode of dress. But parts of the tradition were earned, not bought.

A prominent feature of hunts is hunt members wearing 'colours'. This attire usually consists of the traditional red coats worn by huntsmen, masters, former masters, whippers-in (regardless of sex). Other hunt staff members and male members may also be invited by masters to wear colours and hunt buttons as a mark of appreciation for their involvement in the organization and running of the hunt.
Ladies generally wear coloured collars on their black or navy coats. These help them stand out from the rest of the field.
The red coats are often misleadingly called "pinks". Various theories about the origin of this term have been given, ranging from the colour of a weathered scarlet coat to the name of a famous tailor.
Such was Motte's arrogance, that he had not waited for an invitation from the Master to wear his pink.

Another differentiation in dress between the amateur and professional staff is found in the ribbons at the back of the hunt cap.
The professional staff wear their hat ribbons down, while amateur staff and members of the field wear their ribbons up. John's annoyance with Motte grew as he saw the Tax Collector turn, to show his hat ribbon loose at the rear of his cap.

Robin was distracted from annoyance with Clive Motte as Marion walked into the muster area.

She nodded a brief acknowledgment to her father, but walked straight over to Robin, with a smile on her face. "I hoped you would be here", said Marion. "I'm the Duke", replied Robin. "I'm supposed to be at all the traditional events".

He was pleased to see that unlike her step-mother, Marion wore a plain blue hunting jacket, with her cap ribbon tightly tied.

Then, the Master of the Hunt walked over to Marion, closely followed by Clive and Helen Motte. "Miss Motte, I have something for you", began the Master. He handed Marion a presentation box, covered in red velvet. Robin knew instantly what the box contained, and he was interested in seeing how Marion would react.

It was clear from Marion's face that she did not know what to expect as she opened the box. Inside the box were four brass buttons, cast with the crest of the Loxley Hunt.

The number of buttons on a hunt member's jacket is significant. The Master wears a scarlet coat with four brass buttons while the huntsman and other professional staff wear five. Amateur whippers-in also wear four buttons.

Robin and John were both delighted with Marion's reaction to the presentation. She had clearly learned enough about hunting tradition to know that the highest honour is to be awarded hunt buttons by the Hunt Master. This means you can then wear scarlet if male, or the coloured hunt collar if female. "It's a kind offer", said Marion to the Master. "But would you first let me prove myself on the hunt?"

"That's class'" whispered John.

Robin could see from Clive Motte's face that he was not happy with his daughter's reaction. He knew that Clive and Helen Motte were both yet to ride with the hunt. Marion had also told him that Helen was far from being a proficient horse woman.

The time came to mount up. Horses on hunts can range from specially bred and trained field hunters to casual hunt attendees riding a wide variety of horse and pony types.

Marion had her own horse that she had brought back with her from Cambridge.

Helen had been loaned a fairly mild mannered horse from the estate stables.

But Clive Motte, true to form had spent a small fortune on a traditional hunter, of the type which had become a prominent feature of many hunts.

Hunters must be well-mannered, have the athletic ability to clear large obstacles such as wide ditches, tall fences and rock walls, and have the stamina to keep up with the hounds. This athletic skill required of horse and rider alike during a fox hunt is the origin of equestrian sports including steeplechase and point to point racing.

Since the UK hunting ban in 2005, the hunts have been restricted to drag hunting. This involves dragging an object over the ground to lay a scent for the hounds to follow. There are some exceptions, such as permitting the riders to follow if the hounds pick up a fox scent on their own.

So, 20 minutes in advance of the hunt, riders set out trailing behind them an odoriferous substance, mixed with oil, to lay the scent.

Despite the ban on fox hunting, groups such as the League Against Cruel Sports alleged that breaches of law are taking place in some hunts. With Motte's history of criminality, it seemed inevitable that the Loxley Hunt would become one of them.

Motte's blood lust would not be satisfied with following the scent dragged behind the lead riders. He wanted to hunt a red fox, the traditional prey animal of a fox hunt. The small omnivorous predators live in underground burrows called earths, but during the day foxes often lay up in rough brushy areas called coverts.

As soon as they reached the first covert that the Huntsman confirmed could contain a sleeping fox, Motte became excited. "Cast the hounds in after Reynard", shouted Motte. He was using a colloquial name for a fox, taken from European literature of the twelfth century. Reynard was a human like red fox and trickster figure. His adventures involved him deceiving other animals for his own advantage. The stories, written during the Middle Ages were often seen as parodies of medieval literature such as courtly love stories, as well as satire of political and religious institutions.

Motte's first try for a fox was to be successful. The hounds caught a scent and the startled fox was off, running at speeds of up to 30 mph.

Once the pack manages to pick up the scent of a fox, they will track it for as long as they are able, and the riders follow, by the most direct route possible. Led by the Huntsman, the riders kept pace with the hounds until they were able to overtake and kill the fox.

Since taking possession of Loxley Hall, Motte now saw himself quite the country gent. He had been studying the social rituals, which are important to hunts, including the many which have fallen into disuse. One of the most notable was the act of blooding. Motte seemed determined to resurrect this tradition, which had not happened at Loxley since the nineteenth century. He bent down, covered his hands in the blood of the fox, and then smeared it onto the cheeks and forehead of his wife.
Helen seemed to delight in this ancient ritual for a newly initiated hunt follower.
Motte then turned his attention to Marion, who backed away in disgust. Determined to involve his daughter in one of the more bloodthirsty ancient practices, Motte drew his knife, cutting off the tail, or brush, the feet and head as trophies. He then threw the carcass to the hounds, before trying to present Marion with the brush. Again she rejected what she saw as a disgusting act.

Marion jumped onto her horse and rode like the wind. All she wanted at that moment was to get away from her father and his awful wife. Robin rode after her, having to drive his horse hard to stay with the expert horsewoman.
Already he had in his mind to replace the Huntsman who had allowed this to happen. The Huntsman may have been employed by the estate, but most of the Hunt's operating costs came from its members. There was a certain amount of democracy, into

which Robin could tap. He had just the candidate in mind. The son of an estate gamekeeper, who he trusted with his life; John Little.

Chapter 16.

Something was wrong, but the pilot did not know what. He had made the approach to Gamston Airport, two miles south of Retford hundreds of times before. But this time, his instruments had failed, his eyes were giving him slightly conflicting information to what he was receiving from the control tower and an unforecast fog had started to drift in.

The small plane was owned by one of Clive Motte's arms length companies. The flight into Retford had become commonplace for the pilot, since Motte's move to Loxley.

The tiny private airfield was one of many former wartime airfields in Nottinghamshire. The current private owners bought it in 1993, beginning a program of improvements including a complete runway resurfacing and building a new elevated control tower and fire station.

The improved airfield was now a far cry from its wartime opening in 1942, when Commonwealth and Polish aircrews flew from its runway.

Aircraft as famous as Wellingtons, Hurricanes, Meteors and Vampires have worked from Gamston. Today, Clive Motte's use of the airport was far less heroic than its wartime purpose.

Gamston operates between seven am and seven pm, which worked fine for Sheriff Leisure's routine flights, moving cash and personnel around the country and flying to some of the company's legitimate interests in Europe. But when Motte wanted to move drugs around, he needed his planes to fly much later than the usual seven pm cut off.

With The Tax Collector's power and money, bribing the operators was a simple matter. The trade off was that there were no emergency services available, but Motte himself would never be on a drugs flight, so cared nothing for the risk.

The pilot started his approach towards Gamston. He had the street lights of Retford as a general target, then as he flew closer, the bright lights of the airport's new control tower would line him up for his approach. Pilots call the manoeuvre a "normal approach and landing", as under most circumstances it is quite routine. But this was going to be far from normal.

He started to line himself up, running more on sight than his instruments. He flew lower than his official approaches, as no one but the Gamston tower could know of his landing. Then suddenly, the "normal approach" became anything but routine.

"What's this?" exclaimed the pilot. "The bloody Bermuda Triangle". His instruments had gone dead and the magnetic compass began to spin uncontrollably.

As he composed himself, and realised his instruments were not coming back on line, the pilot realised, "never mind, I can do this landing by sight". Turning his attention from his useless instruments, the pilot could just pick out the distinctive lights of the Gamston Tower. "OK", thought the pilot "let's do this", as he adjusted his flight path to line up with the tower. Then, as quickly as his instruments had failed, a fog bank seemed to come from nowhere, making the tower lights a dull glow.

Just as the pilot was adjusting his eyes to the

dimmer lights, the tower and the lights of Retford completely disappeared. Before the pilot had chance to think, or panic, he heard Gamston Tower though his headphones. "Light aircraft, please adjust approach. You are off course". The voice sounded different than usual, quite sing song and soothing. "Gamston Tower", replied the pilot. "I have no instruments and fog is obscuring visual approach ". Any concerns about what was happening drifted away as the pilot took his lead from the soft voice of the tower.

Listening to the soothing voice of the tower, the pilot started what he believed to be a complete go around of the airport. What he was actually doing was taking a huge curve to avoid Gamston completely, and resume a flight path due north. Such was the soporific effect of the tower's voice, that the pilot lost track of the additional 10 miles he flew.

On the ground, in line with where the pilot was now flying, stood Will Scarlet. He wore the scarlet hoodie, which made him feel like the magician Dynamo.
All around Will was an array of computers, monitors and radio equipment.
Will spoke softly and hypnotically into his headset. This was the soothing voice that held the pilot captivated. After a few minutes of Will's directions, the pilot spotted the control tower and runway lights. He began his approach for the second time.
For a normal approach and landing, light aircraft usually fly the length of the runway, in a downwind

direction, lining up their wing tip light against the runway, giving an indication of height. Then they fly across the base of the runway, before beginning their actual approach.

As the pilot flew across the base and into his approach, he saw the four lights he was expecting near the start of the runway. These lights indicated his aiming point. Speed and angle are critical, as when on final approach, the plane is always close to either a stall, or pulling its nose back up. The pilot must concentrate hard to avoid needing to go around for another approach. Will was hoping the pilot was now in full control, as a go around would ruin the illusion he was creating.

Despite what he thought was happening, the pilot was not on his final approach to Gamston. He was actually bringing his plane into land at another of Nottinghamshire's many former WW2 airfields.

During the darkest hours of World War II, Nottinghamshire was one of England's major locations for training RAF bomber aircrew. To cater for the growing demands the county's pre-war grass airstrips were upgraded and many new air fields were built.

In the latter phases of the war visitors to the county included thousands of American Airborne Troops, their carrier planes and gliders, in the run up to major campaigns including: Operation Overlord (the D-Day Landings) and Operation Market (the Arnhem Campaign).

The airfield the pilot was about to land on was the

disused Bircotes airstrip, one mile West of Bawtry. Bircotes was vacated by the RAF in 1948 and returned to agriculture. Only a few of the former airfield structures remain.

The pilot was not seeing an agricultural field and derelict infrastructure. He saw the very much in use, recently modernised Gamston Airport. The newly resurfaced runway awaited his undercarriage. The new Control Tower was brightly lit ahead of him and the runway navigation lights shone exactly where he expected them to be.

Will had to time his next action to perfection. He watched the descent intently, using state of the art equipment to monitor the aircraft's altitude. The pilot was preparing for a landing on Tarmac, but unknown to him, a soft landing on grass awaited him.

At the precise moment, Will altered the lighting, the Tarmac disappeared and bright lights illuminated the grass below the plane. Will knew that for his trick to work, his change in lighting would need to be too late for the pilot to pull up, but allow enough time to adjust his landing.

Executing a soft field landing isn't a black art, but it is a maximum performance maneuver which most pilots learn in training, but do not practice often afterwards.

Will and Robin knew that Motte's pilots had ample opportunity to practice, while making drug collections for the Tax Collector. So they had confidence in the pilot avoiding a crash.

Within seconds of the changing illumination, the pilot

had reacted and was transferring the weight of his aircraft from the wings to the wheels as gently as possible to keep the nose wheel off the ground for as long as possible.

Just as they hoped, the pilot adjusted his landing to a slightly nose high attitude.

Expertly, he brought in a little power to ease the touchdown and help airflow over the tail. Then, just at the right moment, he used full elevators as the aircraft slowed and he kept the nose off the runway for as long as possible.

The pilot had done his job and landed his small plane safely. But he was in a state of confusion. The same change of lighting which made the Tarmac disappear had also made the airport infrastructure vanish. Gone were the control tower, terminal building and the huge new hangers. In their place were fields, trees and barns.

Before the pilot could properly take in his unexpected surroundings, four hooded figures ran out of the shadows. Each of them waved a vicious looking battle axe, and looked to the pilot like Viking berserkers.

This was precisely the effect Robin had hoped for. His young savant protégé had delivered the plane full of drugs to Robin. Now he and his Outlaws had their part to play in keeping the drugs off the streets of Nottinghamshire.

Robin had chosen his historic mode of combat well. Until the Outlaws gained control of the aircraft, there was every possibility that the pilot could turn and

take off again.
But fixated on the Viking apparitions before him, the pilot could not regain the logic that would fly him out of harm's way.

There were many types of axe that Robin could have chosen from history, as the most common hand weapon among history's warriors was the axe. Swords were more expensive to make and only wealthy warriors could afford a sword.
But Robin knew that battle axes are particularly associated in Western imagination with the Vikings. Scandinavian marauders used them as their stock weapon during their heyday, between the 8th and 11th century. It was this fearsome image that Robin used to capture the pilot's attention.
Robin had chosen a selection of axes for his Outlaws. He and John were the first to run towards the plane. Their own large frames were ideal for carrying their weapons of choice. Theirs were a larger axe, which evolved later in the Viking period. They were specialised for use in battle, with larger heads and longer shafts. The handles were as long as a man and made to be used with both hands. These were the Dane Axe.
The crescent-shaped heads were originally made of wrought iron with a carbon steel edge. But as the centuries elapsed, they evolved to use steel, which was what Robin had made his axes from. The hardwood handles of his military axes were reinforced with metal bands called langets. These were intended to stop an enemy warrior cutting the shaft, but it was for part of the plane, not another warrior that the reinforcement was needed.

Robin and John reached the front of the plane together. Both men raised their huge axes aloft, then brought them down, towards the plane.

They required less swinging power than one might expect, as the large bladed heads allow gravity and momentum to do most of the work. So, the two axe heads simultaneously struck either side of the plane's single propeller. As the propeller shattered into several pieces, the pilot knew that without his plane's only means of propulsion he could not escape in the aircraft.

Panicking, the pilot began to open his cockpit, in the hope of escaping on foot. But Tuck and Much moved forward to prevent any escape. They each carried two very specialised battle axes.

The first of their axes, they would deploy as a deadly projectile.

The francisca evolved as a throwing weapon during the Early Middle Ages by the Franks, from about 500 to 750. It was also used by other Germanic peoples of the period, including the Anglo-Saxons, who brought the weapon to England.

The Vikings later adopted the throwing axe, with its distinctly arch-shaped head, widening toward the cutting edge and terminating in a prominent point at both the upper and lower corners.

With accuracy honed from hours of practice in the forests of the Dukeries, Tuck and Much launched their francisca axes towards the Plexiglas cockpit, shattering it instantly. Then, while the pilot was disorientated by their first axes, they moved forward

with the second of their weapons.
Their follow up weapons were the skeggox, or
bearded axe, so named for their trailing lower blade
edge which increased cleaving power.
Striking together, at either side of the pilot, their
skeggox cut through the aluminium of the fuselage,
providing a door to exit the cockpit. Then, to further
ease the pilot's exit from the plane, Robin again
stepped forward with his Dane Axe. One powerful
blow removed the nose wheel, dropping the cockpit
down to floor level.

It was not just the fearsome sight of the axe, or the
fearless skill of the Vikings that intimidated the
Christians of Britain. Their habit of naming axes after
Norse gods was inadvertently psychologically
intimidating. King Magnus of Norway named his axe
Hel, after the Norse goddess of death. Christians
associated this name to the word Hell.
So famous was Magnus that his axe is still portrayed
in the Norwegian Coat of Arms.
The habit of naming their weapons spread across
most Scandinavian weaponry. Axes in particular
were often named after she trolls. This led to the
modern use of Battle Axe to describe an evil or bad
tempered woman. Robin could not help but take
King Magnus' Hel axe one step further, naming his
axe Helen, after his father's widow.

Once the pilot had been removed from the plane,
the Outlaws set about the process of interrogating
him for information on the Tax Collector's business.
This time they needed far less violence than they
had previously with the street gangsters. The pilot

was not a street tough; he usually had no cause to fight in the service of Clive Motte. The combined terror of what had happened to him loosened his tongue. The pilot had never experienced anything like these Viking warriors coming out of nowhere. Neither could his frightened brain comprehend how he ended up in the field. His last memory was being in the latter stages of landing at Gamston Airport, when suddenly, and magically, he was on a derelict wartime airfield.

Robin obtained everything the pilot knew about Motte's airborne drug routes. He now had many more options to hit back at the Tax Collector.

The Outlaws secured the pilot a safe distance from the plane, while they set about recovering anything of value from the plane.

The drugs were left inside the plane, as the plans they had for them would also bring rescue for the pilot.

As the hooded men turned to leave the plane, they again deployed one of the few modern weapons they were prepared to use in Britain. Four incendiary grenades landed in the broken shell of the plane. The resulting fireball could be seen ten miles away in the Gamston control tower, where they were still trying to regain radio contact with the pilot.

Chapter 17.

The Outlaws had slept late in Robin's cottage after their nocturnal mission. As they drank coffee together around the big kitchen table, they all enjoyed the view out onto the Loxley Estate. Today, that view was added to by Marion doing her daily yoga practice. Marion's skill and flexibility showed the years of dedication she had devoted to the eastern art.

As Robin began to debrief their taking of the Tax Collector's plane, he smiled as he remembered that it was Marion who had provided the inspiration for that operation.

Will Scarlet liked Marion and she had shown enormous patience with the autistic young man. The two of them could happily chat for hours at a time. More often than not, the subject of their conversation was the Sorcar family of magicians. She had seen the Sorcars many times on her regular trips to India. They were well known throughout the sub continent and Marion had sought out their performances at every opportunity.

Pratul Sorcar (P.C. Sorcar Senior) had been a renowned magician from the glory days of Indian magic, which made the Indian Rope Trick so famous. But he was just the latest in eight generations of magicians. The family's practice as illusionists continued with his son, Prodip Sorcar (P.C. Sorcar Junior), who had become an internationally known magician in his own right. Sorcar Junior was no side show charlatan, he had

an M.Sc. in applied psychology from Calcutta University, which assisted him in creating his illusions in the minds of his audience.
P.C. Sorcar Junior had caught Will's imagination, when she told the excited youngster about his talent for making huge objects disappear.
In 1992 Prodip made a train packed with passengers vanish. To add credibility to his illusion, he performed the feat in the presence of Justice Mukulgopal Mukherjee, senior railway officials, and the media.
He is also credited with making Calcutta's Victoria Memorial disappear and an aircraft vanish in Japan. Will decided then and there that he must himself perform such a magnificent illusion.
 Will's determination to learn from P.C. Sorcar Junior grew when Marion told him about Prodip's claim that he will perform magic till he is 123 years old, confident he will remain alive till then.
Will was becoming fixated on the idea that practicing magic might have the same effect on him. Despite having not reached 23 years of age, he very much desired to live a further 100 years.

The magical dynasty of the Sorcar family had continued into another generation, with Prodip's daughter Maneka, who assisted her father with their most famous illusion.
This was the performance that really inspired Will. Marion had been present at the performance in 2000, so she described the experience in detail which enthralled the young savant.

Marion described the magician appearing on stage

dressed in a glitzy robe and turban, looking like a Maharaja of the ancient times. He stood before one of the wonders of the world, the Taj Mahal, built in the 17th century in memory of Emperor Shah Jahan's wife as a symbol of their eternal love. It is often described as the most beautiful building in the world.

Marion vividly remembered being among the onlookers gasping in astonishment as Prodip made the Mughal architectural marvel disappear into thin air.

This time there were even more witnesses than he had for his vanishing train illusion.

Prodip made the Taj vanish in broad daylight in front of a distinguished gathering of the country's elite; prominent dignitaries, veteran politicians, scholars, literary figures and a host of foreign tourists.

But before the viewers could be transported back to the real world from the world of illusions, the Taj Mahal was back in its place. It took P.C. Sorcar Junior, precisely two minutes to perform the trick.

Will spent the following days reading everything he could find about P.C. Sorcar Junior, and watching every recording of his performances. He was determined to learn all he could from this flamboyant magician.

Will took particular interest in an interview given by Prodip, immediately after his grand illusion. Sorcar told the interviewer that he made the Taj Mahal disappear by optical illusion, by stopping the light rays from reaching the spectators' eyes. When pressed about if it was magic or science, he replied "It was the magic of advanced science by using lots of laser beams, heat, sound and other ways of bending light rays". Will particularly liked Prodip's opinion that "science and magic are both the same. The magic of today will become science tomorrow". Will could see himself as a Magical Scientist. Although Sorcar did not give much away, some of his comments did strike a cord with the savant, who was already skilled in the art of illusion.

"It was not mass hypnotism," Sorcar was quoted as saying. "I just kept the Taj away from your eyes. It was a perfect illusion." "There was nothing supernatural in this vanishing act. This is all science, the science of controlling the mind and the willpower to create a psychic balance with the environment." To the lay observer, P.C. Sorcar Junior had not revealed much about his methods. But Will was able to compare what he had learned, with David Copperfield's famous disappearance of the Statue of Liberty.

Will Scarlet had watched Copperfield's recording innumerable times. He had also studied an account of the methodology given in William Poundstone's book of Bigger Secrets. Poundstone says that his book "seeks to explore a number of mysteries, and reveal the uncensored truth about all sorts of stuff you are never supposed to know".

The book describes Copperfield setting up two towers on a stage, supporting an arch to hold the huge curtain that would be used to conceal the statue. The TV cameras and the live audience only saw the monument through the arch. When the curtains closed, David waxed poetic while the stage was slowly, and imperceptibly, turned.

When the curtains opened, the statue was hidden behind one of the towers, and the audience was looking out to sea. Voila! The Statue of Liberty has disappeared!

Even if the stage hadn't completely hidden the statue, the towers were so brightly lit that the audience would be nightblinded.

Copperfield had also set up two rings of lights, one around Liberty, and another set up somewhere else. When the trick "happened," his assistants simply turned off the lights around the statue and turned on the other set for the helicopters to circle around.

So, learning from these two great magicians, Will was able to help Robin divert the Tax Collector's plane to a landing strip of their choosing. He created his own grand illusion, making an entire airport disappear.

Clive Motte's pilot guessed something was wrong with his approach when his instruments failed and an unforcast fog started to drift in. This was Will Scarlet applying some science to begin his own great illusion.

An electromagnetic pulse weapon, provided by the Outlaws had destroyed the small plane's instruments. Then, a military fog machine, also from Robin's unit, provided the evening mist.

The pilot was using the street lights of Retford as a general target to begin his approach towards Gamston. But as the fog started to thicken across his flight path, two huge telescopic aerials rose invisibly in front of him. Strung between the aerials was a closely woven mesh that coupled with the fog, obscured Retford from the pilot's view.

Just as Copperfield had done, Will turned his audience to create his illusion, Will did not have a revolving stage, but he used his voice to turn the plane. The soothing voice that the pilot took to be Gamston Tower, was Will Scarlet, speaking through one of Robin's powerful transmitters.

P.C. Sorcar Junior had claimed that his illusion was not mass hypnotism. But Will had long ago mastered the art of hypnotism. The soft, sing song voice that the pilot heard helped his mind to accept Will's reality. Believing that Will's soothing voice was coming from the tower, the pilot started what he believed to be a complete go around of the airport. What Will was actually doing was talking the pilot through a huge curve to avoid Gamston completely, and resume a flight path due north. The soporific effect of Will's voice, made the pilot lost track of the additional 10 miles he flew.

After a few minutes of Will's directions, the pilot spotted what he thought were the control tower and runway lights. These were actually a scaffolding structure and lights built by the Outlaws, and now controlled by Will's bank of computers.

Aided by Will's hypnotic voice and a second of Robin's fog machines, the pilot began what he believed to be his second approach to Gamston. Despite what he thought was happening, the pilot was actually bringing his plane into land at the now abandoned, former WW2 airfield at Bircotes.

The angle of approach had placed the streetlights of Bawtry precisely where the pilot thought Retford should be. Fog and more mesh obscured other landmarks that Will did not want the pilot to see. Then his final touch was to use coloured lighting to turn the grass runway into Tarmac.

The cumulative effects of unexpectedly landing on grass and listening to Will's hypnotic voice had already put the pilot in a confused state. The sight of Robin and his Viking berserkers completed the effect, adding a final flourish to Will's illusion.

Robin could not have been more proud of what the young savant had achieved for them. In fact, as he looked around the table at his band of Outlaws, Robin realised he had a very special team fighting with him.

In the days that followed it became clear that the pilot did not hold quite so rigidly to the gangster's code of silence, or Omertà. Where most of Motte's thugs and Lieutenants had worked up through the ranks, the pilot had been hired for his skills and was not so entrenched in their ways. He quickly broke under the pressure of police questioning, having already been softened up by the Outlaws.

The problem was, that his story was so outlandish that the police did not believe him. They thought his story of a vanishing airport and reincarnated Vikings was just an elaborate way of saying "no comment". Either that, or he had been sampling his own cargo of narcotics. The account was so ridiculous that some of the investigating officers could not wait to repeat his fanciful tale.

The TV news bulletins treated the incident as a joke story. It was presented in a very tongue in cheek manner by the news team. But there was one reporter, outside of the mainstream media crews, who listened to the story with a more open mind. This was John Prince, the investigative reporter who had first made the link to Robin's historic weapons, and argued against his Outlaws being part of a local turf war.

Prince had not yet learned of the Iron Maiden illusion performed on Carol Wilkinson because Motte's accountant had chosen not to tell anyone about his treachery. But Wilkinson's fear would soon grow when Prince began to tell his version of the story.

Prince was beginning to get air time for his investigation. They were small segments to start with, buried in the local news bulletins. But as he gathered more information, his exposure would steadily grow.

John Prince faced the camera and listed some of the more outlandish element's of Robin's campaign. "Vikings, axes, bows and arrows, mediaeval war clubs and magically disappearing airports". Prince explained these were all the fantastical elements that had emerged in coverage of the latest drug war. "Many of my colleagues would have you believe that these actions are the work of street thugs", continued Prince. "I say no! Guns, knives and fists are their weapons of choice. Why would they suddenly take an interest in history, when the ghettos of America have always provided their influence?"

Prince went on to detail another theory that had found its way into the media. "An alternative view put forward by other journalists, would have us believe these are all hallucinations, caused by a bad batch of drugs". Prince did not like this theory either. "Would they have us believe that every Nottingham gang member has sampled the same dodgy drugs?" he asked. "Have the independent witnesses also, by chance, taken the same hallucinogens? I say, no they have not".

The screen behind John Prince then filled with the artist's caricatures that someone had produced after one of the Outlaws earlier raids. The hooded tops and ancient weapons were surprisingly close to the image Robin had unconsciously created for his team. "I say there is a new team in town", continued Prince. "These are not street thugs, their methods are too subtle and too different. The question is; are they another drug gang, looking to take over Nottingham. Or, do we have a gang of vigilantes working in our city?"

Tony Wilkinson watched Prince's bulletins with growing fear. He had no idea whether the Outlaws were rival dealers, or vigilantes. What he did know, was that they were no hallucination, Robin and his team were frighteningly real.
Wilkinson's mind was even more of a mess now. The information Robin had forced from him led directly to the taking of Motte's plane. He knew the Tax Collector would kill him for his betrayal. But, if he withheld information about the Outlaw's, his death could become much more painful.

Chapter 18.

"It is a great pleasure for me to be here today on behalf of Sheriff Leisure.
I would like to seize the opportunity to congratulate all of my employees and customers on an outstanding fundraising campaign. Our donations this year have amounted to £20,000 towards malaria treatment and prevention in Columbia.
We all know that parts of South America are in a desperate economic condition, many of its natural resources exhausted and different political groups still tearing the continent into separate parts due to their endless conflicts. But common people, victimised by the corruption and the cartels, have a right to live and to enjoy life with their families and kids."

Robin was at a table in Loxley Hall's grand ballroom. As the Duke, he had been invited to Clive Motte's charity ball, raising money for South American malaria prevention. Robin could not believe his ears, hearing Motte talk about the Columbian cartels. "He must be one of the cartels' best customers", thought Robin.

Motte continued with his speech. "However, the conditions are grave. Poor, if any medical care and a high rate of infant deaths. I can hardly imagine that all this may be possible in the 21st century. When I was last in Columbia, I met Albertine. She's three years old. Like the rest of her family, she's no stranger to the symptoms of malaria; fever, headache and feeling weak. Sadly, one of her

brothers had already died from the disease.
Millions of children suffer agonising bouts of malaria every year, and thousands of young lives are tragically lost. Children are most at risk while they sleep. That's why it's vital families use insecticide-treated mosquito nets at night to prevent the spread of malaria. Clinics funded by Sheriff Leisure work with Albertine's community, training volunteers to pass on life-saving advice and show families how to hang their nets. Our workers also teach the use of other controls to help manage the risk: education, better housekeeping, fumigation, drainage works, mossie coils and stocking rainwater tanks with guppy fish to eat the larvae.
But we still need to protect many other children like Albertine from this deadly disease.

John was just as sceptical as his friend about the Tax Collector's motives. "Saint Motte has got to be up to something. It can't be through the goodness of his heart, because there isn't any".
"No", replied Robin. "There's an ulterior motive, and it will be something to do with the drug cartels".

Motte was about to give a hint as to his interest in malaria. "That is why I have decided that I should do even more to help children like Albertine. One of my companies has taken shares in the medical research company Nottingham Science.
They are already working on new drugs and insecticides to combat malaria. With your help, I hope to open a subsidiary company in Bogota, to put help closer to where it is needed".
"Legitimate cover for cocaine smuggling", whispered

Robin. He knew from interrogating Tony Wilkinson, that Motte's holdings in Nottingham Science was nothing new. The shares had been held by one of Sheriff Leisure's shell companies for several years. What Robin wanted to know was; if the lab was already up to no good, or had it been bought in readiness for this project.

Like most pharmaceutical science companies, Nottingham Science is a mixed discipline laboratory, involved in the design, testing and delivery of drugs. They apply knowledge from chemistry, biology anatomy, physiology, epidemiology, statistics, and chemical engineering. A perfect mix for Motte to hide some less humanitarian research.

When Robin started planning action against Nottingham Science it became plain that Much already had quite strong views about the company. Just as he had stayed clear of the Loxley Hunt because of disagreement with blood sports, Much had very strong views about scientific testing on animals.
Nottingham Science was one of many research laboratories that did test on animals. In most areas of drug research, it is a legal necessity.
Robin knew that the extra security to keep out animal rights activists would serve the Tax Collector's purposes very well indeed. He had no doubt that the security elements of Motte's companies would also be profiting from the protection of the site.

Robin too had mixed feelings about animal testing,

not as strongly held as his friend Much, but enough for him to think about the arguments.

Before the 20th century, laws regulating drugs were lax. Today, all new pharmaceuticals undergo rigorous animal testing before being licensed for human use. Supporters of the use of animals in experiments, such as the British Royal Society, argue that virtually every medical achievement in the 20th century relied on the use of animals in some way.

But opponents argue that many of the experiments cause pain to the animals involved or reduce their quality of life in other ways. They claim it is morally wrong to cause animals to suffer by experimenting on them for the benefit of humans. Much was in the camp of the opponents, but Robin trusted his friend to remain professional throughout the operation.

When the Outlaws left the Loxley tunnels, they were again five in number. Young Will Scarlet had earned his place among the team and his deep red hoodie stood out among the greens and blacks of the other Outlaws.

There would be no magic needed on this raid, but Will would be useful to get them through the science building's electronic security.

Robin's choice of historic weapon for this mission was the Crossbow. Its invention in ancient China caused a major shift in the role of projectile weapons in warfare. Robin knew from experience that the longbow was a specialised weapon which required a lifetime of training and great physical strength. In many cultures, bowmen were considered a superior caste, despite being drawn from the common class, as their archery skills were developed from birth. So, it had been a simple task for the Outlaws to master the crossbow, which was simple, cheap, and physically undemanding enough to be operated by conscript soldiers.

In Europe, crossbows became widely used in the early medieval period, and this led to the formation of large mercenary armies of crossbowmen and the eventual demise of the heavily armored aristocratic knight.
The crossbow had evolved into many different forms over the centuries, some still in limited use by today's military. Robin would use many of these differing systems at Nottingham Science.

Two of the military applications interested Robin. He knew that the Peruvian army equips some soldiers with crossbows, to establish a zip-line in difficult terrain.
Robin combined this equipment with his own version of the U.S. Army Launched Grapnel Hook (LGH). This is intended for use in mine clearance, where a crossbow shoots the hook across a minefield, which is then dragged back, clearing the mines. But Robin would use it to scale the wall of the laboratory building, as there was a potentially vulnerable skylight he had identified with a drone flight. Three powerful crossbows shot their hooks towards the roof. Then, within minutes Robin, Tuck and John had climbed the ropes and awaited a signal from Much.

Will and Much were in the shadows at the side of the lab building. Much was protecting the young savant, while Will tapped into the estate's communications box.

All the phone and Internet traffic for Nottingham Science flowed through this box. Will knew that, given time he could access the building's security system and allow the Outlaws in.

The brilliant young man soon had control of the security system and the three Outlaws abseiled through the skylight.

They knew that Will would be interfering with the CCTV feed as they worked their way through the building. But this would itself cause the guards to be suspicious.

Robin had a crossbow solution ready for the inevitable arrival of curious guards.

They carried the smallest type of crossbows, specially prepared pistol crossbows.

Robin had modelled these on crossbows issued to the Indian Navy's Marine Commando Force. They used crossbows with cyanide-tipped bolts as an alternative to suppressed handguns. Robin's bolts were tipped with a powerful tranquilliser, rather than poison. But they would take out their opponents just as quietly as they did for the Indians.

With the first four guards sleeping soundly, the Outlaws found their way into the first of the labs.

"Good thing we left Much outside", commented John. He had spotted the first of the cages and knew that Much would not approve.

They expected to find animals, as the lab was registered for animal experimentation.

They also suspected the experiments would be on a

fairly large scale, as worldwide it is estimated that the number of animals, from zebrafish to non-human primates used in experiments numbers in the tens of millions. It seemed to Robin that most of them were in this lab. Such was the noise coming from hundreds of caged mice.

The fact that the lab used mostly mice as their test animals also made sense. Mice are the most commonly used lab species because of their size, low cost, ease of handling, and fast reproduction rate. They are a good model of inherited human disease as they share 99% of their genes with humans.

Robin would have liked to have done something for the animals, but the Outlaws did not have time to concern themselves with anything but their mission. Motte was up to something here, and they needed to know what.

The Nottingham Science building was divided into many separate laboratories. The Outlaws moved through each of them, with Will Scarlet manipulating the CCTV and security systems as they went. Each change of lab brought more guards, all of whom fell victim to the tranquilliser tipped crossbow bolt.

But every lab they entered seemed completely legitimate. The notes and records in each room suggested genuine UK focused medical research.

Then, the Outlaws reached a floor with a much heavier security presence and the guards soon spotted the Outlaws. Will was able to stop them raising the alarm, but it was up to Robin, John and

Tuck to stop the guards.

To stop such a large force of guards, Robin turned to a Chinese repeating crossbow called a Chu Ko Nu, a historic forerunner of the machine gun. This is a handheld crossbow that accomplishes rapid fire with a magazine of bolts on top. Robin worked the mechanism by moving a rectangular lever forward and backward. The Chinese used the weapon against lightly armored soldiers, since it shot small bolts that were often dipped in poison. Just like his crossbow pistol bolts, Robin had tipped these bolts with tranquilliser. The rapid rate of fire quickly evened the odds, sending the large force of guards to sleep.

"Bingo!" exclaimed Robin as he started to search the lab.
This was another animal testing lab, but the substance on test appeared to be pesticide, not medicine. This fitted with the anti malarial work Motte said the company was performing for Colombia.
About 12,000 mice are used annually to test pesticides in the EU alone. Robin was less comfortable about these tests than he was for the medical drugs. He had read that the tests were conducted without anesthesia, because interactions between drugs can affect how animals detoxify chemicals, and can interfere with the test results.

Boxes addressed to and from the Columbian Malaria clinic were stacked on the lab's benches. The incoming boxes were empty, awaiting disposal or re-use. But the outgoing ones were packed and waiting for the courier. They all looked completely legitimate, packed with mosquito nets and insecticides. But Robin kept digging, and eventually, hidden in the padded waterproof lining of the boxes, he found Dollars. Lots of Dollars, Motte's people had been very clever in constructing the packages. Robin had to cut open the factory sealed padding to find the money, but once he knew where to look, tens of thousands of pounds came out of the boxes. Disappointed they had found no drugs, but happy with the rucksacks full of cash that would be going to charity, the Outlaws pushed on through the building. Will had identified a section of the building that was much harder for him to breach the security. The cameras were on a separate system to the rest of the building and the entry systems were more complex. There had to be a reason for the heightened security, and the Outlaws guessed it was nothing legal.

It took Will time to crack the security in the central area. Just like at Motte's HQ, the area was in the centre of the building, with no windows, only one door and heavily reinforced walls, floor and ceiling. Unlike the HQ, it was not secured with retina identification, but the codes were heavily encrypted. Will had hardly slept in days, studying all the systems he might encounter. He breached the security and got Robin inside, but he had made a mistake which would cost him more sleep after their mission.

Once inside, the Outlaws saw what Motte was

hiding. Robin instantly recognised it as a Crystal meth lab. Crystal meth is a form of the drug methamphetamine, a synthetic chemical, unlike cocaine which comes from a plant.

It is most commonly used as a "club drug," taken in night clubs or at rave parties. Its users know the drug as ice or glass. It is a dangerous and potent chemical that first acts as a stimulant but then begins to systematically destroy the body.

The more serious side effects include memory loss, aggression, psychotic behaviour, heart and brain damage.

Highly addictive, the drug creates a false sense of happiness and well-being, a rush of confidence, hyper activeness and energy. Crystal meth burns up the body's resources, creating a dependence that can only be relieved by taking more of the drug. Many users report getting hooked from the first time they use it.

Robin recognised the labs purpose, because this was the drug that had poisoned Marion's Cambridge boyfriend. After his death, she had studied the process intently and had described it in detail to Robin. Although the process was recognisable, this was a much larger and more professional set up than the one in a Cambridge flat.

Common pills for cold remedies are used as the basis for the drug. The meth "cook" extracts ingredients from those pills and to increase its strength combines the substance with chemicals such as battery acid, drain cleaner, lantern fuel and antifreeze.

Motte's scientists did not have to do anything so

crude as buying up cold remedies. Robin now saw the true purpose of some of the innocent looking labs the Outlaws had passed through. Nottingham Science was able to manufacture its own precursor chemicals under the legitimate cover of selling cold medicine.

Robin and his Outlaws set about preparing to blow up the lab. They knew this would be a simple task, as the dangerous chemicals are volatile and explosive. Amateur meth cooks are often severely burned, disfigured or killed when their preparations explode. Such accidents endanger others in nearby homes or buildings, but Robin was sure that this lab's fortress like construction would contain the blast.

Just as they were finishing their preparations, the mistake that Will had made became known.

Chapter 19.

Will Scarlet had disabled all the security systems linked to Nottingham Science's computers. But here, in the most secret part of the building, there was a separate alarm system, linked only to Clive Motte's headquarters at Sheriff House.

As soon as the alarm came in, Motte's Lieutenants were quickly on the phones, summoning assistance. While the Outlaws were working, all of Motte's thugs in Nottingham were rushing toward Nottingham Science.

The advancing army was a curious mix. Some were uniformed security guards, hired out by Motte to other Nottingham companies. Others were the door staff from Sheriff Leisure's many pubs and clubs. The rest were just street gang members, who knew nothing more than the mythical Tax Collector needed them.

The last of the guards inside Nottingham Science had responded to the alarm, and just like their predecessors, they were quickly dispatched with tranquilliser bolts from the Outlaws' crossbows. Robin and his team did not yet know about the reinforcements rushing towards them, so they continued rigging the meth lab to explode.

When the men started to arrive outside Nottingham Science, Much was left with only young Will to help him fend off the advancing forces. Will was no fighter, but luckily, Much only needed him to help reload the heaviest of the weapons the Outlaws had brought with them.

This large weapon was the only one in today's

armoury which had a recurve bow, with tips curving away from the archer. The recurve bow's bent limbs allow a longer draw length than a straight-limbed bow, giving more acceleration to the bolt and less hand shock. This gave it much more range and power than a standard bow.

Recurved bows also make more noise with the shot, due to increased stress on the bow material. This was why none of their inside weapons were of this design.

But outside, against rising odds, Much was no longer concerned about the noise his huge crossbow would make. Silence was unimportant; power was needed to keep Motte's men at bay.

Robin had designed this weapon of last resort around medieval siege machines. When siege warfare became more common, the size of crossbows increased to hurl large projectiles such as rocks at fortifications. These huge crossbows needed a massive base frame and special systems for pulling the sinew via windlasses.

Robin's specific model was based on the Greek ballista weapon, named Polybolos. This was a replica of an ancient repeating ballista, reputedly invented by Dionysius of Alexandria in the 3rd century BC.

Like the repeating crossbows Robin had utilised inside, this much larger weapon also automated the separate actions of stringing the bow, placing the projectile and shooting. This way Much could accomplish the task with a simple one-handed movement. As a result he could shoot at a faster rate than an unmodified version.

The army surrounding Much and Will was testimony to the Tax Collector's power. Never before had such a huge and diverse mob come together in Nottingham for a single purpose. They looked a strange sight; security uniforms, bouncers in dinner jackets and gang members in street fashion.

Most people would be frozen to the spot at such odds stacked against them. But Much was a decorated special forces soldier, and the autistic young Will was too focused on his task to notice them. Together, these two men and their Polybolos siege machine were holding off an overwhelming force.

The huge crossbow was disgorging its bolts as quickly as Will could load them in the magazine. Unlike standard crossbow bolts, or the tranquilliser tipped bolts the Outlaws had already used, these were softer tipped. Robin had designed them to function as baton rounds, or rubber bullets. Although officially designated as "less lethal" weapons, the baton rounds were extremely painful and were successfully holding back Motte's men.

Inside, Robin and his Outlaws had overcome all of the inside guards and were ready to blow the lab and leave.

Of all the drugs Motte could trade, crystal meth is possibly the most lethal. Robin was determined to make his sabotage of the meth lab complete. He remembered listening to one meth addict talk about his addiction. "I tried it once and BOOM! I was addicted. I lost my family and friends, my profession as a musician and ended up homeless."

Experts say that it is one of the hardest drug

addictions to treat and many die in its grip.

The addict went into say "I started using crystal meth when I was in senior school. Before my first term of college was up, meth became such a big problem that I had to drop out. I looked like I had chicken pox, from hours of staring at myself in the mirror and picking at myself. I spent all my time either doing meth, or trying to get it."

Despite his insistence on historic weapons, Robin still used more modern technology to blow things up. Without reliable timers and detonators, anything could happen in an explosion. So, Robin, Tuck and John carefully set their timers and started their evacuation.

But it was not just the guards who had been attracted by the alarms and commotion at the high security lab. A single researcher had been working late, trying to make up lost time on her project. Like many of the staff and scientists at Nottingham Science, she knew nothing of Clive Motte's illegal activities. Like the others, she was curious about what really happened in the secure lab at the heart of their building.

There were no more guards inside the building to hinder the Outlaws as they ran from the lab. They were heading for the roof, the same way they got into the building.

John led the run down the corridor towards the stairs, where they met someone coming towards them.

The three Outlaws instantly fell into a defensive formation, raising their crossbows to tranquillise the approaching member of staff. But before they could pull their triggers, they realised it was not one of the guards.

This was obviously a scientist, but it took a few moments before they realised the shapeless laboratory clothes hid a female figure. This was the curious researcher who had only secured new funding a few days earlier, and was trying to catch up on the gap in her research.

Realising it was a woman, and a scientist, not a guard, Robin dropped his crossbow onto its leash. He instantly turned to push the researcher out of his way. As he faced her, there was a distinct feeling of deja vu from both of them. Robin had too much to think about for him to properly register the woman's face beneath the laboratory cap. But, looking into Robin's hood, the woman recognised the handsome face she knew very well indeed.

This was Clive Motte's latest attempt to rebuild a relationship with his daughter. He had agreed to fill the funding shortfall that had ended Marion's Cambridge research.

In a specially prepared section of the Nottingham Science building, Marion was restarting her research to test the benefits of yoga in cancer treatment. Hearing the commotion along the corridor, Marion had decided to investigate. So, after Will Scarlet, she became the second person outside of the Outlaws to learn Robin's secret.

Confusion running through her mind, Marion continued on to the secure lab. "What could Robin be doing here?", thought Marion. "Is my father involved with the army in some way?"

The moment she set foot in the lab, Marion recognised it for what it was. The only real love of her young life had died in a lab very like this one. Her lover's Cambridge meth lab was much less sophisticated than the one at Nottingham Science, but it was obvious to Marion what she was looking at.

Then, while Marion was taking in the horror of what she had just seen, two strong hands grabbed her from behind. Knowing that drugs and violence go hand in hand, Marion was terrified. It could only be something bad that was going to happen to her.

"Get off me. Put me down", shouted Marion, kicking and punching her assailant.

The man easily lifted Marion across his shoulder, ignoring her struggles, then ran effortlessly to the staircase.

"Robin", exclaimed Marion, as she was sat onto the stairs. "What's happening? Why are you here?"

"No time to explain", replied Robin. "You will have to trust me. We need to get out now". Despite her confusion, Marion did trust Robin. Her confusion increased when, despite the staircase's fire protection, she heard the woosh and felt the heat of the fire ball behind her.

Taking Robin's hand, they ran up the stairs, meeting John and Tuck on the roof.

The same ropes the Outlaws had used to reach the roof were now rigged for descent.

John slid down the rope first, protecting the landing area for his friends.

Next came Robin and Marion. He had quickly

fashioned a makeshift harness for Marion, out of a piece of spare rope. Now, attached together, they followed John down the rope.

Tuck's job was to rig the ropes to pull down after them, preventing any pursuers from using their equipment. He abseiled down after the others, pulling the ropes through behind him.

Robin's group moved quickly to join Much and Will, who were still holding off the Tax Collector's army. They grabbed fresh ammunition and a new weapon from the van, before starting to work on their evacuation.

Robin had chosen a bullet crossbow, a handheld weapon which rather than arrows or bolts shoots spherical projectiles made of stone, clay or lead. This type of bow used a double string with a pocket for the projectile.

He had packed a range of ammunition for his bullet crossbow. Some were versions of the baton rounds that Much was using so successfully. Others were steel ball bearings, should more powerful projectiles be needed.

But first, Robin was sending specially prepared clay balls into the path of Motte's men. These balls were filled with the same smoke producing chemicals they had used to make the airport disappear. This time, rather than to assist an illusion, the smoke would mask their own retreat.

While Robin was laying down his smoke screen, John and Tuck returned to their Chu Ko Nu, Chinese repeating crossbows. This time, instead of the tranquilliser bolts they had used inside, they now fired volleys of baton rounds towards their attackers.

The huge siege weapon used by Much was fixed to their van, so could not move with them on foot. By using the smaller Chu Ko Nu, the Outlaws could move away from the van, hidden by smoke, with their opponents still thinking they were dug in at the van.

The further the Outlaws moved from the van, the less impact their smaller baton rounds were having. So, the army gradually moved in towards the van. Once Robin thought that Motte's men were close enough, and that his team were far enough away, he pressed his remote detonator. The explosives in the van had been rigged to do two jobs. First to destroy any forensic evidence in their van. Secondly, Robin had added material used in military Flash Bang devices. The noise and bright light would further hamper their pursuers and assist their retreat.

The Outlaws used a similar route of retreat that Robin and John used for their first, unplanned operation in the Lace Market. The old railway infrastructure and industrial decay provided plenty of cover for them to lose their pursuers, who were still disorientated from the flash bang. This time they were also better prepared. Changes of clothing were hidden in one of the derelict buildings.
Out of their hoodies, boots and combat trousers, the Outlaws looked nothing like the raiders of Nottingham Science. Marion had no change of clothes, but with the hood removed from Will's scarlet top and her long hair flowing free, she looked nothing like a raider or a scientist.

The Outlaws waited out the night in the derelict building, then split into pairs to leave the city among the rush hour commuters. John, Tuck, Much and Will used the two cars they had earlier parked for their escape.

Robin chose to catch the train with Marion, as they had a lot to discuss. By the time the train reached Worksop, Robin had brought Marion up to speed on her father's lifetime of criminal activity. What he told her filled gaps and confirmed suspicions that she had tried hard to dismiss.

Marion's first instinct was to have it out with Motte and tell him exactly what she thought of him. Robin managed to convince her that she was much more help on the inside.

The journalist John Prince had been on scene very soon after the Outlaws van exploded. Nottingham Science was in the area of the city which housed most of its media, so he was quickly alerted to the incident.

Prince soon realised this had the Outlaws' hallmark. Witnesses had seen hooded men, crossbow bolts were scattered everywhere around the scene, and the whole incident fitted their unusual ways of working. Princes arguments of a new vigilante force were now starting to gain some acceptance with the police and mainstream media.

Chapter 20.

Over the next few weeks, Marion spent as much time with Robin as she could manage. It was hard for her to pretend everything was well with her father, so she spent very little time inside Loxley Hall.

She did not have the option to continue with her research, as the interior of Nottingham Science still needed a lot of work before the scientists could return. So spending time with Robin provided her with a release. It was not just Robin's company that provided the release. Robin knew Marion would need something more to calm the rising hatred she felt for her father. He had begun to teach her the art of sword play, but the gifted yoga practitioner had taken his tuition and turned it into something of beauty.

The Outlaws watched as Marion stood on a bridge over the Loxley Estate's lake. Her long dark hair flowing around arms and shoulders honed from a lifetime of yoga.

The bridge was a primitive, rustic design. It's walking surface made of rough hewn logs, and it's guardrails also fashioned from a lattice work of logs.

A sword spun loosely in her hand, much lighter than Robins broadsword, the thin curved blade had an elegance about it which matched Marion's movements.

The sword spun effortlessly through her hand and around her head and shoulders. Moving it from side to side and hand-to-hand, the blade never stopped spinning.

A small pommel at the very end of the handle

helped Marion keep the sword in her small hands as it whirled around her head and body. The narrow curved blade seemed to become one with Marion's body. Even the concentration on her face just seemed to highlight Marion's beauty.

She moved down from the bridge into the shallows of the lake, still spinning the sword, its tip just breaking the surface of the lake, before effortlessly spinning back around her head. The light reflecting off the water highlighted the movement of her blades.

Marion began to turn herself round and round as the sword kept spinning, all about her was a kaleidoscope of flashing lights.

All of the movement seemed to blend into one, the graceful movement of Marion's body, the flashing metal of the blade as she spun in the water, and the spray from the sword catching the surface rising around her, adding to the spectacle. No one would have thought such a deadly weapon could be turned into such a beautiful ballet.

Walking out of the water, Marion seemed to glide about the edges of the lake. She now reached a meadow and continued to swirl her blade among the grass, bluebells and dandelions.

Then, Marion performed a forward roll with her sword held aloft. As she came out of the roll she picked up a second sword she had placed there ready. Dropping to her knees, Marion kept both swords spinning about her head and among the wildflowers.

Rising effortlessly to her feet, Marion moved out of the meadow and still appeared elegant walking up and down a flight of stone steps rising from the lake.

Not a step out of place and never halting the whirling of her blades.

Eventually Marion moved from her dance into something more like a more martial art kata. These were the fighting drills that Robin had taught her. Despite the more deadly purpose to her movements, the sword still moved with elegance, looking something more beautiful than dangerous.
Once it was obvious that Marion had finished her dance, Robin moved towards her.
Now that she knew about her father's real business and Robin's secret life, he knew that it was only a matter of time before Marion would face danger.

Rather than try to teach the slightly built young woman in the use of an English broad sword, Robin chose for her an ancient form of scimitar, the shamshir.
Many Islamic traditions adopted scimitars, as a symbol, such as on the Coat of arms of Saudi Arabia. Probably because common belief puts the scimitar as the weapon of the Saracens during the Crusades.
However history suggests that scimitars are actually a lot more contemporary. In fact even during the times of the crusades the Saracens were armed with straight swords, not Scimitars, a fact that Hollywood often likes to ignore. Most antiques are from the 17th and 18th century and are believed to have spread gradually through the Islamic world after unfriendly contact with the Mongols.

Marion's sword was named after the city of

Shamshir, which means "curved like the lion's claw" in Persian. The word has been translated through many languages to end at scimitar.

The shamshir is a one-handed, curved sword featuring a slim blade that has almost no taper until the very tip. It was normally used for slashing unarmoured opponents either on foot or mounted; while the tip could be used for thrusting.

The sword Robin had chosen for Marion was a thing of beauty. With its deep brass fittings, black handle and scabbard, the colour scheme is simplistic, yet the combination worked extremely well.

Marion's shamshir could best be described as lightweight and curvaceous. The curve of these Arab swords opens up several new angles of attack that can be incorporated into a fighting style to deliver fast and unexpected attacks from unfamiliar angles.

Robin's lesson moved from the aesthetic to the deadly, as he worked on the strength of Marion's blow. The traditional test for a cutting sword is tatami mats, the same kind used to test the most popular of curved swords, the Japanese Katana. Tatami mats are used as a flooring material in traditional Japanese homes, made using rice straw to form the core, with a covering of soft woven rush.

Robin took several high quality half mats and prepared them for Marion in the traditional manner. He was sure that the Arab sword's blade would cut through the mats without too much of a problem. The only thing that concerned him was that this was a one handed sword while the Katana was a two hander. He had selected the shamshir for its lightness, but knew Marion would need to train hard

in matching the cutting power of a heavier sword.
Her first cut sailed on through without a problem,
and Marion seemed to enjoy herself as she stalked
the target, slicing and dicing it from various angles,
each time cutting clean through.

Next their practice moved to a duel. Just like the
medieval knights he so respected, Robin had
chosen a straight bladed sword. This time it was not
his heavy broadsword, but a lighter rapier.
Rapier is a loose term for any slender, sharply
pointed sword, generally used as a thrusting
weapon. They were mainly used in Europe during
the 16th and 17th centuries, having first developed
in the 1500s as the Spanish Espada Ropera, or
dress sword. The word usually refers to a long-
bladed sword with a protective hilt constructed to
protect the hand wielding the sword.
Robin's rapier was more of a hybrid with a
broadsword, featuring a slightly broader blade
mounted on a typical rapier hilt. While a standard
rapier blade is broad enough to cut to some degree,
it is designed to perform quick and nimble thrusting
attacks. Robin's was a more robust weapon, making
it weigh a little more than the usual one kilogram.
Some rapier blades are sharpened along one edge
only, from the centre to the tip. Robin's weapon had
two cutting edges, running the full length of the
sword. This allowed Robin to use his more favoured
fencing techniques, without being too heavy a match
for Marion's shamshir.
As he fought, a part of Robin's mind drifted to the
movies he enjoyed so much. As always, he was
very aware of the liberties that Hollywood takes with

history. Despite the rapier's common usage in the 16th and 17th centuries, many films set in these periods, often starring Errol Flynn, have the swordsmen using épées or foils, for their more cinematic lightning thrusts and parry. The director and fight choreographer of The Three Musketeers did attempt to more closely match traditional rapier technique.

With the mix of broader than normal rapier, and straighter than usual scimitar, Robin and Marion's duel was anything but traditional. The style should have been typical east against west, where the knights had rapiers and the Turks had scimitars, but they had to adapt to their slightly unusual swords. Rapiers are a longer distance weapon, while the scimitar is a close quarters slashing weapon. The curved blade can cause more damage than a straight sword, with its cutting edge running the full length of the blade.

Marion moved in close with her blade, resting it on Robin's shoulder, then drawing down, just stopping short of slashing Robin's neck. Robin's rapier needed range, to work from a safe distance to stab with the point, so this put him at a disadvantage when Marion moved in close.

Marion used every part of her scimitar in their fight, using the reverse of her blade along the concave side of the curve to guide away Robin's straight blade.

She had also picked up her scabbard, which she also used to block Robin's rapier.

Then came a move that Robin had not taught, it came wholly from Marion's imagination. She moved in much closer beside Robin, too close even for her own sword. Then, she took the curved blade behind her own back, stabbing backwards into Robin's side. This was a direction of attack that even the master swordsman was not expecting, and it cost him the duel.

"Ouch", exclaimed Robin, as he felt the point of Marion's sword. "I didn't teach you that one".

"It's a yoga posture", replied Marion. "You would be surprised some of the positions I can get into".

Robin knew better than to voice his thoughts, but he could imagine some of the positions that Marion's yoga trained body could manage.

Relaxing after their duel, Robin and Marion returned to the cottage, where they joined the other Outlaws. The TV was turned to a 24 hour news channel, which the Outlaws were barely watching. Their attention was drawn though, when John Prince appeared on screen.

"Is he still banging on?" asked Much. The journalist had been trying for months to convince his audience about the existence of a band of vigilantes using medieval weapons. No one had been taking Prince seriously. His story seemed the stuff of comic books, and Nottingham was used to the regular gang wars on their estates.

But this time, Prince seemed to have found someone who would listen to his theories.

Beside Prince, waiting to have his say was a very young looking police officer. From the pips on his shoulder and the braid on his cap, Robin could tell he was a Chief Inspector. But he looked barely old enough to be an Army Second Lieutenant, or trainee officer. "Fast Track", said Tuck, making the same observation about the police officer's age. "I'd rather follow young Will into battle.

While Prince introduced the police officer, his name scrolled across the screen, Chief Inspector Guy Guisborn, Local Area Commander for City Central. Looking at Guisborn, Robin thought the French ancestry suggested by his name must be a long way back. His slight build, ginger hair and freckles looked anything but French.

Guisborn held a handful of the Outlaws' modified crossbow bolts. "These are not the stuff of the street gangs", explained the Chief Inspector. "I might think that standard arrows could be the gangs. But these were adapted by specialists. There are; flash bangs, baton rounds and tranquilliser darts. I think Mr Prince may be onto something with his theory". Guisborn went onto explain how dangerous vigilantes could be. "They are not confined by the Rule of Law, or under the same scrutiny as the police".

Neither the reporter, or the Chief Inspector could provide any reason for the pitched battle. Nor the apparent burglary of Nottingham Science, who were oddly reticent to become involved in the police enquiry.

Guisborn could only offer up a theory that the Outlaw's action against Nottingham Science was an animal rights protest. John Prince could see the holes in this theory, but he did not voice them to the Chief Inspector. Prince knew the animal rights theory did not explain the involvement of bouncers, security guards and gangsters. This was an angle that Prince wanted to explore further before discussing it with the police.

Robin became a little more comfortable when he learned how far off the mark Guisborn was with his theories about them. He was however, far from happy with being branded as some sort of terrorist on the TV news.

He also, quite correctly suspected that the journalist John Prince did not subscribe to Guisborn's ideas. Prince had been dogging them too closely to jump to such an easy conclusion.

Chapter 21.

"He's up and running again", said Marion.
Nottingham Science now had some of its lower
floors operational. But it was the staff from the upper
floors who were now occupying the workspace. This
meant that Marion's lab was not yet habitable, as it
was on the same floor as the Meth Lab.
"He said that the more profitable areas of business
had to go on line first, to fund the rest of the repairs",
added Marion.
"I can guess what is most profitable", replied Robin.
"I think we might need to do something about it.
Keep your ears open, but don't risk making your
interest too obvious".
Marion had a legitimate interest in Nottingham
Science, as her work could not progress as quickly
without a lab. So she had reason to visit the building
and ask her father about progress on repairs.
Security was now very tight at the building and there
were very few areas to which Marion was allowed
access.
What she was able to find out was that her father
had stepped up security on anything arriving and
leaving the lab.

Motte had already made the same conclusion as
John Prince, that the attacks on his interests were
linked. Motte also knew there were more attacks
than Prince had reported. The journalist did not
know about the ambush of his circus convoy, which
led to the operation at the Goose Fair.
He therefore considered road transport to be a
particular vulnerability. A vulnerability he could avoid

by the close proximity of the railway station to Nottingham Science.
All Motte's shipments were now travelling by specially chartered trains.

Nottingham's ornate railway station serves as a hub for both railway and tram systems. The station was first built by the Midland Railway in 1848, and rebuilt by them in 1904, with most of the current buildings dating from that later rebuild.
 The station runs roughly east to west, at the southern edge of the city, with Station Street to the north and Queen's Road to the south. This gave Motte's staff a very short road transfer from Nottingham Science to the station's freight entrances.
At the western end of the station, the tracks are spanned by Carrington Street, which forms an artificial tunnel for trains arriving and leaving to the east. The station's main entrance is on the eastern side of Carrington Street, adding the width of the entrance concourse to the tunnel's length.

The Outlaw's had been working relentlessly for the last week, getting ready to take out one of Motte's trains.
Nottingham Station is one of the city's busiest thoroughfares, so a pitched battle like the one at Nottingham Science was out of the question. Even using their less lethal crossbow bolts, Robin would not take such risks with the public.
Planning this operation was one of the toughest Robin had faced in both his long military career and shorter time as a vigilante. Somehow he had to pull

off a train robbery in a busy public area, against the best of Motte's security and within minutes of the police response base at Riverside.

Marion and Will came up with the solution. This time it would be the public and the police who would be subject to the illusion. Motte's people would be under no illusion that anything other than a robbery was happening to them.

Marion first suggested two of PC Sorcar Junior's most famous illusions. The Indian magician has twice made trains disappear as part of his spectacular magic shows.

Sorcar's signature trick is using light refraction to give the impression that large objects have vanished. His past performances included the "disappearance" of the Taj Mahal. He also made the Victoria Memorial disappear on the 300th anniversary of Calcutta. But it was Sorcar's use of this technique on trains that interested Marion and Will.

In 1992, Sorcar vanished a train full of passengers before a large crowd at Bardhaman Junction in West Bengal. Then, in 2013, he developed the illusion to disappear the Indore–Amritsar Express, a bi-weekly mail express train which runs between Indore and Amritsar, in the Punjab.

Marion had been present at the Khana Junction station in West Bengal, on July 12th 2013 when Sorcar performed his grand illusion. Will had watched the recording more times than he could count

The exotic showman performed his illusion in front

of 2000 local people, a few judges from Calcutta, railway officials and a TV crew.

The 10-bogey Amritsar Express drew up, packed with passengers just as it did twice in every week. Dressed in his maharajah regalia, P.C. Sorcar Junior instructed a few people to squat on the tracks on both ends of the train so 'it couldn't run away'. Then, exhorting his audience to have one last look, he waved an eight by ten feet banner emblazoned with his name in front of them, counted to three, and as fireworks detonated deafeningly, the train vanished.

During a post show interview, the reporter asked if it was an optical illusion.

Optical illusion? "But then it is not possible to sustain an optical illusion forever, is it?" Sorcar Junior quizzed smiling at the interviewer. The only thing he disclosed was that the Eastern Railway authorities arranged a special train resembling the Amritsar Express. "The joy of magic", he insisted, "is in not telling its dark secrets, in leaving people hanging, on the threshold of reality." Sorcar Junior went on to explain that, offstage he is just another human, but people think he is a magician there too. A family in Allahabad brought their son who had been bitten by a poisonous snake to him. They pleaded with Sorcar to save the boy through magic. After the magician begged them to take the boy to the hospital, an argument followed and precious time was lost and the boy died. "It's frightening. People in this country have placed me on such a pedestal".

Despite his repeated viewing of Sorcar's Amritsar

Express performance, the Indian magician had given very little away about his technique. What did strike Will, was the spectacle of his whole performance. Will knew that illusion was about misdirection, so Sorcar's flamboyant stage presence would go a long way toward captivating his audience's attention.

The Sorcar show is a grand exercise in psychological hoodwinking, helped by the 108-member troupe, nearly 60 tonnes of equipment, mirrors, brocade dresses, psychedelic laser lighting systems, an ingenious smoke machine, and his two pets Samrat, the lion, and Badshah, the elephant. The backdrops are the results of painstaking creativity: a pharaoh's tomb, a collage of Picasso prints, a Calcutta street. The soundtrack is provided with original music by his own orchestra.

Will had only six people, but he did have access to military equipment and massive funds raided from Clive Motte.

PC Sorcar Junior was not the only magician to make a train disappear in front of a huge TV audience. American illusionist David Copperfield performed the disappearance of a 70-ton Orient Express dining car In 1991.

Although very much American in style, Copperfield is every bit as flamboyant as PC Sorcar Junior. He is described by Forbes as the most commercially successful magician in history.

Copperfield has so far sold 40 million tickets and grossed over $4 billion, which is more than any other solo entertainer in history. In 2015, Forbes listed his earnings at $63 million for the previous 12 months and ranked him the 20th highest earning celebrity in the world. Copperfield holds 11 Guinness World Records, including earnings and attendance records, and largest stage illusions. But, crucially for Will Scarlet, Copperfield is much less subtle in his magic. Will had been able to work out how he made the Statue of Liberty disappear, and was able to replicate the illusion to make an entire airport vanish. Young Will now set about studying Copperfield's Orient Express illusion.

Will played a DVD of Copperfield's illusion over and over. This was one of the benefit's of Will's autism, if something interested him, he would never bore of it. Through his repeated viewing, Will took in everything the audience was meant to see, as well as much that they should not have seen.
The televised illusion was performed in a huge WW2 blimp hanger. A large metal circle, shaped like Stonehenge, supporting the lights surrounded the train track.
Then, to dramatic music, an ornate Orient Express dining car was wheeled in to the center of the circle. Observers verified the floor was solid concrete and the track was 2" square stock steel anchored to the concrete.
80 people surrounded the car, joining hands in a circle around the train carriage. These were all employees of a company rebuilding passenger cars for The Orient Express. Then, to more dramatic music, Copperfield walked through the car, filled with more employees of the rail stock company, to show that it was real.
Moving back outside, Copperfield, assisted by his

staff on the coach roof, pulled a tan coloured sheet over the car. Lights from the metal structure shone through the sheet showing the silhouette of the train car under the sheet.

Intense concentration filled Copperfield's face as the sheet raised up, with the form still showing through the sheet.

With more of Copperfield's trademark flourish, He pulled the sheet off. As the sheet moved it appeared to follow the form of the car which seemed to have remained stationery as the sheet was pulled off. But, as the sheet fell to the floor, everyone was amazed as the ornate carriage was no longer there.

Eventually Will pieced together how he could replicate David Copperfield's illusion and make Clive Motte's train vanish.

The Outlaws were lucky in setting up Will's illusion. Under most circumstances they would trigger a security alert in setting up the scaffolding, lights and other infrastructure needed to make the illusion work. But Nottingham Station was undergoing a major phase of renovation. The builders had tower cranes, scaffolding, floodlights, screens and fences all over the site. Will was able to adapt these to serve the purposes of his grand illusion.

Normally, the Outlaws began every one of their operations with stealth. This time, it began with; a fanfare, music, fireworks and bright lights. This was the start of Will's misdirection. Just as Will began to draw the attention of everyone at the station, Much crashed a truck though a safety fence onto the tracks west of the Carrington Street tunnel. This blocked anything from entering the station through the tunnel.

With his truck on fire, Much ran forward to join the other Outlaws.

Floodlights turned skywards as two figures were lowered from the booms of the overhead cranes. The first was dressed as an Indian Maharaja, complete with turban and white feather. His long, red silk jacket flowed in the breeze of the descent and the floodlights reflected from his jacket's gold decoration.

Then shortly after him, on a parallel rope dropped a stunning young woman. She was dressed in an elaborate costume reminiscent of an Arabian Knights princess. Loose black trousers billowed around her legs, subtle gold decoration catching the light, looking like stars in a night sky. A tiny red and gold waistcoat to match the Maharaja's jacket showcased the woman's figure and drew the gaze of every man on the platform.

Will and Marion landed softly on the roof of Motte's train and began their performance. Perfectly synchronised, they leapt from the roof of the train's single carriage. They performed a forward somersault before landing faultlessly on the platform. This had been Marion's first contribution to the performance. The young savant had made an excellent student in learning the gymnastic moves that Marion had choreographed.

Will had taken the practicalities of his illusion from David Copperfield's performance, but his showmanship was all PC Sorcar Junior. Marion loved anything Indian, and Will was always keen to please his friend. But Will also wanted to see something of himself in the Indian mystic. He particularly liked Sorcar's claim that magic would bring him long life, as Will wanted his time with the Outlaws to last forever.

While Will and Marion were making their exit from the train roof, a package was being lowered behind them. This was a carefully folded sheet, which as it hit the roof, spilled cords down each side of the carriage.

By now, camera crews were rushing from the nearby BBC and Nottingham Post buildings, to record what they thought was an unannounced show. Almost everyone at the station had also made the assumption that they were part of a surprise TV show. The only people not taken in were Motte's guards inside the carriage. They knew that the Tax Collector would never have agreed to participate in such a stunt. With the amount of cash and narcotics on board they had too much to lose by drawing attention to themselves.

With the gathering crowd disoriented by music, lights and fireworks, Will and Marion danced around the carriage, pulling at the numerous cords. This brought the specially prepared sheet down around the carriage. Only the carriage's distinctive shape was now visible under the sheet.

This was Robin, John, Much and Tuck's cue to move forward.

Will and Marion continued to provide distraction, aided by the music and lights. Their exaggerated movements and flamboyant costumes drew the eyes of everyone around as they moved about the carriage. While they kept the audience's attention, the other Outlaws provided the behind the scenes parts of Will's illusion.

Precisely in time with firework detonations, Robin used shaped charges to blow off the carriage door. Robin and John moved swiftly through the carriage, dispatching Motte's guards with the same tranquilliser bolts they had used inside Nottingham Science.

The only people not taken in by Will and Marion's performance were now sleeping soundly. So the Outlaws could move to assist Will with the next stage of his illusion.

Tuck slipped in between engine and carriage, uncoupling the two. The sheet was then able to fall all the way to the floor, completely covering the carriage.

Then, with Will and Marion drawing the audience's attention to the front of the carriage, the Outlaws moved to the rear. Aided by John's huge size and strength, they rolled the carriage out from under the sheet, and into the darkness of the Carrington Street tunnel.

Moments before moving the carriage, Robin had switched on a powerful compressor. This blew air under the sheet, which had been sewn precisely into the shape of the carriage. In the same way that some advertising banners are held aloft, the blown air held the sheet in shape, despite there no longer being anything underneath it.

While John, Tuck and Much searched the carriage, Robin continued to act as Will's technical assistant.

Another switch activated lights he had placed under the now empty sheet. The lights were specially designed to cast a silhouette of the train carriage onto the insides of the sheet. The audience now had the evidence of their own eyes that the carriage remained where it had been parked.

Tiny electric motors powered a multitude of cables strung between the sheet and the tower cranes above. The cables had been fixed to enable the sheet to keep its shape as it began to rise. To the audience's eyes, the carriage was now beginning to levitate above the track.

The maharajah and his beautiful assistant continued to dance around the now floating carriage, keeping the audience's attention where they wanted it. Marion had brought her scimitar with her, the hours of practice she had put in added another dimension to her dance. Each elegant movement of her blade reflected the fireworks and light show.

Chapter 22.

In the shadows of the Carrington Street tunnel, The Outlaws were moving through the carriage like a tornado. There was no time for a careful and tidy search. They needed to remove cash, drugs and precursor chemicals before Will ended his show. Their search was made easy by Motte's people using the same packing technique they had seen at Nottingham Science.

A small fortune in cash was hidden in the packaging of boxes full of anti malarial products heading for South America. This was quickly transferred into rucksacks, to find its way anonymously to a charitable purpose.

In other boxes, the Outlaws found meth amphetamine and other designer drugs created in the Tax Collector's labs. The drugs were packaged for shipment to Motte's South American clinic. But they knew this was only to fool any inspection of the cargo. The narcotics would be removed and distributed long before the cargo was loaded for shipping across the Atlantic. The Outlaws also knew that this particular shipment would never reach the street dealers and drug users. One of Robin's military incendiary devices would see to that.

Their final act inside Motte's railway carriage was to remove his sleeping men. Every one of the Outlaws had killed many times over. But their kills were at war, under rules of engagement set for them by their Generals. They would not kill on British soil, and certainly not a group of sleeping men. The carriage needed to be cleared before they could burn it and its cargo of drugs.

When the Outlaws' work in the train carriage was finished, John alerted Robin and Will through their earpieces. This gave them the signal to wind up their performance.

Will and Marion were still dancing around the floating sheet when they received John's message. The next few steps of the performance had been carefully timed and choreographed. Will and Marion ended their dance, then, with a flourish, they spread their arms, directing the audience's attention to the sheet.

Robin pressed another switch on his tiny control panel, stopping the compressed air and releasing the cables. The sheet fluttered to the floor, showing the carriage had disappeared.

Then another switch started a much bigger pyrotechnic display than anything that had gone before. This was partially to aid Will and Marion's escape through the tunnel. But it was also to mask the incendiary device that was now destroying the Tax Collector's train carriage.

The van that blocked the tracks into Nottingham Station had served another purpose before its deliberate crash. It had carried six compact dirt bikes, which Much had pre-positioned in the trackside shrubbery. The four Outlaws, plus Will and Marion soon had the motorcycles out and running. The automated firework display was still entertaining the crowd at the station, so no one noticed them race up the embankment and through the hole Much had punched through the fence.

Will and Marion had paused briefly to put on overalls

that Much had left for them. The sight of a maharaja and an Indian princess riding motorcycles through Nottingham would be sure to attract attention.

Robin had chosen the Meadows Estate as their escape route. The estate sits immediately south of the railway station, and the Outlaws had already studied the paths and alleyways for their assault on the cycling dealers. They had learned the routes for the mountain bikes they had used previously, but the paths suited their small trail bikes equally well.

Back at Nottingham Station, the audience was left confused by the end of Will's illusion. The disappearance of the carriage was celebrated by the most spectacular part of the sound and light show. But the performers were no longer there to take their applause.
The audience surged forward onto the tracks to inspect the sheet which now lay across the rails. Railway officials and British Transport Police also moved onto the tracks to begin an official inspection. It did not take them long to find the still burning carriage and the unconscious guards.
British Transport Police, or BTP, have very limited numbers based at major railway stations and only have jurisdiction over the rail network. So, they very quickly put out a call for assistance from Nottingham Police.
The urgency of their alert was raised when the Outlaw's tyre tracks were found leaving the railway, confirming that those responsible had made their escape.
All of BTP's updates were reaching the ears of Chief

Inspector Guy Guisborn. He was showing a particular interest in anything out of the ordinary that happened on his patch. Guisborn still did not fully understand what was happening in his city, but he was certain this impromptu magic show was a part of it.

The City Police have a small off road motorcycle unit, intended to stop anti social behaviour in the city's parks and open spaces. Guisborn was in luck today, as three of their team were just leaving Nottingham's Central Police Station, to begin a patrol of Wollaton Park. It was a small detour for them to ride south towards the railway station. Tyre tracks, witness reports and the city's CCTV unit led the bikers towards the Meadows, in hot pursuit of the Outlaws.

"Five O", shouted Will, who was first to spot the police.
"He's been watching too many cop shows", thought Robin. The youngster's reference was to the Hawaii Five O to show, the title of which had become a street colloquialism for the police. Robin looked back and saw the three powerful motor cross bikes gaining on them.
The police bikes were much faster than the motorcycles Robin had chosen. But his choice had been for agility, not speed. Robin knew that to fully take advantage of their escape route through the Meadows, the motorcycles would need to be as manoeuvrable as their mountain bikes had been. The Outlaws all clicked down a gear and began to push their motorcycles harder. They needed to

reach the Meadows' network of footpaths and tunnels before the police caught up with them. They made it just ahead of the police, but the police motor cross bikes were now right behind them.

Just as they had when chasing the young drug couriers, the Outlaws began to make full use of the tunnel walls and changes of level in the maze of footpaths. As they entered one cylindrical tunnel, they turned their motorcycles onto the tunnel side, wall of death style.

The police were still powering their bikes in pursuit of the Outlaws. As the smaller bikes rose up the wall, the police passed though beneath them, unable to stop in time.

Marion reached down with her scimitar, slicing the rear tyre from the last of the police bikes. The seemingly endless training Robin had put her through made the curved blade move as one with her body. In a single movement she had disabled the police bike, then replaced the scimitar in her belt and rode on.

"Then there were two", thought Robin as his own tyres landed on the Tarmac behind the remaining two police bikes. The other Outlaws landed neatly behind him, as they sped off towards the next underpass. The two remaining police bikes remained on their tail, this time keeping a respectful distance from Marion's scimitar.

The little convoy of motorcycles powered through the Meadows' rat run, dodging the few people out and about. Small gangs of youths stood drinking and smoking, single mums who were out walking their babies to sleep, and a few reckless BMX couriers had started to return. Robin allowed himself a smile, knowing the Outlaws would have to return and finish clearing out the estate's drug couriers.

By now, all of the available police resources had crossed the River Trent and were searching the Meadows Estate. This allowed Robin to move to the next phase of his escape plan. The Outlaws had built a small earth ramp beside the river. They had practiced hard in the depths of the Dukeries to perfect their next move.

Each Outlaw hit the ramp cleanly, sending them soaring to the other side of the Trent. They were right back where they had begun their escape, close to Nottingham Railway Station.

The two police bikers showed no fear as they followed the Outlaws, to emulate their stunt. But the police did not have the benefit of the Outlaws' practice and preparation.

The first police officer misjudged his speed, falling short and landing his motorcycle in the river.

The second officer learned from his colleague's mistake and opened his throttle a little wider. This took him across the water, but his landing was not so clean, falling from the bike as the wheels slipped from beneath him. Luckily the officer was unhurt and remounted his motorcycle, losing a little more ground to the Outlaws.

"And then there was one", thought Robin.
The police motorcyclist was skilled and was soon back in hot pursuit of the Outlaws. They needed to lose him quickly before back up arrived, and before they could start the final part of their escape plan.

The Outlaws started to follow the wet grass alongside the Trent, but soon realised the police bike was much better suited to fast off road riding. So, taking advantage of their lighter, more manoeuvrable bikes, Robin led them back onto Tarmac and into the maze of retail and industrial estates. Their nimble bikes wove through the parked cars and side streets, cutting from one estate to another.

As Robin rode, an 80s Eddie Grant reggae number began running through his head. "We're gonna rock down to Electric Avenue, and then we'll take it higher". If the police motorcyclist could have heard Robin, the song would have given away their destination. One of the roads on the Riverside industrial estate was lined with electrical infrastructure. If the planners had not officially named it, the locals would probably have come up with the name Electric Avenue themselves.

Robin had parked a truck in one of the Avenue's bays. As soon as he was happy they had lost sight of the police biker, Robin led the Outlaws towards the truck. A remote control activated motors, which lowered the rear ramp. Then the Outlaws rode up the ramp, closing the truck behind them.

Minutes later they heard the noisy motor cross bike, as the police officer conducted a search pattern. They sat quietly in the van, waiting for the police to move on.

Before long, they were able to calmly drive the truck away, towards Loxley Hall.

It had taken some doing to keep the excitable Will

quiet while the police were searching. He was so full of adrenalin from his magic show and the motorcycle chase.

Despite everything that had happened, Will was most fixated on one aspect of his day. In studying PC Sorcar Junior, Will had learned that some of his detractors accuse him of mindless repetition. Will knew that K. Lal, a Calcutta-based magician, had said "Sorcar Junior is more stunt and less magic." Lal had in fact thrown a 50,000 Rupee gauntlet to Sorcar to repeat the train vanishing act. Will became fixated about whether Lal might pay him the reward for the illusion that he had just completed.

Chapter 23.

Robin kept Will's mind off Lal's offered reward by keeping him busy preparing the Duke of Loxley's fleet of classic cars. The annual Loxley Country Fair was approaching and Robin always took the opportunity to show off some of his collection. The Loxley fleet and Robin's luxury car business was officially Will's job. He had been away from it for a while, preparing for the grand railway illusion, so the young savant had a renewed vigour for his tasks, putting right all the things he found to be less than perfect with the cars, trucks and motorcycles.

There are many among the public who argue against old money families like the Loxleys owning so much land in the Dukeries. They use events such as the Hunt and the game shooting to argue the irrelevance of the landed gentry. But the Loxley Country Fair was undoubtedly the most inclusive event in the Dukeries' calendar.
Visitors travelled from far and wide to enjoy the Fair's many attractions. But it was the local people who played the biggest part in many of the weekend's events.
Residents of villages in and around the Dukeries had been preparing all year to make their mark at the Loxley Fair. Dog owners had been training their dogs. Gardeners had been preparing the best of their flowers and vegetables. The Women's Institute had made cakes, jams and chutneys. Athletes had been training themselves on the area's hills and forest trails. Some, like Helen Motte had just been working on their appearance in an attempt to turn as

many heads as possible.
The Fair had always provided something for everyone; rich, poor, young and old.

On the weekend of the Country Fair, the Outlaws were out in force to support Robin with his duties as the Duke. Most had been training for the weekend's flagship cross country race, but Tuck was relying on his catering skills to take on the Women's Institute. The other Outlaws joked that Tuck had been watching too many TV baking competitions, as he was taking his "showpiece" very seriously indeed. Francis Friar had stuck to his military background in creating his competition piece. The intricate creation of cake, biscuit and chocolate depicted the British Army's D Day landing on Normandy's Gold Beach at Aromanches. Crumbled biscuit formed the sand. A blue, green sugar depicted the English Channel. Chocolate shaped the supposedly temporary mulberry harbours, which still survive 70 years after their deployment. But it was the soldiers on which Tuck had lavished the most attention. Even in moulded and carved sugar, Tuck felt for the young squaddies who had taken such huge risks and endured such hardship.

"They'll never let him win", commented John. Most of the competitors in the baking competition, and all of the judges came from the WI.
Robin replied "he took on the Taliban, but I don't fancy his chances against the WI mafia".
"We'll fare better against the running clubs", added John.

One of the Loxley Fair's flagship events was The Chase. This was the first year the whole Outlaw unit would enter the race as a team, and they hoped to defeat all the local athletic clubs.

The Loxley Estate had its own equestrian cross country course, which Robin had ridden and competed on many times before. Recently it had become a challenge to take on with Marion.

Today Robin did not have the benefit of a horse and the Outlaws would have to take on the high fences and water jumps under their own power.

At the sound of the starting claxon, the Outlaws shot away together. Their plan was to intimidate the civilian athletes from the start. Many of the club runners wore gloves to protect their hands from injury on the rustic equestrian jumps. But the Outlaws were hardened from their years as commandos. They reached the first jump as a single unit. The fence was high, designed for the local Hunter horses, but the Outlaws attacked it as they would any assault course obstacle.

The drop down the jump's opposite side was into water. Most horses would easily clear the water, but the humans had no chance of avoiding a soaking. Cold water held no fear for Robin's warriors, who dropped straight from the top of the jump into the water trap. Many of their opponents hesitated at the top, allowing the Outlaws to gain some distance on their pursuers.

After the first few fences, the course left the equestrian track and sent the runners over open ground. This gave the athletes a chance to regain some ground, as the Outlaws were not sprinters. But the sprinters advantage did not last. The

Outlaws and the top runners came together just as they reached the corner of the Loxley Lake. The whole field knew they had to enter the lake for a short water crossing. What many did not know was that a cargo net had been fixed across the water's surface, forcing the racers to submerge themselves. Here, once again, Robin's team gained advantage while the elite runners hesitated. The battle hardened Outlaws did not hesitate at all. They dived straight under the net and swum strongly across the lake, emerging with clear distance ahead of their closest rival.

The route took the runners back onto the equestrian cross country course for a further lap. The elite runners fought hard to pull in the advantage the soldiers had gained in the lake. But the Outlaws were not going to give up their lead. Robin and his men seemed to take flight each time they reached an obstacle. Pumped on adrenalin, the Outlaws leapt at each fence, clearing them with gymnastic ease.

For the first time ever, someone who was not part of a running club had won the Chase. Robin burst over the finish line to a riot of applause from the estate workers and residents. Not only had first place been denied to the running clubs. But Robin was followed across the line by John and Much.

Marion had entered the women's race, which ran simultaneous with the men's event. Robin had coached her in the lake dive, which had brought his team to victory.

Fired up by seeing her friends so far ahead of the field, Marion too began to feel the buzz of adrenalin. She began to power past many of the young women in club vests. But, along the final straight, Marion was missing the killer instinct the Outlaws had honed in times of war. Marion did better than any other woman from the estate, but the top three elite women had too much reputation to lose and just beat her over the line.

While the runners were finishing the Chase, the WI were judging the baking competition. Just as predicted, Tuck's military masterpiece had not been able to swing the judges away from a WI win.

After the race, Robin and Marion wandered off from the other Outlaws. They had all been training hard for the race and needed a little time to themselves. While the Outlaws amused themselves with very typical and exuberant military celebrations, Robin and Marion's mutual congratulations and commiserations went unspoken.
For a while they just walked, taking in the beauty of the Loxley Estate and just enjoying the closeness of each other.
It was Robin who broke the silence, asking about Marion's research. "Forgive me", said Robin. "We've been so preoccupied with the missions and the race that I haven't asked about your work".
Robin knew that the Outlaws' raid on Nottingham Science had damaged Marion's laboratory and set back her research.
"Slow", replied Marion. "My father is trying to buy back my favour by funding me. But we've badly affected his short term cash flow ".

The Outlaws had spent more than a year attacking

every aspect of Clive Motte's businesses, legal or otherwise. It was only since their raid on Nottingham Science that Marion had known about their campaign. But she was so set against the narcotics trade that she immediately threw in with Robin and his team.

But there was a side effect of their campaign which had almost halted her medical research. Marion had been researching the medical benefits of practicing yoga during cancer treatment. Researchers before her had long ago shown that the relaxation techniques helped calm some patients. The reduction in anxiety without doubt helped many to deal with their devastating diagnosis. But none had shown any proven medical benefits.

Marion had been on the verge of a breakthrough when the Outlaws blew up her lab. She had been getting some tentative results, showing that relaxation and mental focus may have helped the action of chemotherapy on a small sample of patients.

As with any research, sustained and repeated results were needed to prove any theory. Marion had continued to work with her research subjects, but without her lab, she could not analyse any of her samples and observations.

"I might have an answer", replied Robin.

A puzzled look passed over Marion's face. She knew Robin would not joke about anything as important to her as her work. But she did not know how Robin could help.

As Duke of Loxley, Robin had a generous trust fund. But it was too restrictive for Robin to personally provide much funding. Neither could Marion figure out how the Outlaws could help through their steal from the drug dealers and give to the needy policy. Her's was serious medical research which could not be funded with a bag full of cash.

"I can practically read your face these days", said Robin. At which Marion's cheeks flushed a little red. "OK clever Dick", she replied. "What am I thinking?" "How?" said Robin. "It's written all over you. How can we legitimately pump money into building you a lab?" As Marion nodded her confirmation to Robin, he continued "you can thank your pal Will Scarlet". Robin explained that Will had been putting his energy into studying money laundering and the discrete movement of funds. This had started as research into further ways of hitting the Tax Collector's cash flow. But as he studied, Will realised the same techniques could be used to help Marion. Motte was struggling to fund his daughter's work because the Outlaws were stealing his money. Will needed to create a false, but legitimate entity to pass some of the money back to Marion.

While the Outlaws were enjoying the Country Fair, journalist John Prince was once again on the television. So far, no one had linked the railway station incident to any of the Outlaws' earlier incidents. But Prince had been digging hard. He had started on the basis that the train was carrying cargo for Nottingham Science. The same company the Outlaws had inexplicably attacked a few weeks earlier. Prince could still not find any reason for the science company to be targeted. He still ruled out animal rights activists, because no group had taken credit for the attack. All this left in Prince's mind was theft of pharmaceutical products.

Such a theft fitted with Prince's theory, that this was a new gang trying to take over Nottingham's drug trade from its established gangs. Prince did not know that Clive Motte was actually at the top of Nottingham's organised crime pyramid. Neither did he know that the train was carrying a huge quantity of cash, which was now hidden in the Loxley Tunnels.

Prince made a huge thing of the hooded tops that Robin and his team used as disguise. Similar hooded men had been seen at many of the incidents involving the city's drug dealers.

A "source within the police", who was widely believed to be Chief Inspector Guy Guisborn, had given Prince some useful information about the aftermath of the disappearing train illusion. The statement from one of the motorcycle officers described Marion using her scimitar to disable his motorcycle. Prince quickly linked the scimitar to the magician's beautiful assistant. He also made a tentative link with the other historic weapons that were seemingly in regular use against the dealers. Prince was weaving a very convincing case for a gang of hooded men using historic weapons against Nottingham's established drug trade.

Robin had not been difficult to pick out as the leader. Although shorter than John Little, Robin carried himself with an aristocratic bearing and the men clearly deferred to him. Prince had begun to call Robin "the hood".

This gave Marion just the name for her fictitious benefactor. And so, because Prince had been making a big thing about the hoods that Robin and the Outlaws wore to conduct their missions, Robin Hood was born.

Now it was up to Will to create the many layers of shell companies which would hide the true source of Robin Hood's wealth. Robin and Marion worked on the back story for their character. The reclusive businessman could never be seen in public, but he needed a believable history. Their character was to be a self made millionaire, who's roots were in Nottingham. He had made his fortune around the world, but mostly in India. Then, following the death of his wife from cancer, he wanted to help a Nottingham based cancer research project.
The link to India gave them the opportunity to build an awareness of yoga into Hood's back story, and so a reason to fund Marion's work.

"What!" exclaimed Clive Motte as Marion finished explaining her new funding package. Motte was slightly embarrassed about not being able to properly fund his daughter's work. But his temper grew from the caveat that Marion work from her own lab, away from Nottingham Science. Not only had someone stepped in with money he did not have, but the mysterious benefactor was taking Marion away from his company.
Marion could not help but wonder how mad her father would be if he learned the money had been stolen from him and his dealers.
Motte vowed there and then to track down Robin Hood and make him suffer. Marion did not hear her father's silent vow. But if she had, it would likely

have made her smile at the irony of him being the source of her new funding.

Chapter 24.

With a legitimate outlet for the money they stole from the Tax Collector, the Outlaws now needed another cash rich target to hit.

Losing his train put Motte on the back foot with transportation for a while. Despite being wary of road transport, he had very few choices left open. So, Motte fell back on his travelling showmen to move his merchandise and cash.

Because of the Outlaws' previous raids, Motte dramatically increased the security on his fairground convoys, making Robin think carefully about another hijack. But Robin was lucky with the time of year. His need for another raid to fund Marion's research coincided with Nottingham's annual Goose Fair.

The previous year, the Outlaws had beaten information about the Goose Fair from one of Motte's travelling convoys. That information had led to their assault on the Ghost Train and the drug dealers hidden inside. Of course, the travelling showmen had not let Motte know they had given his secrets to Robin. So the Outlaws were free to use more of the information at this year's fair.

Robin's new target was the Dodgems, or Bumper Cars. The way the staff moved from car to car lent itself perfectly to the dealers' methods. Standing on the outside of the cars, they jumped from car to car, making small drug deals along the way. The ride's cash desk hid the larger packets of drugs, and the cash they generated. Robin had all the information he needed, now he just needed a plan.

With the fair operating over several days, Robin had

the chance to do a little surveillance. Together with John and Much, he wandered through the site. To anyone watching, they were just a group of young men, wandering aimlessly, checking out the many young women at the fair. But anyone skilled in surveillance would have realised that their wandering made repeated passes of the Dodgem Car ride.

The Goose Fair Dodgems were a fairly typical bumper car ride. They used the oldest and most common method for power, with a conductive floor and ceiling. Contacts under the vehicle touch the floor while a pole-mounted contact touches the ceiling, forming a complete circuit.
On Motte's ride, the metal floor is set up as an oval track. The ride's operators sprinkled graphite on the floor to decrease friction and allow the cars to travel more smoothly around the track. Just like most other Dodgem rides, a rubber bumper surrounds each car and drivers ram each other as they travel.
Robin remembered riding them as a young boy with his grandma. She would insist on keeping control of the accelerator and steering wheel, despite not being a very good driver. The cars can be made to go backwards by turning the steering wheel far enough in either direction, necessary after his grandma's multiple crashes.

On the evening that the Outlaws' chose for their operation, they again wore wigs and false beards or moustaches. The hoodies they usually wore as disguise would attract suspicion at the crime prone Goose Fair. The Outlaws mingled with the crowds around the Dodgems, and even took a few rides on the attraction. They were waiting until customers started to arrive for their drugs.

The wait was tactical on two levels. Robin wanted to be sure the dealers stash was still in the same place. But he also wanted to take as much money from the Tax Collector as he could, so waiting for the lower level dealers to part with their cash made sense.

Robin watched the ride's operators moving about the track, jumping from car to car, holding onto the rear poles which powered the cars. Dependant on how distracted they were with trading their drugs, the operators sporadically enforced the "no bumping" signs posed around the track. Although the idea of the ride is to bump other cars, safety conscious, or at least litigation conscious owners now routinely put up signs reading "This way around" and "No bumping". In general, and depending on the level of enforcement, these rules are often ignored by bumper car riders, especially younger children and teenagers.

While they waited, Will Scarlet had, as usual, memorised facts about the Dodgems, which he eagerly shared with the Outlaws. "The heyday of the Bumper Car ride was in the late 1920s through the 1950s", he began. "The name Dodgem, was the trade name used by Americans Max and Harold Stoehrer for their funfair ride. Their competition, the Lusse Brothers, came up with the much less catchy Auto-Skooter".

Will's favourite Bumper Car fact was that in the mid 1960s, Disneyland introduced hovercraft-based bumper cars called Flying Saucers, which worked on the same principle as an air hockey game. The autistic young man was disappointed that the ride was a mechanical failure and closed after a few years, as he could imagine himself piloting a flying saucer.

Will's parents had once taken him to the Fairground Heritage Centre in Devon, while they were on a family holiday. The Dodgems were the first ride that caught Will's attention. The elaborate ride was built in 1932 for showman Robert Edwards.

Edwards took delivery of a standard 60 feet by 40 feet square-ended track. But over the years, competition with other showmen led him to expand his ride to one of the biggest sets ever to travel, with a 96 feet long track.

One of the main fairs at which the Dodgems appeared each year was on Hampstead Heath. When Robert Edwards heard that his main competitor, Tommy Benson, was having a new set of painted boards for his Dodgem Track, he immediately ordered an even grander set for his ride. The impressive painted scenery was added over the winter of 1953-54.

The Goose Fair Dodgems was a large and elaborately painted ride, but it seemed an anticlimax against Will's memory of the Heritage Centre. He could not help trying to redesign it in his mind. He was so deep into his thoughts that he did not hear Robin say "ok, let's do it". Robin had to physically grab Will by the shoulder to break him out of his thoughts.

The Outlaws moved forward in pairs to claim their

Dodgem Cars. Robin kept Will with him, hoping to keep the young man's mind on their mission. Much and Tuck rode together, while John and Marion teamed up. Robin could not help but doubt his pairing of John and Marion, as they stood out from the crowd as a couple. John was well above average height, while despite her disguise, Marion always looked striking. The young Showmen began to take interest in Marion, jostling to ride on the back of her car. But a hard stare from John soon sent them away, assuming the giant was her boyfriend. The showmen might have been put off going near "little" John, but there were others whose stupidity transcended their bravery.

The Goose Fair's location at the edge of Radford and Hyson Green put it at the heart of Nottingham's gang tensions. So there were plenty of young men looking to prove themselves to their gang's hierarchy. Already high on testosterone, many of them were also buzzing on cocaine or amphetamines. So, it was no real surprise when some of the dodgems started to collide with John and Marion's car.

After the first of the cars had bumped John, Will started to explain the science behind it to Robin. "Newton's third law of motion comes into play on the bumper cars", explained Will. "This law, the law of interaction, says that if one body exerts a force on a second body, the second body exerts a force equal in magnitude and opposite in direction on the first body. It's the law of action-reaction, and it explains why you feel a jolt when you collide with another bumper car."

Robin tried to appear interested in his young protégé's explanation, but the gang members' cars were now heading thick and fast towards John and Marion.

Will continued to explain that when bumper cars collide, the drivers feel a change in their motion and become aware of their inertia. Though the cars themselves may stop or change direction, the drivers continue in the direction they were moving before the collision. He went on to say that this is why it's important to wear a seat belt while driving a real car, since you could suffer injury being thrown forward in a collision.

As Robin watched the cars colliding with John's, he noticed that Marion seemed to be suffering much less than John, who was being thrown about the inside of his dodgem car. So much so that he was unable to react. "What's the matter with John?", asked Robin. He spoke more to himself than anyone else, but Will had an answer for him. "

The masses of the drivers affect the collisions. The difference in size between John and Marion means that John experiences more change in motion than Marion, or more of a jolt."

Robin was barely listening to Will as he leapt from the dodgem car. The young gangster's actions had forced Robin to show his hand earlier than planned. The Outlaws wanted the benefit of surprise when they robbed the cash desk of its stash of drugs and money. But now, they would be on alert as the Outlaws fought with the gang members.

Tuck and Much had reacted almost instantly to Robin's move. Will was a few seconds behind, but remarkably quickly for one not trained in warfare.

Just like their last visit to the Goose Fair, the
Outlaws were armed with knuckle dusters, which
were easier to hide than their usual weapons. Blow
after blow rained down on the gang members,
keeping them in the seats of their dodgems. Robin,
Will, Tuck and Much easily handled the first four,
then the next four. But by now, their friends were
starting to run onto the ride to help and looked like
they might get the better of the Outlaws by sheer
weight of numbers.
But Marion and John had started to recover from the
repeated impact of the other dodgems.
Marion was first out of her car. She did not have the
physical strength to do much damage with a knuckle
duster, so she carried a telescopic steel baton,
similar to police issue. She was able to wield this in
the same way Robin had taught her to use her
scimitar. The swing before the blow put much more
power into the blow than Marion could manage with
her fists alone.
John had no such trouble putting force into his
punches. The giant man was now swinging
repeatedly at the gangsters, angry that they had
momentarily got the better of him. "If in doubt, knock
em out", shouted John as he put several of the
gangsters unconscious onto the floor.

The Outlaws were soon surrounded by the
unconscious bodies of the gang members. But they
were also becoming surrounded by showmen. The
dodgem operators were loyal to Clive Motte. But the
other showmen were loyal to their own kind. There

is a close bond between those who live their lives on the traveling fairs and men rushed in from the surrounding rides to help the dodgem workers. Robin's strategic mind could see past the obvious danger to draw some advantage from their situation. "Will, Marion, do the job", shouted Robin. He realised that while all the showmen were concentrating on the Outlaws, their attention was away from the pay booth with its stash of cash and drugs. Will and Marion were the obvious ones to slip away and raid the pay booth. Will was not a natural fighter and although Marion was skilled with a sword, she was less proficient at hand to hand combat. But both of them were fast and stealthy, ideal traits to get in and out with the cash and drugs quickly and unseen.

As soon as Marion and Will made their move, the Outlaws started work on breaking the stand off with the showmen.
By necessity of their trade, they were all bigger, more powerfully built men than the gang members. They would take much more force to overcome than was needed for the up and coming gangsters. But the Outlaws were skilled in behind the lines warfare, they had faced overwhelming odds many times before, and had not been found wanting.
The Outlaws were seriously outnumbered, but as each showman hit the ground, the odds got slightly better. They did not need to defeat all of them, only keep them distracted until Marion and Will completed their task, then all six of them could escape together.
Time after time the Outlaws' fists fell on the

showmen. Some fell easily, particularly when faced with the strength of John's punch. Others took more stopping. Like most travelling communities, the showmen had a tradition of bare knuckle boxing and the older men had a lifetime of experience taking hard knocks.

But the Outlaws had survived many times in situations where losing meant death, so was not an option for them.

Marion was first to slip away with her rucksack filled with cash. Will hung back to signal Robin that their robbery was complete. This meant the Outlaws now had to turn their fight into an escape, so gradually they began to regroup on one side of the dodgem track. Their manoeuvring was so subtle that the showmen never realised their moves were being choreographed to allow the Outlaws an avenue of retreat.

Once everyone was where they should be, Robin and his men made their move, vaulting the barrier around the track and making their way into the crowd.

Here Will's keen mind once again helped out his friends. He had studied the science of the dodgem ride so closely, that he saw a weapon no one else had considered.

To ease the bumper cars' progress across the metal floor, dodgem operators had always sprinkled graphite around the track. Will knew well the lubricating properties of that particular form of carbon. He also knew that bigger quantities under the showmen's feet would hamper their chase. Will's liberal handfuls of graphite did the trick as the showmen slid about as if on ice.

A few of the showmen had spotted Will and did their best to reach him. But without a firm footing, they could not catch the fleet footed young man.

All six Outlaws were now back together and heading through the Goose Fair crowds towards freedom. But in the excitement of their mission, they had missed what should have been a familiar face in the crowd surrounding the dodgem car ride.

The camera sat on the man's shoulder was big by amateur standards, but was tiny for a broadcast quality camera. John Prince had travelled without a film crew, on a hunch the Outlaws might show. The Goose Fair had a reputation for crime and gang tensions. Prince had gambled correctly that his targets would appear.

Chapter 25.

John Prince now had what he had been wanting, good quality footage of this new gang in action. Something he had been chasing for months on end. He was disappointed the Outlaws were not wearing the hooded tops that he had built up as their trade mark. But Prince could tell from their distinctive silhouettes that these were indeed the gang he was interested in.

Prince was still convinced they were just another gang muscling in on Nottingham's rich organised crime network. But the truth that they were actually philanthropic vigilantes was a difficult concept for anyone to consider.

Any good investigative reporter relies on contacts from both sides of the law. In Prince's case, he had become close to Chief Inspector Guy Guisborn. The fast track police commander was not to many people's taste, but Prince had found him willing to exchange information where there was a mutual advantage to doing so.

The reporter immediately saw benefit in tipping off Guisborn to the Outlaws presence at the fair. The police officer would be grateful for the tip off, and the police response would give Prince something else to film.

Guisborn was the police Bronze Commander at the Goose Fair, so he was close at hand, with officers available to him for deployment. It took no time at all for him to arrive at the dodgems with a Police Support Unit, or PSU, behind him. A PSU is the standard police formation for any operation where pubic order tactics might be required.

Under Chief Inspector Guisborn's direct command was a Police Inspector and three Sergeants. Each Sergeant had six constables and could operate as a small unit, or come together as one large team of 22 officers. While theoretically under Guisborn's command, the inexperienced commander would only set their objectives. The far more experienced Inspector and Sergeants would actually put the tactics into operation and attempt to achieve their boss's objective.

Guisborn's objective for his PSU was simply to catch the Outlaws. The PSU supervisors translated this into using the individual groups of Sergeant and six PCs, known as a Serial, to attempt a pincer movement on the Outlaws.

The officers quickly deployed to positions around the Outlaws' last sighting, like the feet of a huge tripod. Then, under the direction of their Inspector, the three Serials began to close in. Each officer within the Serial was in sight and shouting distance of each other. The ends of each Serial were in sight of their adjoining Serial and the Sergeants were in constant radio contact with each other, directing the pace of their advance.

Prince too was an experienced operator. He had been a reporter for decades and instantly spotted the advantage of the nearby helter skelter to him. Prince ran quickly up the spiral staircase, to gain the elevated viewpoint at the top of the ride. Prince trained his powerful video camera on the crowd below, and before long he had spotted the retreating Outlaws. A quick call to Guisborn allowed the PSU to reposition their serials, closing in more efficiently on Robin and his team.

The Outlaws had a distinct advantage on the encroaching police. Modern police bosses' insistence on hi vis jackets made the officers very easy to spot. While Robin and his friends looked much like everyday funfair customers. Only Prince's trained eye was keeping the police on track in their search. Each time the Outlaws turned towards a weakness in the police lines, Prince pointed them back in their direction.

As he watched the police and the Outlaws play cat and mouse, Prince was trying to make sense of what he had seen. Everything about the Outlaws was an enigma. Here again, Prince was puzzled by what he had seen.

The fight with the young gangsters fitted Prince's hypothesis perfectly. The new gang in town was taking on members of the established street gangs. But why, he wondered, had they hung around to take on the showmen. Surely, he thought, they would have run off as soon as the gangsters were taken care of.

That was when the penny started to drop, that maybe the showmen were in on the drug trade. "What a perfect cover for drug smuggling", thought Prince, the thought coming over a year after Robin made the discovery.

Prince was snapped out of his thoughts as one of the police serials closed in on John.

There were countless occasions where the giant's size had worked to his advantage. But there were also many times, like this one, where his huge presence had been a disadvantage. John would stand out in any crowd and the Goose Fair was no exception. Head and shoulders above the tallest in the crowd, he made an obvious target for the police to home into.

Guisborn could not help but involve himself in the operation. His role should have been to coordinate from a distance, leaving his Sergeants and Inspector to do their job. The enthusiastic, but inexperienced senior officer was now amongst the crowd, shouting at the police serial. "There, there! The tall one!" shouted Guisborn. As he shouted, he began pushing constables towards John. Often the Sergeants will push their Constables into formation, but this is only done to reinforce the supervisors' directions in a fast moving situation. All Guisborn was doing was creating confusion. The Sergeants were trying to maintain a cordon, through which the Outlaws would be unable to escape. But Guisborn had become fixated on a single member, to the exclusion of the other five.

The Outlaws had spotted the police confusion and reacted almost instantly. They had stayed alive in some of the world's most dangerous war zones by being at the very peak of their profession.
Seconds after two of the police broke ranks to grab John, Robin and Much shot out of the crowd, knocking the two officers to the ground.
Guisborn was now incensed that his officers had not held onto John. "Cretins! Useless fools! Get after him", shouted Guisborn.

"Yeh, that will work", thought Robin sarcastically. The experienced commander knew that kind of outburst would not bring the best out of Guisborn's men. In fact, it was likely to do the opposite and make them less likely to try and please. Which was exactly the effect that Guisborn had on his PSU officers. As the Outlaws slipped through the gap in the cordon, Robin heard one of the Sergeants say, "tosser! won't someone get rid of the boy wonder?" Robin knew instantly that the Sergeant meant his youthful looking fast track senior officer. Robin could not help chuckling, thinking of the many keen Second Lieutenants he had moulded over the years, as they left Sandhurst thinking they knew it all, but actually knowing very little.

"Hey, Rube!" went up the shout from the Dodgem operators. Quickly the cry echoed as it passed from ride to ride, repeated by the Goose Fair Showmen. Soon the repeated cries of "Hey, Rube!" had drowned out Chief Inspector Guisborn's outbursts and drawn the attention of John Prince.
Prince knew that "Hey, Rube!" is a slang phrase used by circus and traveling carnival workers, with origins in the 19th century. It is a rallying call, or a cry for help, used by showmen in a fight with outsiders. The journalist was not to know that Motte's Showmen had just discovered their drugs and cash had been stolen. They were rallying the other showmen to draw on their misplaced loyalty.

These days it was usually the city's gangs who did the fighting at fair grounds. But, during the 1800s, in the early days of traveling shows in America, it was very common for showmen to get into fights with the locals as they travelled from town to town.

The fairgrounds of old were rowdy affairs, where country people could gather and blow off steam. Even Mark Twain described them as violent in his Adventures of Huckleberry Finn.

Apparently, the origin of the expression hey rube can be traced to 1848 when a member of circus pioneer and clown Dan Rice's troupe was attacked at a New Orleans dance house. That man yelled to his friend, named "Reuben", who rushed to his aid. Or, alternatively, it has been said that the name "Rube" is a slang term for country folk, or "Rustic Reubens", often shortened to "Rubes".

Whatever the origin of the phrase, it was now ringing out across the whole Goose Fair. Dan Rice, whose troupe coined the phrase, used to call it "a terrible cry", explaining that no other expression has the same meaning, that a fierce deadly fight is on, and that men who are far away from home must band together in a struggle that means life or death to them.

In one sense, Motte's men were crying wolf by using "Hey, Rube!" for personal reasons. But, on another level, they knew that losing so much of the Tax Collector's cash and drugs really could be a matter of life or death for them.

The Showmen ran in from all corners of the huge fair. But unlike the police, they did not have the benefit of direction from Prince's lookout on the Helter Skelter. Despite their good intentions to help their fellow showmen, all they were doing was

adding to the chaos that Guisborn had created.
The three Sergeants were running back and forth, regrouping their Serials in an attempt to correct Guisborn's damage.

The Showmen were racing about, trying to join a fight which was not happening.

The Dodgem operators were shouting descriptions of the Outlaws, trying to convince the other showmen that their takings had been stolen. Cries of theft drew the police attention too, distracting them from their efforts to track Robin and his team.

Above it all on the helter skelter platform, John Prince shook his head. What should have been a text book operation, was now becoming a comedy of errors.

Prince now had the dilemma of how to report what he had seen and filmed. The incident had been a long way from the police's finest hour. But he needed the Chief Inspector's cooperation too much to show it for the catastrophe that it really was.

All Prince could do for now was edit together the better sections of his video for broadcast, and analyse the rest for clues to what was actually going on with the various gangs.

"Please leave the police work to the experts", began Guisborn for his TV interview with Prince. "It is commendable that the Goose Fair showmen tried to stop the robbers", he continued. "But they just ended up getting in the way of my officers".

"Unbelievable", said John, as he watched the interview at Robin's cottage. "That buffoon shouting the odds and interfering let us slip away."

"Maybe he should take his own advice", replied Robin, "and leave policing to the experts".

Guisborn was trying his hardest to move the blame for the failure of his operation. Left alone, his experienced PSU officers could well have caught the Outlaws. But Guisborn's interference really had scuppered his officers' tactics.

The Chief Inspector also pleaded for information from the public about the reported robbery of the dodgem ride takings. "I will not have this sort of lawlessness in my city", he said.

"It's a long way from being his city", commented Robin. "At the moment, it's still Motte's city. But I think we are turning the tide".

Despite letting Guisborn have another 15 minutes of fame, John Prince was still sceptical that this was as simple as Guisborn was saying. Too much did not fit. The Outlaws were much older than the members of Nottingham's existing street gangs. Their methods were too unorthodox, with their use of historic weaponry and the many gangsters who had been left captive for the police to arrest.

The following evening, Prince was to gain another piece of the jigsaw. Like many of his other pieces, it was for a different jigsaw to the one Chief Inspector Guisborn was building.

"Sheriff Building at midnight", was all the distorted voice had said. But it was enough to intrigue Prince. The experienced journalist had an almost sixth sense for when a tip was worth following. This tip especially interested him, as the reporter was still trying to figure out how Motte's Nottingham Science company, and its train, fitted into the Outlaws' story.

The first firework went off at exactly midnight. It was the first detonation of Will Scarlet's most complex pyrotechnic show so far.

Fireworks use many forms to produce their four main effects: noise, light, smoke, and floating materials. The floating material is often confetti, but Will would use something very different later in his display. Will's fireworks were burning with colored flames and sparks of red, orange, yellow, green, blue, purple, and silver.

The citizens of Nottingham had seen many Displays at cultural and religious celebrations, but they had seen nothing the like of which Will was about to unleash.

Will's first volley was just to attract attention. With the exceptionally loud bangs and brightly coloured displays, they performed that function perfectly.

Will had created all the fireworks himself, while hidden away in the Loxley tunnels. He had built the pyrotechnic stars, which produce the intense light, using five basic ingredients: a fuel which allows the star to burn, an oxidiser, which supports the combustion of the fuel, a range of colour-producing chemicals and a lightweight binder to hold everything together and lastly, chlorine, which strengthens the colour of the flame. Together, these ingredients created a very attention grabbing display.

Then, with everyone around Sheriff Leisure's HQ building watching the display, Will moved into his second phase.

Will had created an elaborate display on the pitched roof of Motte's building. Huge, brightly coloured letters spelled out "Drug Dealer".

Simultaneously with the roof display, Will detonated hundreds of smaller fireworks. Each of these carried aloft, not the usual confetti, but tiny hypodermic syringes, which at the peak of the fireworks travel, began to rain on the gathering crowd.

The syringes were clean, without needles, but they helped reinforce the message about Motte.

The finale to Will's display was a recreation of the Yellow Brick Road in fireworks. Very slowly, ground based fireworks began to paint the famous icon from the Wizard of Oz movie.

When, eventually, the road reached its destination on nearby waste ground, another set of fireworks were ignited. Forming a perfect circle, These were designed to burn long and hot, preventing the crowds reaching inside the circle of fire.

For this effect, Will was using large shells containing several smaller shells of various sizes and types. The initial burst spread the shells around the perimeter before exploding. These are called bouquet shells and their effect is usually referred to as "Thousands". Very large versions of bouquet shells, of up to 48 inches are frequently used in Japan. But Will's were significantly smaller, as they only needed to deny access to the circle's centre.

Robin could not help thinking of the origins of Fireworks in ancient China, during the 12th century to scare away evil spirits, as a natural extension of that Great Invention of ancient China; gunpowder. Here, Will was scaring people away,

and they were fighting an evil man. But there were no spirits involved.
China remains the largest manufacturer and exporter of fireworks in the world, for festivities such as Chinese New Year and the Mid-Autumn Moon Festival.

Chapter 26.

Robin knew it was only a matter of time before the police attended such an obvious display. Just the display alone would draw the police to have a look. But they would also have to check if the display was safe and legal. Will was breaking several firework laws, but compared to the carrying of swords, longbows and other weapons, these were minor offences.

In Britain, fireworks cannot be set off between 11pm and 7am with exceptions only for: New Year, Bonfire Night, Chinese New Year, or Diwali. Will's midnight display breached this rule, so the police would have to take an interest.

Robin also knew the police would want to check out the insurance cover for the display. Category 4 professional fireworks, of the type Will had built, must have adequate insurance and storage. Will had neither, but he did not plan on sticking around to answer any police questions, or to produce any documents.

Once the police arrived, Will turned off his fiery ring, allowing the police to find what the Outlaws had placed within. What the police found, was samples from every haul of drugs the Outlaws had taken from Motte.

They destroyed most of the drugs soon after they were stolen. But small amounts were kept back in the hope they could be forensically linked to the Tax Collector and his companies. Robin knew this would take time for the police to complete. But he had also provided additional clues in the form of packaging from Nottingham Science.

Because of his tip off, the journalist John Prince had a front row seat. His camera was capturing Will's firework display for broadcast. He also recorded the gathering of the crowd and the arrival of the police. Nottingham had never before seen such an intricate pyrotechnic display, so irrespective of its purpose, Prince knew he had a winning story. But the seasoned newsman knew there was more to this than just a fancy light show. It could not be coincidence that Prince had been directed to the Sheriff Group headquarters.

Prince had been developing suspicions about Clive Motte throughout his coverage of the Outlaws' story. Motte was always depicted as a millionaire philanthropist, to whom Nottingham owed its gratitude. But none of Motte's public image fitted properly with the shadowy world that Prince had seen develop around Motte and his companies. Far too often Motte's supposedly legitimate interests had become embroiled in the continuing drug war. "There's no smoke without fire", thought Prince.

Chief Inspector Guisborn had responded to the high profile incident on his area. The young, fast track officer was always keen for media attention, so he made a bee line for John Prince. Guisborn always referred to the older journalist as his "friend". But for Prince, their relationship was simply a convenience. Prince began to brief the police officer on his suspicions about Clive Motte, and on what he thought the elaborate display signified. But Guisborn still seemed fixated on the Outlaws being just another gang. "If they're helping us, it's only to hurt the competition", said Guisborn. Then, remembering that Motte was one of his benefactors, Guisborn added "besides, Clive Motte is too good a man for all this".

"His funeral", thought Prince, as it seemed clear that the Chief Inspector was not going to be open minded about where Motte's wealth had come from. Prince would continue to trickle information to Guisborn, in the hope that he would take action. But, Prince was not above throwing the police officer to the wolves in the ending of his story. "You're either with me, or you're a target", thought Prince. His story could cast Guisborn as either crusading police officer, or as a corrupt or incompetent collaborator. Only time would tell which direction Prince would go.

By the time the police decided it was safe to approach the pile of evidence, the Outlaws were long gone. Will had detonated one last burst of loud and smoky fireworks to cover their escape. The Crime Scene Investigators, or CSI, would find plenty of forensic evidence pointing to Motte's companies. But they would find nothing to suggest the Tax Collector had handled the merchandise himself. Neither would they find anything pointing to the identity of the Outlaws.

Robin and his team were safely back on the Loxley Estate when the TV companies started to play catch up on the fireworks story. Most networks, except the nearby BBC, relied on John Prince's footage. But the wily journalist had only released video showing what the crowd had already seen. He shared none of his suspicions about Motte.

Chief Inspector Guisborn had given an interview urging the public not to take the allegations at face value. Motte was, he reminded them, a "great friend and benefactor of Nottingham".

"Benefactor my arse", said John, as they watched the interview. "How much evidence must we give the young twit?", he added.

"One must think of ones career", mocked Tuck, mimicking Guisborn's upper class accent.

They were still making fun of Guisborn when Marion walked into the cottage.

"Looks like father is getting his big tournament", said Marion. Ever since Motte opened Loxley Hall as a casino, he had been manoeuvring to host one of the world's biggest poker tournaments.

Grosvenor Casinos host the annual Goliath tournament, which is the largest Poker Tournament held outside of Las Vegas.

Motte had pulled in favours, issued threats and paid bribes to bring this year's tournament to Loxley Hall. Marion told the Outlaws that, the previous year, 2,764 players took part in the £120 buy-in Main Event. This meant that the Tax Collector would be responsible for the total prize pool of £421,000. Motte was taking great pride in offering the players the opportunity to turn their £120 stake into life changing sums of money. He had begun to call the Goliath "The Recreational Player's Main Event" Over £200,000 in cash prizes was awarded to the final 9 players. Some had invested one or two buy-ins at £120 a go and some had qualified online for only a few pounds.

He had excitedly told Marion that the previous year, after nine days of non-stop play, and with poker fans watching from all around the world, the Goliath Main Event drew to a close when a 27 year old Finnish player defeated the last of the remaining competitors winning the Goliath trophy and £70,800 in cash.

Motte particularly singled out bus driver Andrew James, from Newcastle as his Working Class Hero. James had finished sixth in 2015, winning £8,400. This was the sort of story Motte was hoping to boast across the world's media. It fitted well with Motte's image of himself as a rich philanthropist, so he made quite a fuss about James to Marion.
"It would be good to stop his boasting then", said Robin. To which the other Outlaws nodded their agreement. Bringing Motte down with something he held dear appealed to all of Robin's team.

Marion went onto explain that the Hall's main casino room would host the finals, but qualifying games would be held in a huge marquee outside the Hall. Also in large tents would be the week's other attractions, such as the David vs Goliath Bootcamp, run by professional poker players to improve the skills of the newer players. There would also be a series of other imaginatively named events in the tents, such as: Blind Man's Bluff, Deep 'n' Steep, the Open Dealer's Championship, Win the Button and a Tag Team event.
Will Scarlet did not hear the names of any competition after the first. The young man's imagination was intently piqued by images of David and Goliath. He brought himself back into the room

at the sound of Marion's voice.

"The tents should be a piece of cake to hit", said Marion.

"I'm sure they would be", replied Robin. "But we would only damage his image in the tents. The cash will be safe inside Loxley Hall".

"Then, we do something spectacular in the tents, while we're robbing the casino", declared John. The Outlaws all agreed this would be a good idea. A spectacle outside the Hall would draw the media and damage Motte's credibility. But it would also provide a distraction for the team working inside the casino.

Will Scarlet was quickly at attention when John suggested a spectacular event. The young autistic savant was naturally shy, except when he could hide behind one of his characters. Will had proven his worth to Robin's team as a hooded warrior, a pyrotechnic expert and a brightly costumed illusionist. He would have to decide which of his alter egos to become and how he planned to draw everyone's attention.

With so much at stake, Robin suspected that Will would need aspects of all his many characters.

No matter how hard Will thought, he could not bring his thoughts away from David and Goliath. But, for now, he could not figure out how these images could help him.

Just as he always did when he found a new interest, Will began to obsess over David and Goliath. He read various bible versions, including versions found in Jewish and Islamic texts. But he also scoured the

Internet for all the academic interpretations he could find. Each time he learned something new, he eagerly updated whichever of the Outlaws were in the tunnels.

Will already knew from his schooldays that Goliath of Gath, one of five city states of the Philistines, was a giant warrior defeated by the young David, the future king of Israel. Like the rest of his classmates, he knew that the story is told in the Bible's Books of Samuel, and the original purpose of the story was to show David's identity as the true king of Israel. Will's school had a Christian tradition, which gave the story a distinctively Christian perspective, seeing David's battle with Goliath as the victory of God's king over the enemies of God's helpless people. But today, the phrase "David and Goliath" has taken on a more secular meaning, denoting an underdog situation, or a contest where a smaller, weaker opponent faces a much bigger, stronger adversary.

The book of Samuel's account of the battle between David and Goliath has Saul and the Israelites facing the Philistines near the Valley of Elah. Twice a day for 40 days, Goliath, the champion of the Philistines, came out between the lines and challenged the Israelites to send out a champion of their own to decide the outcome in single combat, but Saul and all the Israelites were afraid.

Will saw himself as the underdog David in the story, bringing food for his elder brothers. When David heard that Goliath had defied the armies of God and of a reward offered by Saul, he accepted the challenge. Saul reluctantly agreed and offered David his armour, which David declined, taking only his staff, sling and five stones from a brook.

In his imagination Will saw himself confronting Goliath, Goliath with his armor and javelin, Will, as David, with his staff and sling.
The bible stories show Goliath curse David "by his gods", with David delivering a very religious reply that "This day the lord will deliver you into my hand, and all the earth may know that there is a God in Israel". Will knew that few of the Outlaws openly worshiped, but he could not help but deliver David's speech to his audience with the emotion of a Hollywood epic.
David hurled a stone from his sling with all his might and hit Goliath in the center of his forehead, Goliath fell on his face to the ground, and David cut off his head.
The Philistines fled, pursued by the Israelites, while David took the head of Goliath to Jerusalem.

Will's first instinct was to see Little John in the role of Goliath. But accounts of Goliath's hight varies among ancient manuscripts: the Dead Sea Scrolls and 1st century historian Josephus, give his height as four cubits and a span, or 6 feet 9 inches. While later texts have him as six cubits and a span, or 9 feet 9 inches. Even the more realistic 6'9" was a few inches taller than John.

Will's wider reading revealed more about how the phrase "David and Goliath" has taken on a secular meaning, describing an underdog situation, or a weaker opponent facing a much stronger adversary.

It arguably remains the most famous underdog story.
His studies had also thrown up many differences between the modern telling and the story's historic beginning. Modern versions suggest it is about a weak shepherd defeating a mighty warrior. However, Will had read that was not necessarily the case and began to lecture the Outlaws on his theories.

"Let's start with the fact that Goliath is a giant", said Will. "a mighty, 6 foot 9 Philistine warrior. He would be a big guy by modern standards, bigger even than Little John. So, he would have been absolutely colossal in Biblical times." Will described how scientists have debated for decades whether Goliath might have had a disorder called acromegaly. This condition leads to a person growing extremely tall, but also leads to double-vision and severe nearsightedness. Will, conscious of his own autism, was always keen to see disability in well known figures.
He realised that, in the Biblical story, Goliath had to call out to David in order to fight him: "Come to me that I might feed your flesh to the birds of the heavens and the beasts of the field." The scientists speculated that this was because he could not see David. Will explained the moral of this part of the story, saying that "A big opponent's perceived advantage can often mask their even bigger disadvantages".

Will was also keen to challenge the accepted wisdom that David was either brave or foolish to go against Goliath with such light armourment. The stories show Goliath outfitted head to toe in glittering bronze armour, with a sword, javelin and a spear. He is so terrifying that none of the Israelite soldiers want to fight him.

On the other hand, David, a lowly shepherd boy, is the only person willing to fight Goliath. He also refuses to wear armour. Will saw something of his own intelligence in David and said that, rather than being foolish, David was the only person in the story who realised that heavy armour weighs a warrior down. Goliath could easily kill David with his sword, but only if David were foolish enough to walk right up to Goliath. Of course, that was the last thing David planed to do.

Chapter 27.

The final part of Will's telling pricked Robin's interest, as it dealt with historic weapons. Modern readers think of David's slingshot as a child's toy. However, that is not what David had at all. His sling was a simple but effective weapon. Armies used it in battle, and shepherds like David used it to protect their flocks from wild animals. Will urged the Outlaws to look at the story again. The lesson, he said, isn't simply that when a powerful competitor takes on a smaller one, the smaller one might nevertheless win. Instead, great leaders understand that the real keys to battle are sometimes obscured by our misconceptions. "Perceiving them correctly can amount to a Goliath-sized advantage", finished Will.

"That's fascinating", said Much. "But how does it help us take down the Tax Collector".

"I'm not sure", replied Will. "But I'm working on it". Robin knew that his young protege would more than likely pull something useful out of his studies, because he always did. "The lad's mind moves in strange ways", thought Robin.

While the Outlaws were plotting how to upstage Motte's poker tournament, John Prince was also busy plotting. In some respects, he was already involved in a David and Goliath contest of his own. The information Robin had leaked about Nottingham Science had caught Prince's interest, because he was already working on projects to expose the misdeeds of big pharmaceutical companies. For many years, Prince had been a member of the

Bureau of Investigative Journalists. Stories he had worked on with them had shed some much needed light on the vast corruption within the pharmaceutical industry. His articles had suggested that a large number of pharmaceutical companies are guilty of fraud, cover-ups of fatal side effects and huge kickbacks paid to doctors.

Prince and the BIJ had seen so many stories about pharmaceutical companies promoting the misuse or abuse of their drugs that their products complicated names seemed to merge.

He had been involved in a case concerning an anti-diabetes drug linked to heart attacks. At the end of the investigation, and on the strength of Prince's evidence, the European Medicines Agency recommended its suspension from the market, while the US Food and Drug Administration made it all but impossible for doctors to write prescriptions for the drug. With sales worth over $3 billion in 2006, this was the world's best-selling diabetes drug until May 2007, when The New England Journal of Medicine published a study linking it to heart attacks. Reporters, led by John Prince, circled, and the US Senate investigated, forcing the manufacturer to hand over internal documents.

Prince had argued vigorously on the need to penalise executives when companies are caught committing illegal acts. Since 2004, pharmaceutical companies have paid over $7 billion in fines and penalties, but these figures barely dent profits. The $2.3 billion fine Pfizer paid in 2009 for the way it marketed drugs, was the biggest ever paid by a corporation in the US. Yet the fine was just 14 per cent of $16.8 billion revenue from the drugs from 2001 to 2008, little more than the price of doing business.

Prince knew that Motte's Nottingham Science would be no different. If left purely to the regulators, profits would continue to exceed any fines levied. Motte himself would also evade prosecution, as he remained at arms length from the company.

Prince would not go straight to the regulators, as he wanted to collect enough evidence to be sure of forcing their hand.

Britain's regulator is the Medicines and Healthcare Products Regulatory Agency (MHRA), which is an executive agency of the Department of Health. It is responsible for ensuring that medicines and medical devices work and are acceptably safe.

Among its roles are: Post-marketing surveillance for monitoring of adverse drug reactions to medicines and incidents with medical devices; Assessment and authorisation of medicinal products for sale; Sample and test medicines to address quality defects and to monitor unlicensed products; Investigate internet sales and counterfeiting of medicines; Regulate clinical trials of medicines and medical devices.

Prince was well aware of some of the Agency's alleged failings, as one of his reports led to the MHRA being criticised by the House of Commons Health Committee for, among other things, lacking transparency, and for inadequately checking drug licensing data.

But it was not just the UK regulator who had received criticism. Both the MHRA and US Food and Drug Administration, have been criticised in the book Bad Pharma, for advancing the interests of the drug companies rather than the interests of the public.

The Netherlands Institute for Advanced Study summed up the problem, stating "the industry has shaped the rules of the regulators, funded their operations, and lobby them constantly".

In compiling his stories on Big Pharma, Prince looked at trends in state actions against drug companies and the impact of their shady activities. Among other findings, he reported that, while the defence industry used to be the biggest defrauder of government, the drug industry has now overtaken them.

Taking action seemed easier in the US, where they make regular use of qui tam. This is a legal process where a private individual who assists a prosecution can receive part of any penalty imposed. Its name is an abbreviation of the Latin phrase qui tam pro domino rege quam pro se ipso in hac parte sequitur, meaning "he who sues for the king as well as for himself."

The writ fell into disuse in England but remains current in the United States under the False Claims Act, which allows a private individual, or "whistleblower," with knowledge of fraud committed against the government to bring suit on its behalf. The False Claims Act provides incentive to whistleblowers by granting them between 15% and 25% of any award or settlement amount. In addition, the statute provides an award of attorneys' fees, making qui tam actions a popular topic for the plaintiff's bar

Such actions are less common in the UK, where whistleblowers are only granted employment protection. English whistleblowers should not be treated unfairly or lose their job. There is no reward, but they are protected by law if they report: a criminal offence, such as fraud; someone's health and safety in danger; risk or actual damage to the environment; a miscarriage of justice; or someone is covering up wrongdoing.

Without a reward, Prince knew he would have to find a way of incentivising someone to come forward Against Motte. Luckily, his previous investigation had uncovered links between one of America's big pharmaceutical companies and Nottingham Science. If he could reactivate one of his previous sources, he could bring pressure on Motte's company.

Robin and his team were unaware of how much Prince was up to behind the scenes. But they had noticed an increase in media coverage about the alleged crimes of Big Pharma, particularly focusing on the travel medications that Nottingham Science specialised in.

"Is this coincidence", asked Marion. "Or do you think they are onto my father". Motte used travel medicines, especially anti malarial products, to cover the export of his designer drugs and importation of cocaine.

"May be, may be not", replied Robin. "I'd like to think someone has taken the corn we have put down. Goodness knows we have scattered plenty. But let's not get ahead of ourselves.

John Prince had taken more of Robin's "corn" than he could have imagined. The veteran journalist had also uncovered plenty through his own investigation. Prince was now convinced that Clive Motte and his science company were rotten to the core. He still needed to figure out exactly where the rot lay and how to expose it.

That was why Prince was again working away in the United States. If he could find a trail that led to an American company, his lawyers could use qui tam to make it worthwhile for a whistle blower to come forward.

Which is exactly what happened. The search was much easier than Prince could have hoped for. Motte's delusions of invincibility made the American trail easy to follow. His US subsidiary was called Sheriff Science. Of course the Americans envisioned Wild West gunslingers, rather than the medieval barons of Nottingham. But the links were very easy to find.

Prince had learned that although Sherif Science was run by Motte's people, most of the investment came from one of America's biggest pharmaceutical companies. If he could get a whistleblower to evidence these links, Prince would be able to get the British regulators interested in Motte, and sell some very lucrative journalism.

It was one of Prince's off the record sources who found him the key. May Cambridge's working life was very different to Marion's, in that she was an accountant at Sherif Science. But their college lives had been uncannily similar. Just like Marion, May had met her first real love in college. The young lovers were on very different courses, May was a gifted mathematician, while her young man was a promising chemist. It was their shared shyness that brought the two of them together, giving each other confidence among the cliques of American college. But May's boyfriend had found a way of buying popularity among his fellow students.

Their college days were a generation behind Marion's, when celebrities like the Beatles were making drugs such as LSD popular. The young chemist had been supplying the other students with drugs at very low prices, making him and May a very popular couple on campus.

But, just like in Marion's story, they were not to live happily ever after. Her beau was testing a new batch on himself, when things went wrong. The psychoactive drug had an unexpected effect, making him believe that he was the comic book hero Superman. The young chemist leapt confidently from the roof of the college. But, rather than flying like a bird or a plane, he plummeted straight to the hard concrete below. It took several hours for May's boyfriend to die from his injuries. When he finally passed in May's arms, she turned against drugs forever.

His source had told Prince that May Cambridge had thrown herself into her work and had never taken another lover since the college tragedy. Dedication to her work had taken her to a senior post in the company, and she remained vehemently anti narcotics. If she was shown evidence of her company's involvement in the illegal drug trade, there was a good chance she could turn whistleblower.

Prince played May very carefully. He learned which gym she used and slowly, over a couple of weeks built up conversation with her. At first very generally, then gradually moving into his work against some of the huge pharmaceutical companies. Never, in those first few weeks did Prince mention any of his suspicions about Sheriff Science.

Slowly, Prince managed to lead the conversation in directions which made May suspicious about her employer. Prince was a skilful journalist and he had manipulated May into discovering her own smoking gun.

Like all of Sheriff's employees, May knew about the malaria clinics in Columbia. Motte had his executives practically shouting about them from the rooftops.

She regularly paid the freighting bills between the US and Columbia, and between their UK and US subsidiaries. Prince's revelations had been carefully constructed to tempt May into looking more closely. Things just did not add up. The amount of freight fitted the busy philanthropic project publicised by the company, but the journeys did not make sense.

May charted where the raw materials were bought from and what products were shipped to their Columbian clinics. There were too many unexplained packages coming out of Columbia. "What could South America be shipping to England and the States?", thought May. "Could it really be the narcotics suggested by John Prince?"

May started to examine the size, weight and quantity of the packages being shipped around the Sheriff

Group. The official business plan was for most of the shipping going into Columbia. Anti malaria drugs went from both Britain and America, into Columbia. Some products, like mosquito nets were manufactured in other South American countries, then shipped direct to the clinics.

The only things coming out of Columbia should have been medical and entomological samples, for analysis in the labs. But the weights being transported were far too heavy. Especially those between Columbia and the States.

Prince had suggested that designer drugs were being sent from Nottingham to America, via Columbia. He had also told May that very pure cocaine had been coming through the clinics, for delivery to the UK and USA.

When she examined the manifests, Prince's allegations began to make sense. The pattern fitted the journalist's explanation far better than the company's version.

With both protection and payment promised by the False Claims Act, May was easily convinced to turn whistleblower.

The release of documents ordered by the American courts had exactly the effect that Prince had hoped. They caught the attention of the British regulators.

Prince had often reported on the perceived failings of the Medicines and Healthcare Products Regulatory Agency (MHRA). The regulator was renowned for being slow to act and a little toothless in enforcement. But this time, Prince was ahead of the game. He had stories and press releases readily prepared. So as soon as May's evidence became public, Prince flooded the media with the story. Day after day, the U.K. and US media were flooded with stories about Sheriff and the pharmaceutical industry in general. The plot of international intrigue and drug smuggling, with Big Pharma cast as the villain, caught the viewers and readers' attention. Prince could barely produce updates fast enough to satisfy the networks.

The MHRA was forced to rumble into action much faster than would usually be the case. The papers and TV channels were full of demands for action. Politicians, eager for a sound bite jumped on the story. Many, quick to defend Motte who funded their campaigns, called for a "robust investigation by the MHRA to settle the matter".
Listening to the politicians, Robin thought "a robust investigation would be great. I don't think they realise what is under that particular rock".
What the politicos and the public did not realise, was that both Robin and Prince had, independently of each other, been providing the police with evidence to complement the MHRA investigation.
As is often the case with bureaucracies, the allegations crossed into both police and regulatory nets. It had always been Prince's plan to feed both beasts. But Robin's information served to bolster the journalist's case and drive the investigation onward.

Within months, rather than the expected years, Prince was live on national TV, talking about his investigation.
The Outlaws watched expectantly as a series of

experts were rolled out to dissect the scandal of Nottingham Science and its bogus malaria clinics. Despite the distaste for her father, Marion felt some pangs of sadness as the TV anchormen joined Prince in condemning the Tax Collector.

But Motte had been true to his clean hands policy. His reputation was in tatters from his very public backing of the project, but there was no evidence tying him directly to any crime.

For now, the Outlaws had to settle for a huge hole in Motte's cash flow and an end to his philanthropic crowing. "His time will come", thought Robin. "We haven't finished yet".

Chapter 28.

The Outlaws did not have long to gloat on the Tax Collector's misfortune, as the Goliath Poker Festival was fast approaching. With the damage Prince had done to his name, Motte was determined this would be a spectacle that people would talk about for years to come.

Robin had very similar thoughts, although the spectacle he intended to put on would not please Motte in the slightest.

This mission would test every member of the Outlaws to their limits. Every one of Robin's team had something unique to bring to the operation, which would be one of the most complex Robin had ever planned.

True, his men had faced great danger on many occasions, deep behind enemy lines. But they were military operations, where extreme force was accepted, or often expected.

At Loxley, the risk of collateral casualties was huge. With the massive amount of cash on site, Motte would put on equally massive security. Without doubt, he would also flout firearms law by arming his men.

Robin needed to destroy the tournament, without killing innocents, or damaging his family's ancestral home.

Marion knew that she would take the lion's share of risk in the preliminary phases. As residents of the Loxley Estate, Robin and his Outlaws had easy access to the public areas of the Hall and casino.

But only Marion could get behind the scenes to plant equipment, or conduct surveillance. As the tournament got closer, the risks grew greater, with her father steadily increasing and improving his security.

Robin had taught Marion well and slowly, but surely, cameras, explosives and weapons were secreted around Loxley Hall.

Outside the Hall was a different story, although security was tighter than usual, Robin's team were able to go about their preparations. With no reason to suspect the Outlaws, Motte hired the men to help put together the tented village which would host the tournament's fringe events. The burley soldiers were ideally suited to heaving canvas, setting up lighting and hauling tables and chairs.

Snob that he had become, Motte assumed the soldiers were badly paid and taking advantage of some extra beer money. But the Outlaws all had rank and earned generous bonuses for their specialist skills and dangerous deployments. They were taking advantage of Motte, but not in the way he thought.

Will's imagination had been working overtime to decide how his latest obsession with David and Goliath could help with their mission. Eventually and almost in a flash, it had become clear to Will. Going days without sleep he prepared the technology he would need to pull off a massive distraction in the marquees, allowing the Outlaws to rob the casino. Every lighting rig and sound system the Outlaws fitted carried something of Will's design. A year ago they would have doubted that someone so young could pull off such a feat. But they had all seen over and over just how capable the young savant could be. Will took on nothing that he did not believe was possible and, with his endless drive and focus, the seemingly impossible happened anyway.

The sight that smashed into the biggest marquee certainly seemed impossible. The students and professional poker players in the David vs Goliath Bootcamp all sat open mouthed as a giant tore through the canvas wall of the tent. The nine foot tall giant wore ancient armour and bellowed "bring me your champion", as he threw tables aside.
Anyone who knew him well would have spotted the giant's resemblance to Little John. But John was nothing close to nine feet tall and the face, though like John's, was subtly different.

Waiting in the wings, while everyone's attention was on the giant, Will Scarlet knew the story behind the sudden and catastrophic disturbance.
Will knew that it was actually hidden motors and cables which tore through the already weakened tent wall. He knew also that compressed air had launched the tables across the room. Most importantly, Will knew that the giant was not actually inside the tent. Little John was ten feet below Loxley Hall, in Robin's tunnels, acting out his role.
Today's spectacular illusion was the absolute pinnacle of Will's secret career in magic. A huge amount of the money stolen from Motte had gone into creating the appearance of Goliath. But money was just the start; Will had pulled on the tricks of

Hollywood, powerful computers stolen from Nottingham Science and expertise of Marion's alumni from Cambridge.

Will's autistic mind very quickly linked his image of Goliath with one of his childhood obsessions, the Incredible Hulk. The shy young boy had often imagined himself changing into a giant monster to punish his tormentors. So, Will saw the Hulk as a way of bringing Goliath to life at the tournament. Just like all his previous obsessions, Will studied long and hard to learn everything he could about how the SFX teams brought his hero from the pages of a comic book to the big screen.

Will knew the 2012 Avengers version of the Hulk was what he needed as his model for Goliath, but he desperately wanted to know what the SFX teams had learned from each other along the way. Ignoring the TV series, where body builder Lou Ferigno was covered in green body paint, there had been two previous attempts to CGI the Hulk.

Ang Lee made a first attempt in 2003, then Louis Leterrier's 2008 reboot, The Incredible Hulk, improved the process.

Will knew that nine months of pre-production design were needed to create the Hulk and his opponent, the Abomination in 2008. Now, he had nothing like that much time in hand, but he had a wealth of information to study on all three movie versions.

Lee's 2003 Hulk had been in the works for nearly 12 years as the studio waited for digital-effects technology to reach a point when such a project was even remotely viable.

Star Wars' creator George Lucas' who brought the Hulk to life for Ang Lee, said it was one of his company's most taxing projects, taking 200 technicians a year and a half to create the Hulk that eventually appeared on the screen. The entirely computer-generated character was intended to reproduce actual human movements, with personal trainers, not bodybuilders, serving as the models for various actions. The animators used similar technology to that which was used to bring the elf Dobby to life in Harry Potter and the Chamber of Secrets, and a cardboard standup was used during most scenes with live actors to indicate where Hulk would be located in the finished scene.

There was actually very little that Will could use from the 2003 techniques, as he needed a much more realistic Goliath, who could interact with the environment of the tournament.

Cut to 2008 and there was a new face for Bruce Banner, Fight Club actor Edward Norton; and a new studio tasked with making Hulk a more lifelike, believable character on the screen. This time around, a blend of motion-capture and animation were used by effects studio Rhythm & Hues to bring the man and the monster closer together, using more of the former and less of the computer-generated latter whenever possible.

Norton filmed more than 2,500 different takes in front of 37 digital cameras and used phosphorescent paint and lighting techniques to record facial expressions and mannerisms.

Will liked the way that this version of the CGI-driven Hulk was more expressive facially. He also liked how the Hulk's muscles and skin reacted throughout the film. The studio had developed computer programs to mimic inflation of muscles and the flushing of skin. Will knew he had to find a way of copying this part of the process to turn Little John into Goliath.

For the 2008 film, animators used 80 motion capture cameras, recording a performer wearing a special suit with 50 digital markers running across the stage. As he ran, he flipped over large wooden boxes, which appeared as cars in the film. Will could not use post event CGI, as his Goliath would have to appear in live time. So, he could only use parts of this technique, explaining his use of compressed air cannons in the tables.

Though the 2008 Hulk seemed to address many of the issues critics had with the 2003 model, The Incredible Hulk still failed at the box office, reaping only marginally better ticket sales than its predecessor. Despite generally positive reviews, Hulk's climactic battle with Abomination was cited as one of the elements that relied too heavily on digital effects, with much of their clash lost in a whirlwind of computer-generated carnage. Again, Will realised that he had to put much more live action into his performance.

Will was determined that John would act out his character's part. He thought that "No one's ever played the Hulk exactly; they've always done CGI". He knew this was the hurdle he needed to get over. So, he studied Marvel Studio's third attempt at their monster.

The bar may not have been set very high for Hulk in

his third attempt in a decade, but Marvel, like Will, paid close attention to what worked, and more importantly, what didn't work in previous projects. For The Avengers, a new actor, Mark Ruffalo played both Bruce Banner and the monster, relying on a motion-capture suit and four motion-capture HD cameras, two for his body, two for his face, to bring man and Hulk closer than they've ever been on the screen.

Will borrowed software from some of Marion's former university friends to aid his illusion.
The way that Marvel merged Mark Ruffalo into the Hulk was exactly what he wanted to do with Little John. Using enough of John to be realistic, but creating something larger than life to grab his audience's attention.
He created his own version of Marvel's light stage, a dome with lights and cameras, which captured John's movements and postures. A digital model was created as a base for everything Will was to create afterwards. Will took detailed casts of John's face, hands and even teeth. Once scanned with lasers, these casts added incredible detail to the digital projections of Little John as Goliath.
Of course Goliath could not look too much like John, or both Motte and the police would be on his case. So, while scaling up the digital model of John, Will gave his features a more North African appearance as well as adding a helmet to cover part of his face.

Will was very pleased with what he had created in his Goliath, but he still needed a way for him to interact with the poker players. All the big screen versions of the Hulk were added to the live action after the actors had been filmed. This could never work at the tournament, as Goliath had to appear before a live audience, not on a movie screen.

It was Marion who brought him the solution, care of her former university friends.

The Cambridge based team, which focused on 3D-sensor technologies and machine learning had been engaged by Microsoft to help their researchers create something called holoportation, that they believed would change how we communicate over long distances forever.

Holoportation, as the name implies, projects a live hologram of a person into another room, where they can interact with people in real time, as though they were actually there. In this way, it actually one-ups Star Wars' R2D2, in which a recorded message appeared in hologram form. Holoportation's real magic is in what basically amounts to a holographic livestream.

Will started his experiment with Holoportation by placing high-quality 3D cameras strategically around the Loxley tunnel. Those cameras captured every possible viewpoint of John acting out Goliath's rampage. Will then used custom software to stitch them together into one fully formed 3D model. The accumulated data resulted in an incredibly lifelike hologram that could be transported into the tents above, or indeed anywhere in the world that had a receiving system.

The commercial version is not too far away, but Will was sure that few of those present would be aware of the technology's capability. Microsoft had created a promotional video, but it had not seen too much viewing outside of the United States.

There are still some hurdles to overcome before holoportation becomes a part of our everyday lives, though. The furniture seen in the video's two rooms is identical, making interaction much more seamless than it would be with the furniture from two rooms overlapping, or people walking through desks, and so on. Will had to replicate this by copying the layout of the marquee in the tunnel. The position of tables and chairs were subtly marked, so that John could move around them. But the background of canvas and the position of lighting had to be copied exactly.

Will and John had obviously made their illusion believable. Tournament competitors scattered as Goliath rampaged through the tent, with tables and chairs taking flight in his path. John waved Goliath's sword about his head, as he shouted for a champion to be brought to him.

The software and pre-production modelling worked perfectly. John's menacing facial expressions were amplified into Goliath's ferociousness.

While competitors ran away, TV crews and Motte's security were running towards Goliath. The Outlaws wanted the media attention, but they needed to take some of the guards out, preventing them from interfering with their robbery of the casino.

This was where Will Scarlet entered his own illusion as something other than the illusionist.

So obsessed had he become with the David and Goliath story, that he could not resist taking the part of David for himself. Unlike John, who needed Will's wizardry to increase his size and alter his appearance, David was able to appear inside the marquee in real life. Just like his current hero David, Will appeared dressed in the simple clothing of Old Testament times. And just like David he rejected the armour worn by Goliath and carried only a simple sling.

Simple though his weapon was, Will had approached his mastery of the sling with his usual obsessiveness. His biblical predecessor had a lifetime of practice in which to develop his skills. In fact, the people of the Balearic Islands, where slings were invented, were trained in the use of slings from childhood. They would not so much as give bread to their children unless they first hit it with the sling. But Will had become expert in its use in a matter of weeks.

Chapter 29.

The gamblers did not know which way to look, as the two very out of place characters both demanded their attention. Goliath waved his sword and roared for a champion, while David began an almost rapid fire salvo of sling bullets.

The first volley of projectiles was aimed straight at Goliath. The interaction of real life and hologram was a fantastic example of Will's mastery of SFX. Will had one end of his sling looped around his middle finger. He placed a sling bullet in the pouch at the middle of the cord. The tab at the other end of the cord went between his thumb and forefinger. Almost instantly, the sling began to swing in an arc, and the tab released moments later, freeing the projectile to fly at Goliath.
Sling bullets can be either ordinary pebbles, or specially made projectiles of lead or clay. For this volly, Will had chosen a very fine clay that fell apart during flight to disguise the fact that there was nothing for them to hit.
But, attached to Little John's armour were dozens of tiny SFX squibs. These detonated in a tiny explosion, sending a puff of powdered clay into the air. The explosions were perfectly timed, giving the impression that, despite being in different places, David's sling bullets had repeatedly hit Goliath.

Just like the classic slings, Will's was braided rather than using twisted rope, as a braid resists twisting when stretched, improving accuracy. The traditional materials are flax, hemp or wool; those of the

Balearic islanders were said to be made from a type of rush. Flax and hemp resist rotting, but wool is softer and more comfortable. Wool was also much easier to obtain in modern day Nottinghamshire, so Will used a woollen sling.

Will had put a lot of time into braiding the several slings he carried with him

At the end of one cord, called the retention cord, he braided a finger-loop. At the end of the other cord, the release cord, Will braided a complex knot, adding weight and bulk to the end. The finger loop remained around Will's finger. The release cord was held tightly between Will's finger and thumb to be released at just the right moment. The extra weight of the end knot allowed the loose end of the discharged sling to be recovered with a flick of Will's wrist.

Practice allowed Will to loose many of his adapted sling bullets before the security arrived. When they did arrive, they came en mass, forcing Will to quickly move to the next phase of his distraction.

The disintegrating clay sling bullets were replaced with ones more like their historic predecessors. The ones he began propelling at the guards were moulded from lead.

Will had copied Ancient Greek lead sling bullets with a winged thunderbolt moulded on one side and the inscription "ΔΕΞΑΙ", meaning "take that" or "catch" on the other side. Will liked the irony of sending a message to Motte's men, even if they could not read the speeding projectiles.

The media had attended the tournament in huge numbers and like the security, they took very little time responding to the disturbance.

Will had specially prepared sling bullets for them too. The first were modified versions of his disappearing bullets. These clay projectiles did not disintegrate in flight, but were designed to cause irritation, not injury on impact.

The sole purpose of Will's performance was to distract Motte's men from what the Outlaws were doing inside Loxley Hall. So Will needed to keep up the intensity of his distraction.

His next trick used Whistling Bullets, with holes drilled in them. When archaeologists first found examples, they thought the holes were to contain poison. But later research on holed Roman bullets excavated at Burnswark hillfort, proposed that the holes would cause the bullets to "whistle" in flight and the sound would intimidate opponents. The holed bullets were small and not particularly dangerous, but several could fit into the pouch of Will's sling and he produced a terrorising barrage. Will had studied experiments with modern replicas, demonstrating that they produced a whooshing sound in flight, which is exactly what Will was now doing with them, alternating the type of projectile he used.

Inside the Hall, Robin and his team were making full use of the David and Goliath show outside. Seemingly safe behind the walls, alarms and cameras, Motte sent away most of his guards to deal with the massive risk to his publicity, which was unfolding outside.

Unlike John and Will's performance, the rest of the Outlaws were using stealth and guile. Devices placed by Marion were systematically opening locks and fooling the CCTV. The security was weakest from above, as all the experts predicted a frontal assault through the casino to be the most likely scenario. Robin had no intention of being predictable and took his Outlaws to the roof.

The domestic part of the security system was much easier to bypass than those in the casino. Marion was soon leading the men through a skylight, down an abseil rope and into the building which had been her home.

Once through the minimal security of the skylight, Marion knew that CCTV was sporadic through the residential areas of the Hall. It took her no trouble at all to get the Outlaws to the edges of the secure zone surrounding the casino. Here, Marion knew they would face much more difficulty. But it was in these areas that she had put in most preparation. First to be defeated were the numerous CCTV cameras. Robin had provided Special Forces grade equipment to do this. When alone in Loxley Hall, Marion had cut into the cable leading from the cameras and tiny computers were now feeding pre-recorded footage to the operators.

Outside, Will was starting to become overwhelmed by the extra security rushing to the marquees. Little John's Goliath performance was keeping the gamblers and media completely transfixed. But the security guards needed more physical attention than a hologram could provide. This was Will's cue to change ammunition. Up till now Will had used a mixture of clay sling bullets and his whistling bullets. But now, he needed to even the odds by using more serious projectiles.

The best sling ammunition had always been cast
from lead. Leaden sling-bullets were widely used in
the Greek and Roman world. Lead, being very
dense, offers the minimum size and therefore
minimum air resistance. In addition, lead sling-
bullets are small and difficult to see in flight.

In some historic accounts, the lead was cast in a
simple open mould made by pushing a finger or
thumb into sand and pouring molten metal into the
hole. But Will had copied a more sophisticated
process, casting his sling-bullets in two part moulds.
Such sling-bullets came in a many shapes, but Will
had chosen an ellipsoidal form resembling an acorn.
The Romans knew these by the Latin word for a
leaden sling-bullet: Glandes Plumbeae, literally
leaden acorns, or simply glandes, meaning acorns.
Being much smaller than the clay projectiles, Will
could load his sling with a greater number of Lead
Acorns. This effectively gave him a rapid fire
weapon, which he was using to devastating effect
against the advancing guards.

Some slingers rotate the sling slowly once or twice
to seat the projectile in the cradle, but Will had
become skilful enough for just one rapid rotation.
Like most slingers, he favoured an overhand throw,
using the sling to extend his arm in a motion similar
to bowling a cricket ball.

Standing 60 degrees from his target, with his non-
throwing hand closest to the guards, Will stood at
the centre of an imaginary circle with Motte's men at
the 12 o'clock position. In a smooth, coordinated
motion Will moved every part of his body, legs,

waist, shoulders, arms, elbows and wrist in the direction of the guards to add as much speed as possible to the bullets. Releasing the projectiles near the top of his swing, the Lead Acorns followed an arc parallel to the surface of the earth, heading towards his target's legs.

As more of the guards were injured, their radios squawked repeatedly for back up. This further emptied Loxley Hall, but it widened the forces now advancing on Will.

To answer this new threat, Will altered the technique of his throw to one more suited for grouped or massed targets, the underhand throw, similar to throwing a softball. Range is increased with this method, but at the sacrifice of accuracy. Historians believe that this was the most commonly used method in ancient warfare due to its practicality. The method also proved practical in Will's modern battle. The increased range and spread, coupled with the quantity of tiny Leaden Acorns, left every one of the attending guards injured and in great pain.

With the immediate threat neutralised, Will and Little John could turn their attention to helping Robin, Marion and the other Outlaws.

John deactivated the hologram device and made his way through the tunnels to one of the hidden entrances, built to secretly enter the Hall. This was the way that Robin intended to get the cash out of the building.

The secret entrance had long since been bricked up. This would cause John no difficulty, as he had ready access to the explosive Method of Entry, or MOE equipment the Outlaws used in their missions. It would create a lot of noise, which needed covering so as not to alert the remaining guards and casino staff.

Will had prepared an answer to this problem too. So far, his sling and projectiles had been quite small, intended to target men. But Will knew that a bigger sling could hurl much more explosive projectiles. Palestinian fighters had made recent use of slings against modern army personnel and riot police, to launch both stones and incendiary devices, such as Molotov cocktails. Rebels used slings to throw grenades during the Spanish Civil War, sending them over buildings into enemy positions on the opposite street. Finns also made use of sling-launched Molotov cocktails in the Winter War against Soviet tanks. It was these techniques that Will had improved upon for the explosive projectiles he now launched towards the Hall.
He could not risk damaging Robin's ancestral home unnecessarily, so his bombs landed near doors and windows, allowing the noise to resonate though the building.
Working alone, Will needed to completely surround Loxley Hall with noise, smoke and flash. For this, some of his projectiles needed enough range to completely clear the Hall's roof.
Will switched to a much bigger, 130 cm long sling and came very close to beating the Guinness World Record of 437 meters, set in the USA during 1981.

This gave John the cover he needed to blow the secret entrance from the Loxley Tunnels. The tightly focused explosion from John's shaped charge was easily disguised by the noise of Will's bombs. John quickly set about preparing a slide for the rapid transfer of Outlaws and cash into the tunnels. They were not expecting much resistance, as so many of the guards had gone outside to deal with David and Goliath. But now the show had ended, those who were able would make their way back inside.

With the cameras still fooled by the Outlaw's technology, Robin's team were able to work on accessing the secure cash area. Again, Marion had pre placed MOE technology to assist them. Her devices were much more subtle than the one John had used to blow the wall. Marion had placed tiny charges on the hinges of every door she had got close to in the build up to the event. Now, Robin was systematically breaching each security door, working ever closer to their prize.

Then, as the last door fell away, the Outlaws found the remaining guards who had not rushed out to the David and Goliath show. These guards with closest responsibility for Motte's cash had not dared to desert their post.

The guards swung around in shock as the security door swung open. It should only have been operable from inside the room. Supposedly the most secure room in Loxley Hall.

The Outlaws now had a tried and tested way of incapacitating men at close quarters. Their crossbow pistols raised in unison, spitting tranquilliser bolts at the guards. The fast acting drug barely allowed the guards a single expletive before they slumped to the floor asleep.

Luckily, the theatrics of the Goliath Tournament saved the Outlaws some time. The TV crews demanded the huge sums of cash be paraded in front of the viewers at regular intervals, to maintain their short attention spans. So, the cash was already packed into elegant leather travel luggage, in which it could be both moved and displayed.

With the classic leather trunks already loaded onto trolleys, the Outlaws soon had it rolling along the corridors to where Little John and Will Scarlet were ready to defend the tunnel entrance.

While waiting for Robin, Will and John had been moving furniture to temporarily disguise the opening. They could not cover the hole until the cash had gone through it, so they stood ready, John with quarter staff and longbow, Will with his sling and Leaden Acorns.

As the Outlaws rolled the trolleys full of cash towards them from one direction, the few guards who could still walk were approaching from the other side. John and Will turned their attention to the guards. As always, their intention was to stop, rather than kill. With the speed of the guards' approach, they could not risk a slow reaction to the tranquillisers, so launched a volley of arrows and sling bullets at the approaching men. Will aimed for their legs, using his smallest sized acorns to replicate shotgun pellets taking out the guards' legs. John was more surgical, his arrows were finding their mark destroying the guards' pistol hands.

In a matter of minutes, the guards were all crawling

along the floor, unable to stand or shoot their guns. With the guards out of action, the Outlaws set about lowering the trunks full of cash into the tunnel.

It was too late for them to disguise the entrance, as Motte's men had seen the hole that Will and John were defending. Luckily, part of Robin's preparations had been to complete works inside the tunnels, making it appear a much smaller system than it really was. Motte would send men into the tunnel, but they would find only a secret passage into the landscaped grounds outside. They would not find the huge rooms, passages and apartments in which Robin had made his headquarters.

Robin knew that Motte's creditors, from higher up the criminal underworld, would want their money back. But Robin cared little about that, his charities would benefit from the theft of Motte's cash. One other person would benefit unexpectedly from Motte's misfortune. Soon after the Outlaws made their escape, the journalist John Prince received an email from an untraceable account.

Attached to the email was CCTV footage from Loxley Hall. As well as disguising the Outlaws' presence from security, their devices had recorded actual footage of the robbery. At the end was a specially recorded message from a hooded Robin, standing next to a fortune in cash, explaining why they had taken such action against the Tax Collector.

Motte had hoped to delay the underworld godfathers finding out about the theft, but with Prince's report playing on every network, there was now no chance of keeping it quiet.

Chapter 30.

The next few months did not go well for Clive Motte.
He was now desperate for money, both in his
legitimate businesses and in his criminal dealings.
Nottingham Science and its American offshoots had
been closed by regulators. Motte had not been able
to hide the extent of his science company's drug
dealing.
Motte had too much invested in the science
subsidiaries to easily recover. He had hoped that
playing the philanthropist in malarial South America
would provide the acclaim that he and his trophy
wife craved. Playing Lord of the Manor always
seemed a little hollow when he did not have the title
to go with it. Motte's coming out of the shadows was
intended to put him on the Honours List, with a
Knighthood to rival Robin's Barony.

"I want them dead", bellowed Motte. He was
torturing himself by watching news reports of the
Outlaws over and over. Everyone close to Motte
knew this was driving their boss slowly out of his
mind, but the Tax Collector could not see what was
happening to him. "Who is he?", screamed Motte,
repeating the question every time he replayed the
tape, trying to see the hooded man's face.
But, just like the thousands of teenage boys
replaying Sharon Stone's famous leg crossing
scene, there was simply not enough detail to be
seen. This too fed Motte's almost insane anger,
which rolled out to the lieutenants closest to him.

All that was left of the Sheriff Group's legitimate

companies were his nightclubs and security guarding. But even these previously lucrative businesses were now in difficulty. Motte had sold many of his more valuable properties to clear immediate debts. But the haste of the sales had not produced the best prices.

It was also a very manpower intensive business, needing staff to run the bars and clubs. But also muscle, to keep at bay the ever circling competitors after picking apart the remains of his empire. The assault of Loxley Hall had cost Motte many of his best men. Huge numbers of his security staff were either too badly injured, or too afraid to come back to work.

Helen Motte had not come to terms with the Tax Collector's cash flow problems. The former Lady Loxley had endured the affections of the old Duke to help Motte gain control of Loxley Hall. She was not about to relinquish the trappings of nobility and continued spending Motte's money far faster than he could make it. This too added to Clive Motte's ever increasing rage. Where previously, he could rely on Helen's deviousness to work for him, now she focused only on herself. This fuelled the inevitable spiral of the husband's temper driving the wife further from him. Helen Motte was not someone you wanted working against you. Despite knowing that she was slowly killing her golden goose, Helen could not help herself becoming ever more reckless with her husband's money.

Most ruthless of all were the criminal godfathers to which Motte owed so much money. The Tax

Collector was at the top of the organised crime tree in Nottinghamshire and across most of the Midlands. But in national and international terms, he was still small beer.

While Motte was trying desperately to collect in any debts that were owed him, those higher up the food chain were squeezing him harder and harder.

Motte was having to tap every source of income open to him. He used fewer staff to secure his night club doors, he squeezed the victims of his protection rackets harder. He took greater risks in cutting his drugs for resale, using synthetic substitutes to disguise the weaker narcotics.

Most dangerous to his licensing businesses was when Motte's managers started watering down the alcoholic drinks to boost profitability. This provided instant short term rewards, but the risk of being caught was immense.

Gradually, Motte's world was falling apart at he seams. His wife was spending his legitimate income like water. All the corners he cut in his businesses began combining to bring him down. Academics describe what was happening to Motte as a "Swiss Cheese Model", where holes in planning line up like the holes in Swiss Cheese, eventually allowing disaster to happen. Which is exactly what did happen. By squeezing his victims harder, they and his competitors began to push back. By cutting back on his security staff, he had less muscle available as enforcers. Flouting licensing regulations caused some of his premises to be closed, which caused a further loss of income. Inability to pay his debts to the national crime bosses led them to support

Motte's competitors in taking his territory.
All in all, things were going very badly for the Tax
Collector.

Robin's Outlaws continued harrying Motte around
the edges of his criminal dealings. Where they
identified a drug or cash shipment, the Outlaws
picked it off.
But Robin was also working behind the scenes as
the Duke of Loxley, rather than as the Hooded
Man. Most of the Loxley Estate was held in a trust,
to which Robin was the current beneficiary. Because
of the trust, the estate, its jobs and tied housing
were all safe from the excesses of Robin's father.
But Loxley Hall had been a different matter, as the
Hall had always been in the ownership of the current
Duke. This enabled the late Duke to borrow against
the Hall, allowing it to fall into the hands of the Tax
Collector. Together with the trustees, Robin had
slowly been buying up some of Motte's debt on the
Hall. When the right time came, the Trust would be
well placed to buy Loxley Hall very cheaply indeed.

The Loxley tenants had known Robin from long
before he left the Dukeries to join the army. They
had all grown to love the lively young boy and had
followed his military adventures as closely as
security had allowed. All were convinced that Robin
would be an excellent landlord if he regained control
of Loxley Hall. They all banded together to help
Robin and the Loxley Trust raise the necessary
money.
It was a day of celebration when Loxley Hall came
into the ownership of the Loxley Trust, with Robin

taking up his birthright as the Duke of Loxley, living as a tenant in his ancestral home.

Robin moving into the Hall created a vacancy in the Keepers Cottage, which had been Robin's home during the Tax Collector's residency in the Hall. This tenancy passed to Little John, who's father had served Robin's parents so well on the estate. Robin had planned on offering the cottage to Marion, in order that she could remain at Loxley after her father's departure. But circumstances were to develop which would change Robin's plans.

Lots of people, on both sides of the law were hunting Clive Motte after his sudden departure from Loxley. What assets could be quickly liquidated had disappeared with Motte. It was rumoured that he had fled to South America, where the remains of his fortune would go much further, but no one had been able to locate him.

The police wanted Motte to discuss the evidence of large scale drug dealing provided by Robin and John Prince. Lawyers for the former employees of the Sheriff Group wanted back pay and redundancy payments. The underworld hunted for the Tax Collector, attracted by a bounty rumoured to be in seven figures. But Motte seemed to have disappeared from the face of the earth. Robin and Marion cared little for Motte's whereabouts, so long as he was out of their lives.

During the living memory of the older Loxley tenants, there had been three weddings held inside the Hall. None of them had proven to be happy marriages for the people of Loxley.

The late Duke's marriage to Robin's mother began well and produced a much loved son. But the Duke's drinking, gambling and womanising could not be hidden from his tenants. They saw his behaviour slowly wear down the Duchess, who they had grown to love.

After the death of Robin's mother came the Duke's marriage to Helen. Everyone but the Duke could see her for a gold digger. Sadly the old Duke was besotted and could see no wrong in his new, young wife. The Loxley people could only watch as the Duke's health suffered and Helen took more and more control on the estate.

Then, soon after the death of Robin's father, wedding bells again rang at Loxley. This time with Helen marrying Clive Motte. The marriage cost Helen her title, but it secured her the money and privilege that she had become used to.

With such a checkered history of Loxley weddings, you could have forgiven the people of Loxley for being wary of another marriage in the Hall. But this time, the tenants and estate workers had much better hopes for the union.

Robin had always been loved by his tenants, while his chosen bride, Marion Motte had proven herself to be very different from her father. The beautiful young woman had thrown herself into every aspect of estate life and was loved almost as much as Robin. Marion had also moved some of her cancer and yoga research into estate buildings, which was providing work for some tenants and experimental treatment for those who needed it.

Robin and his Outlaws were still needed for military operations overseas, but they spent the majority of their time passing on their skills to a new generation of Special Forces in the Dukeries' Proteus Training Area.

Robin, Marion, John, Much, Tuck and Will could often be seen practicing with their bows, swords and other historic weapons in the picturesque grounds of Loxley Hall.
Occasionally Robin would descend into the tunnels, where he still kept several of his green hoodies.
The Hooded Man had served his purpose in ridding Nottinghamshire of the Tax Collector. Robin hoped that his days as a vigilante were over, but he could not bring himself to throw out the clothing, just in case Nottingham ever needed his alter ego again.